By the same author:

The Lost Traveller
Dealer's Wheels

13

STEVE WILSON

St. Martin's Press
New York

Grateful acknowledgment is made for permission to quote from "Bob Dylan's Dream," © 1963 Warner Bros., Inc. All rights reserved. Used by permission.

Library of Congress Cataloging in Publication Data

Wilson, Steve, 1943–
    13.

    I. Title.   II. Title: 13.
PR6073.I47T45   1984   823'.914   83-24489
ISBN 0-312-80042-8

First Edition
10 9 8 7 6 5 4 3 2 1

This is for R.K.H.

Also with grateful thanks for the hospitality that allowed this book to be written, to Keith and Wendy Fisher, John and Frankie Shrapnel, and Sylvia Mann; and for technical assistance, to Keith, Dr. John, and to Robin Batchelor of the Hot-Air Balloon Company.

Finally, out of several books that helped, special mention of indebtedness must be made of Barry Coleman's *Kenny Roberts*, a calmly thought and deeply felt opus, and a must for anyone remotely interested in sport on two wheels.

Let's you and I
get one thing
straight

We did it right,
you in your leather
cape,
I in my lonely
boots

Didn't hesitate.
You were old
enough to know.
I was younger
than you.

Let's fade quickly
like dim, morning
candles.

—Anon., San Francisco, *1967*

1

Kansas, 1982, Sunday

"La treizième revient, c'est encore la première."
—Gerard de Nerval

Cleaver saw the hill before he saw the posted signs, and he heard the thunder of the motorcycle before he saw it hurling up the steep slope, a rooster-tail of dust and scree flying out behind it into the still blue midwestern sky.

He eased the rented Ford in among the pickups and campers clustered haphazardly in the dirt at the base of the hill, then switched off and sat for a moment. The last town had been over twenty miles back. The afternoon sun slanted through a haze of dust settling after the previous run. Flat fields of corn, spring green, stretched away from the bulk of the hill on all sides. The crowd was all white, and not predominantly young, mostly country-looking people, sitting on the ground or leaning in the shade of their vehicles quietly.

The machines made up for that. As Cleaver left his car, another fired up. The ground literally shook beneath his feet. He smelled the tang of nitro, and as the unmuffled engine ran up the rev scale, felt its howl in his ears and his chest, as well as the tug of memory. It had been a while since he had spent time around competition iron.

He walked through the crowd, feeling a little conspicuous.

He had picked up a cheap dark-blue STP windbreaker at a gas station, and his Klein jeans would probably pass unnoticed, but there was nothing to do about the styled hair and Bally shoes. He walked on, and people watched him. He was a man in his late thirties, with gray beginning to show in his full black hair, though not in his bristly mustache. He was not overly tall, a little under six foot, but muscular and still close to lean, with gray-blue eyes and tanned, clear features, softened slightly with age, that were recognizably capable of hardness, even cruelty, but above all conveyed something thoughtful as well as forceful.

He stopped close to the base of the hill. The next machine, crackling as the rider blipped the throttle, edged up to the start line, at the bottom of the two rows of fluttering white tapes marking the run up to the finish at the crest high above them. Cleaver had time to take in the flames popping from the open exhaust pipes, the chromed fuel-bearing rail where the gas tank would have been, as well as the kicked-out rear end of the long, low, specially adapted machine. It was a different scene, he thought, from the way they used to run their road bikes at the slopes, often losing power before the top—which meant comical, expensive, and occasionally bone-shattering backward somersault descents for man and machine. Listening to the ear-splitting crackle of the bike on the line, he could not imagine lack of power would be a problem now.

Then the signal went and the stripped machine rocketed forward, assaulting the hill at an unimaginable pace, bucking and skipping up the one-in-four slope like some bouncing missile of war. This is vertical drag-racing, Cleaver thought, and the next moment he was gasping with the rest as, four or five seconds in and already halfway up the run, the bike's nose suddenly plunged after one leap, as its front wheel hit wrong and dug in solid, catapulting the rider over the bars in a flurry of limbs and crashing him into the ground. Several thousand dollars worth of machinery went over noisily, tumbling back down the hillside. Helpers rushed to the rider, who seemed shaken but intact. When this was clear Cleaver heard a man near him chuckle and say, "The famous flying W," which was the shape the rider's legs had adopted as he passed over the bars. The more it changes, Cleaver thought, the more it stays the same.

The next machine had approached the line, and Cleaver glanced round at it. The rider was bulky in the padded motocross gear they all wore, this one with a bright red jersey bearing the number 2. He was slipping on his white full-face Bell helmet, but just before he did, Cleaver, with a shock of recognition, caught a glimpse of the baby face beneath a cowlick of fair hair. He had found the man he was looking for.

Bill Krass eased the big BSA twin up to the line, the helmet only partially muting the insane din as he constantly ran the bored-out 750 engine up to the red line and beyond. The motor forming the basis of his machine was ten years old, but Krass, like many of the other serious hillclimbers, preferred the previous generation of twins for their lightness and strength over modern Japanese multis.

The bike felt right, but with nitro it was a knife-edge thing; none of his motors had ever blown, but he had seen it happen too often with others to be complacent.

Too late for that, he thought, and centered on the white-lined track rising ahead of him, reducing his world to just that and the feel of his red and chrome machine. In the center of the maelstrom, calmness descended on him, and when the signal came he felt a leap of spirit as the eighteen-plate nitro-proof clutch bit and the BSA leapt forward, the cow-horn bars fighting to wrench from his grip as they hit the hill and the endless power rising to lift the front wheel up and back, threatening to somersault machine and rider. But Krass was on it instinctively, crouched up on the footpegs, his long body canted far forward over the bars, holding down the front end as the bike aviated, skipping like a stone, banging down hard again and again and jarring his body as the rear wheel's knobbly tire with its single chain bit into the dirt and hurled them on and up.

The blur of tapes to the left suddenly swung in, but Krass instinctively corrected the shock of the howling, smashing machine, eased off a fraction when the ridges' surface feedback spoke of the threat of the front digging in, guiding the bike's bars like a dowser's wand for a moment, and then pumped the throttle, gunning it hard, to aviate clear over the finish line.

Throttling back in the run-off, feeling the machine transmute back from a projectile to something approaching a regular motorcycle again, he knew even before the backslappers closed in that he'd cut eight seconds, but could he have gone harder right off? Maybe, he judged. But damn, as his heart's pounding subsided and his aching body threaded the bike down the run-off track, not bad for pushing forty. Like the bike, an oldie but a goodie, he grinned. And damn, there were still worse ways to spend a Sunday.

As he reached his pickup, a figure detached itself from the front fender. Still bemused by the run, Krass took long seconds to recognize the man he had not seen in over ten years, a man from another life.

He pulled off his helmet and, propping the bike against the back of the trunk, called out, "Cleaver?"

"No one but, old buddy," and then they had closed on each other and were shaking hands warmly, Krass taking in the changes in his old friend, the effects of age and what at a quick scan he took to be affluence. Then he realized Cleaver was doing the same, and smoothed his cowlick with embarrassment.

"How did you find me?" he asked.

"I called the last college you taught at, and they put me on to this one. When I got through to your home, Karen said you were out here. At least I guessed it was Karen."

Krass nodded and Cleaver went on. "That was pretty fancy riding back there."

Krass started to say something modest and then stopped. His friend's unexpected appearance, and something in his face, brought him up short. He stood half a head taller than Cleaver, and looking down at him now said, "Yes, but you're not here for the show, are you?"

Cleaver shook his head, saying nothing. In anyone else this silence would have been irritating, but Krass recalled with a rush Cleaver's laconic way with words, and how he could turn his attention on or off in a way that made you both listen to him and want him to listen to you. Which was one part of why he'd been their head honcho, Krass realized.

"It's the guys, isn't it?" said Krass with certainty. "Someone in trouble."

"Yeah, and worse," said Cleaver.

"That . . . Graduation?" said Krass. A pit opened in his stomach and the sounds and sights of the bright day around him vanished. He felt like a man who had buried something hated, dead and putrescent deep underground and piled up rocks above it, only to see the mound stir.

Cleaver nodded.

"The Judge has got Baby Duane and his family down south," he said simply. "He wants us all. He'll kill them if we don't go."

Krass's mind protested just once.

"But it was all so long ago. Like another planet. How many years?"

Cleaver grinned tightly.

"Just thirteen. Hell, it would have to be, wouldn't it?"

2

California, 1967

"That endless blacktop was my sweet eternity."
—*The Loveless*, Kathryn Bigelow and Monty
Montgomery

The 13 only rode together for a little over two years, but in that time they became a kind of legend. Some of the people then were as hot for the latest 13 story as they were for a new Dylan album.

More than just a bunch of friends who rode together, they had been less than a full-house bike club like the Satan's Slaves or the Angels—but in some ways this had helped their legend to grow. For bikers, they were different from the usual tattooed hoods in several ways. They were multiracial, most of them were individually bright and talented, and they avoided larceny and violence when possible, though if pushed they came back massively and effectively. And they were very fast indeed. If any one thing bonded them, it was the feeling that riding was life, and most everything else just waiting around.

Few knew the origin of the "13" tag, which street talk sometimes rendered as the Teen, or Teen Gang. The water was muddied further by many bikers then carrying a 13 patch, meaning the thirteenth letter of the alphabet, *M*, meaning marijuana. That was all right by the boys, who survived in a hologramic box of partly fact, partly fiction. The truth of the tag was simply that eventually there had been thirteen of them. Any superstitious objection to the number was brushed aside one night by Tor, their 290-pound chief head-breaker, when some greasers on the prod unwisely sneered at their title.

"Thirteen?" jeered one, "that's unlucky, ain't it?" To which Tor had rumbled,

"Unlucky for you, suckers," just before proving it in the knuckle-buster that followed. The 13 had remembered and cherished that one, unlike many of the things that were said and done in the swirling madness of their three summers.

They had no turf outside the Californian coastal highways, and no colors; though they did each wear a 13 ring that the Dude, their resident artist and mystic, had designed and executed for them in silver. They didn't even all ride Harley-Davidsons. Two of them were black (and identical twins), one was Mexican, and they were all young and a little weird, from the start distinctively inclining to North Beach rather than Oakland. Some were native Californians, and some had drifted to the coast in the summer of '67, the summer they had come together.

Cleaver himself had grown up in San Francisco, on the edge of the Hunter's Point ghetto. His father had been a merchant seaman, killed off Okinawa in the last days of World War II, and as the eldest son Cleaver learned permanent responsibility early. None of that had emerged from his rebellious school days and drifting late teens. It waited on what was to prove the substantial joy of that time, like minds and kindred spirits breaking out of isolation and discovering one another. For it was Cleaver, above all, who welded them from a bunch of loners hanging out in garages, crash pads, and flop boxes to the brief, bright legend they were to become, before the night they called Graduation.

Cleaver rode a Triumph Bonneville, and both he and Krass, the baby-faced dropout from UCLA, for a while affected gleaming white high-necked Russian tunics edged with red and black embroidery under their leathers, and were grimly amused to see something similar turning up soon after in the movie *Easy Rider*, as art gasped along behind their raven-

7

ing lives. Levon and Leroy, the two blacks, at a time of Afros and garish dashikis, clenched fists and Panther logos, wore black from head to toe, and completed the beat sax-player look with minimal Left Bank berets that the wind never succeeded in dislodging.

The Dude, tall, cadaverous, with an alarmingly bony face and big, very brown eyes with the whites showing clear around them, rode something that was typically both far-out and po-tent—a twenty-year-old Vincent Black Shadow in an Egli frame, the only one of their street machines that would shade 130 mph. Lettered on the tank's glowing black enamel in mod-est white Gothic characters was the legend "The Lord gives me grace, but the Devil gives me style." The Dude wore black pistol-legged pants, and draped a collection of old dark-colored waistcoats, culled from the Free Store, over the collarless work-ing-man's shirts that hung from his bony torso. By contrast, Kemp, the rich boy who doubled as their dope dealer, favored a dark blue U.S. Cavalry tunic, though sweet Baby Duane, the southern charmer from Louisiana, called it Yankee trash.

Tor, their mountainous enforcer, rode a Harley with a big customized saddle for what Six, the bucket-mouthed gun nut, called Tor's two-stool ass. But Tor never rose to the squat gun-man's hazing. When Six got on his case, the big one would just flip his thick wavy shoulder-length black hair out of his dark-complexioned face, pout his thick lips and mumble quietly, "One day, man, I'll be thin, and I'll be rich, and you'll be sorry."

It was easy to misjudge the gentle giant until you had seen him send muscular opponents flying across a room with what looked like just a nudge of his thick hips or belly, before his meaty fists pounded them down like fence posts going in under a steel hammer. Six knew what the fat man was capable of but he didn't care, about that or much else. "I'd tell you to haul ass," he would jeer, "only it would take you two trips."

How Six had come to be with them was a long story and full of flavor. One of the first things the 13 were known for was their hard riding on the various unofficial street events that went down on the Coast, like the street races on Mulholland and the Sunday morning run from Mill Valley to Point Reyes station. But their specialty lay farther south, on a downhill stretch of the coastal highway outside Carmel known as the nerve curves, where at night, or on early weekend mornings, speed-minded gentry would gather to street-race, hurling down the tree-lined turns and laying small wagers on who would reach the ocean first. The embryonic 13 had an edge there, beyond a balls-out approach and their natural rhythm. One, Dance, was already a semipro rider on the way to being a local hero on the So Cal flat-tracks; though as he had started out underage and a fugitive from his Okie Holy Roller parents, he raced under another name. And there was Bob, a raw-boned red-bearded Tennessean, Dance's expert wrench on weekends, who also had regular work as a mechanic with the West Coast BSA–Triumph race teams. This meant factory power parts for himself, Cleaver, Krass, and later the Mexican, Cooch, since they all ran British twins—but Bob was equally well connected and adept when it came to tuning Harleys.

So Team 13 often scooped the pool on the nerve curves, all of which soon came to the attention of the local heat. Cautious scouting by Cleaver and the street people who set up these events and held the money had kept them out of trouble for a while, but they took to switching plates for the runs themselves.

Then one night out of nowhere appeared two motorcycle patrolmen (Six called them "pigs on hogs"), charging into the middle of the pack with lights and sirens going. One was quickly left behind, but his partner had done some work on his Harley and by really trying found himself directly behind the leader (which was Dance) and closing fast.

Then with the steep winding road unreeling in his head-light, as the crouched rider ahead snaked his machine through the turns, the cop snapped a glance left and saw alongside him a long low machine, with less than three feet separating them. Thunderstruck, as far as the road would allow, he edged into the side until another razor-swift glance revealed a third bike running level with him to the right. Some subliminal flash told him that the rider (it was the Dude) had smiled at him.

The officer's long-held conviction in his own skill and efficiency began to crumble like wet plaster in a shower of rain. As the road continued to unwind he braked gingerly, trying to drop back from the box. But the sudden flare of a fourth headlight close behind in his mirror let him know that there was no way out.

And then the riders around him began to go faster.

The cop started to scream and mumble curses through clenched teeth. The night became a tear-streaked blur, an impressionistic jumble compounded of the white spark-showers every time the leading rider's footrests grounded, the sickening yawp in his stomach each time the curves dictated a fast shift from hard left lean to hard right, the howl of their engines on the synchronized down-change, the awful blinding light so close behind, and the worst moment, when his overladen machine lurched outward on a tight right-hander and the tip of his handlebars just kissed the bars of the rider on his left.

When he finally reached the bottom, the one on his left accelerated away around a long right-hand curve. As the gap opened out the officer shot through it too fast, failed to make the curve, crossed the center line and left the highway on the high side, parting company with his machine in the ditch beyond and ending up on his back, no worse than winded, gasping for breath as he watched the riders' tail-lights snarl off into the darkness.

The boys were not magicians or superheroes and once or twice they had been as scared as the cop, but he had caught them in their one area of expertise, something others might do once for a dare with themselves or with their friends, but which each of them had discovered in himself the impulse to do, and do again to tighter limits, and then come back next time to do again, faster. Ask them about the big questions, like life or the war, or whether they'd want to marry a girl who had been with a lot of other guys, and they would have no more sense or certainties than most other kids their age. But about their riding they were serious enough to have reached a point where their young reflexes, nerve, and attention to detail had come together and been transmuted into a highway song. They were no day trippers.

None of this was of interest to the local smoky as his partner arrived and helped him out of the ditch. His back hurt, but his pride hurt worse, and furthermore something in him *knew* that what had just happened was what was going down all over the country, and that right here was where he drew a line and took a stand against lawless punks everywhere.

Both sides kept a low profile for a while, but the story got around the coast, and it could not be long before the riders returned to the nerve curves in force. The first time they did, nothing happened. The second, a pack of a dozen riders, including Dance the racer, the rich boy Kemp, and Cleaver had started their run when a police cruiser burst on to the road behind them. And this one was loaded for bear, with a race-tuned suspension and a Cobra 427 Magnum V-8 engine. A well-liked Hell's Angel had recently gone down for good under suspicious circumstances involving police vehicles, and as the red lights, flaring headlights and squealing tires of the hopped-up black and white closed on the riders' rear fenders, anything seemed possible.

They were coming to a two-hundred-yard straight before two tight Z-bends. Cleaver, riding near the rear of the pack, glanced back to see the cruiser's grille hit the straight and roar down on them like a shark's maw. He checked front and looked behind once again just in time to catch a glimpse of the tail-end rider pulling something from his leather jacket and pointing behind him. There were two sharp cracks as close together as two fast hand-claps, and the cop car's headlights blew out just as they hit the end of the straight and heeled over into the first fast downhill bend. In the momentary blindness that followed this, the police driver failed to negotiate the first curve, left the road and crashed down the slope into a madrone tree, which brought him to an abrupt halt and ripped the hot engine from its mountings, leaving it shoved up through the hood. The two shaken officers sat contemplating it for long moments in the ringing silence before scrambling clear of the wreck.

The riders reached the bottom of the run and scattered, but Cleaver fell in beside the tail-end biker's Harley. Up till then he had only seen shooting like that in the movies. When they pulled up outside a low-life Monterey bar, the short, stocky rider jerked goggles off a face that Duane was later to compare to a pig hunting lunch, and remarked, "Those fuzz weren't just fucking around, I think."

"I ain't seen you there before, man," said Cleaver.

"I ain't been there. My name's Six."

"Six, like, number six?"

"Nah, six like guns," said the short one, patting his waistband and leering like a malignant gnome. Remembering how when he had fired the rider had kept his right hand on the throttle, Cleaver said, "You're left-handed, huh?"

"Nah. Left, right, don't make no difference to me."

"I'm hip," said Cleaver, thinking, unbelievable. But he recognized expertise in any field, and before long Six was riding with them. The fabric of society seemed to be burning out like a piece of film that gets too close to the heat, the tedious images dissolving outward in black-fringed white light. The movie had gotten so boring that at first many welcomed the dissolution as a spectacle in its own right, but with his background, Cleaver had fewer illusions than most about the what would go down when the movie house itself seemed threatened and straight society got frightened enough. So Six was in.

But for the time they felt free. There were long days riding the coast when they merged with the blown spray and the sunlight shooting off their chrome, long hair whipping in the wind, their spirits at one with the purr and howl from their mufflers as they wound among the sun-dappled tree-lined roads south from Carmel. That was where Kemp the rich kid hung out; with his mother and stepfather almost always away in Rapallo or Maui, the 13 had the use of the mansion on the hill, hard by that of Stuyvesant Fish, the little town's patriarch. Ever well connected, Kemp had been at Berkeley long enough before he dropped out to make the acquaintance of San Francisco's legendary synthesizer of high-grade LSD-25, Augustus Stanley Owsley III and his lady, Melissa. The best acid was only one of the benefits of knowing Kemp; his own travels some time previously had begun taking him to Peru and Colombia for cocaine at an unfashionably early stage, and from Mexico he brought in boxes of the *dexedrinas* that were still legal there—"redeyes and midnight flyers," as Six would call the speed, chomping a handful of the pills as if they were M & Ms.

But it was the acid that patterned their early year, from the first chaotic night trip when the stuff hit while Cleaver and Duane were riding in Kemp's pickup truck and Duane saw the road as carpeted with writhing, hopping frogs, red- and green-eyed, from the swamplands of his Louisiana boyhood. Later, in a moment's lucidity, he wanted to lower the window and get some air.

"But not too damn far," he howled. "'case the little fuckers jump right in here with us!"

But as the Dude was to say, "The mind is like a parachute. It only works if it's open," and that was largely what acid did for them.

The pills that made a paint-shaker of the insides of their heads, the driving or fairy-tale San Francisco sounds, Steve Miller and Country Joe, the Doors, the Dead and the Airplane, weed that was as ever-present as *Sgt. Pepper,* all bonded them to the heads on the street, so that as well as Kemp's mansion, there were crash pads from Ukiah to Berdoo where any of them were welcome at any time. And there were the girls; girls from Liverpool and girls from Saigon, surfer girls and dolly girls, barefoot Mexican *braceras* and vague, haughty princesses from Manhattan, or the dirty side as they were already calling the East—but all eager to get off on some authentic (and not too brutal) American outlaws. It was a good time to be young and healthy, and none of them held back. The life they were leading never encouraged long-term attachments.

They trusted and were trusted, buzzin' cousins to the hippies, and only once was this misinterpreted as weakness. In San Diego in the early hours, three of them were roused rudely when one of Kemp's bikes was stolen off the street.

The next week they stayed at the same place and parked another of Kemp's machines, older but still ridable, lightly chained up in the same spot. But this bike had been worked on by Ariel, the newly arrived brother who serviced Kemp's plane out at the airfield where the rich boy was learning to fly, a mechanic by whom a motor could be rigged more ways than a small-town election. Now he and the others watched in the darkness of the crash pad, as out on the street three grimy figures in cut-offs swarmed over the old machine, rapidly taking out the cheap padlock with cutters and only bothering to push it a short way down the street. Then one of them hot-wired the ignition, switched on the gas, straddled the big twin and kicked it into life. What they did not know was that Ariel had wired in a third sparking plug—which was located inside the half-empty gas tank. When the spark came there, the tank blew, the vapor and gas igniting in a sheet of flames between the thief's legs. The story circulated, and the 13 never lost another machine.

By the time of the Monterey festival there were twelve of them, and Dance had already teamed with Krass to win the first of the unofficial nonstop round-trip road races from San Francisco to L.A. and back; they were to become increasingly famous, both for their wins and for the positive thinking they brought to the problem of outguessing and outrunning the CHP.

All that summer the high times continued and word of the group spread, but the madness in the Haight was rising with the unstoppable influx of underage pilgrims, and in the country both race tensions and fear and feeling against war grew. So by October Cleaver had acted on a suggestion from the Dude, who knew the cactus lands, and headed them for the first time away from California, out to New Mexico; again unlike the bike gangs who stuck mostly to their own turf. It was the best month, warm and temperate, yet with little chance of a desert downpour to spoil the run. When they reached the lazy town of Santa Fe, they rented a rambling adobe house some miles out of town from friends of the Dude's. Then they worked on their bikes and lazed away the days, sometimes partying with the girls who worked at La Fonda inn after hours.

In the solitude the Dude, a dazzling, ageless rap-artist and a master of country blues, from Cajun fiddle to twelve-string bottleneck guitar, wove his view of the world into their vision— a witty, life-loving mysticism whose theme tunes were the songs of the legendary bluesman Robert Johnson: "Born Too Late," "Love in Vain," "Steady Rolling Man." He had gotten them to be patient with the crackling of the old recordings and to hear the strength, pain and poetry of the songs. Only Six resisted. The Dude persisted with him.

"He was round about your age, man, when he went down. Some lovely lady fed him a cupful of poison, and the music stopped. Except it didn't, 'cause it never does if you really mean it. . . ."

"That's just like a woman," said Six, scratching his crotch. "I believe that coffee-colored bitch left me some visitors last night. Like, 'Don't look for me with the fishing boats, baby, I'm coming home with the crabs.'"

"Aw, man," said the Dude despairingly, "if you'd just open your mind to the music, man, this stuff could really do you some good on the Karmic level. . . ."

"Karma? I prefer the high-speed kind," said Six, winking as he fished out a rattling pill bottle from his pocket.

"But with them things you have to come down again. I'm talking about the kingdom of delight. . . ."

"You're talking about cloud fucking cuckoo-land," laughed Six as he swallowed a handful.

But it was a girl who inadvertently brought them up against the racial situation that simmered beneath the sleepy bohemian atmosphere of the area. This was a three-way pull: Anglo, Hispanic, and Indian. Duane, the Southern charmer, was seeing a Mexican girl named Luana, and one night he, Krass and Cleaver rode out to a freewheeling party at the house where she lived.

At first they were wary of the all-Hispanic youth gathered there. The Mexicans were nervous, too, initially; there had been an incident recently when an Anglo farmer claimed some Hispanics on trail bikes had taken a shot at him, and there was tension. But big pitchers of margaritas and some good local grass got everybody nicely loose and sociable, and dancing to guitars.

They left after midnight, pulling on their leather jackets and stepping out into the desert chill. Another rider, a young Mexican, came out at the same time, and they wandered over slightly unsteadily to check out his machine. Off-road riding was a big thing in those parts, and the Mexican ran a hairy street-trail monster, a 650 Triumph engine in a Rickman frame. They were clustered round admiring this, when suddenly they were caught by a blinding spotlight from a truck parked away from the house.

By the time they realized it was not a joke, saw the shotgun held on them by the figure standing tall in the flatbed and raised their hands to the stars, two more burly white youths were coming at the Mexican, the glint of long knives in their fists.

"Stay out of it," one of them yelled at Cleaver. "We're going to cut the greaser's guts out."

The three bikers were fanning out, all talking at once, when the Mexican dropped his hand to the collar of his jacket. A blade appeared between his fingers, and with a single fluid motion, he hurled it spinning into the chest of the man closest to him with a clearly perceptible thud. Then he was leaping forward as the body collapsed to wrench the knife out and close with the second attacker.

But the man was already slashing at him: the two blades met, rang and sparked, and the Mexican's was knocked spinning off into the darkness. With a bellow his assailant pulled back his arm to strike again. But in the bright circle of light, the slighter figure of the Mexican closed with him, his right hand flashing a pass once across his own stomach and coming out with a stubby spike of blade protruding from the fingers of his clenched fist. The other man's slash went wide over his shoulder, as the Mexican pulled him in close and ripped the belt-buckle knife backhand hard across his belly.

They disengaged, and in silence the attacker fell to his knees, the big knife tumbling from his hand into the dust, his fingers clutching his shirtfront and stomach, both torn open. He went down, and the Mexican was exposed in clear view of the shotgun in the truck. Cursing, the man there brought the gun up to his shoulder, but then the barrel continued in an upward arc over his head as the dark figure of Cleaver, unnoticed during the fight, had swarmed up the side of the truck behind him, threw an arm like an iron bar across his throat and now wrenched him off the flatbed crashing down on to the ground, straddled him and took him out with two fast right-hand punches.

Quickly Cleaver rose and switched off the spotlight. In the

darkness they could hear the music from the party and the groan of the man with the stomach wound, who lay on his side now, still holding his belly.

Duane swallowed and broke the silence nervously.

"Well, looks like someone did get his guts cut out," he muttered quickly.

"Jesus, will they live?" said Krass wildly.

"Si, *señor*, because I mean them to," came the Mexican's voice, clear and controlled.

"I'd say this cat has a feel for steel," said Duane hoarsely.

"Their buddy can take care of them when he comes around," said Cleaver decisively. "We have to haul ass. You ride with us if you want to," he told the Mexican. "What are you called?"

"Cooch."

Later they found out that the baby-talk sound was short for *cuchillo*, the Spanish word for knife. But at that point no one was asking. They rode off, and before sunrise next morning Cleaver had them over the state line and heading back west. At Williams, Arizona, they turned north again and rode up through piñon-covered slopes.

They left the bikes in the half-empty parking lot at the top, and Cleaver led the way forward on foot. They came to a tree-fringed rim, and halted.

Before them lay the gorge of the Grand Canyon, the Colorado river unimaginably far below, the wrinkled sandstone castellations beyond the canyon walls, seamed with vast tongues of dust and rubble, layering upward majestically in the soft afternoon light of autumn. They felt diminished, yet also enlarged by the quiet, absolute statement of the endless canyon and the mountains.

In the moment of silence, Cooch whistled softly. Cleaver turned and briefly smiled.

"Stick with us," he said.

The Mexican did, and they were thirteen.

3

California, 1982

"Better men than I have gone to grease in L.A."
—Raymond Chandler, *Letters*

It was the business with the dogs that brought home to Cleaver, with some force, the way that his life was going.

He was head of the media buying department of a large advertising agency in downtown Los Angeles. That meant he had responsibility for placing campaigns in magazines and newspapers, billboards and radio, and the big one, television, where a prime-time slot of thirty seconds could set you back $100,000 or more.

His clients ranged from stores and a freezer concern to at least one corporate giant, and also film companies. With the latter, the organization he worked for was diversifying from simply publicizing movies to putting together production packages, financing, setting up and making them. This was what interested Cleaver now, and it could not happen quickly enough to suit him.

In the meantime, on both sides of the fence there were people to wheel and deal with, the businessmen and producers with something to sell, and the deejays, station managers and TV national sales managers who sold the time, space and sound to them. Since a number of these positions were filled by women, as well as the majority of his department being girls, if he wanted, Cleaver did not need to go short of female companionship.

He was married with two children, a girl of six and a boy of eleven. He had married a year after the thing they called Graduation, when the 13 had abruptly dissolved. He had found himself in L.A. drifting, alone for the first time in over two years, for even his sidekick Krass had gone his own way, starting school again. Cleaver himself was still in mild shock.

One of the street people he would sometimes see was a girl with a trail bike whom he had known from before. A year previously she had been something of a 13 groupie, but Cleaver had never slept with her, and now she was just one of a parade of faces that he would encounter, tooling the Triumph aimlessly around the neon boulevards, the glass-walled fast food shacks, and the bars. His money was nearly exhausted, and sometimes he found himself hanging out with junk buzzards, guys who slept on the streets and had little further down to go. It was a possible direction for him: the charisma of street life had gone for good and nothing had replaced it.

But the same thing that had put him at the head of the 13 craved order in his life, even if currently there seemed little point to it. And he saw that at this time, money was the key to order. So when the girl with the trail bike mentioned that there was a job where she worked, Cleaver went for it, and found himself in the mail room of the agency.

From there he took stock quickly of the company's structure. The accounts, creative and production sides were closed to him by lack of qualifications, and traffic was a dead end. But the media buying side looked possible. It had required some imagination to see this, since at his agency the only man in the twenty-strong buying department was the one who ran it. But that seemed good to Cleaver, as did the gossip he picked up on male buyers with other outfits—media queens, untalented older or much younger guys whose energy was mostly expended bitching about where they were being taken to lunch. Cleaver kept his ears open, and the fact that most of the agency's mail was opened in the mail room, where he could read it, didn't hurt either. He also paid some attention to his image, keeping his long hair but getting it styled for the first time, wearing a sports jacket over the right T-shirt, and jeans still, but well-cut black jeans that gave the impression of regular pants but with an interesting difference.

He was punctual and willing, and even in the laid-back atmosphere of the agency, this counted for something. After eleven months, when he had let them know he was interested, he was offered a slot as assistant media buyer, beginning at $750 a month.

The night it happened, Cleaver felt himself flooded with an unaccustomed, slightly guilty pleasure. After a moment he realized it was relief—that the years of living all the time on the edge truly were coming to an end for him. He felt the force of the strain as it lifted.

Not that Cleaver went soft in any sense. He worked out and ran, as well as getting into handball and tennis with colleagues. From the start at the job he overdelivered, taking responsibility, finding out who was seeing to all aspects of deals where he was only the buyer, bringing in buys not just on budget but under. And he made a point of getting inside his clients. He knew how to be nice, but people were never quite sure with him, they were careful not to get caught in a lie by Cleaver, not only because he was obviously smart but also because he retained, carefully unexplicit, the faintest aura of menace.

The national reps, middlemen between the agency buyers and the TV stations, were the worst people he had to deal with; supposedly impartial, but always looking after the station more than the buyer. The first time he was double-dealt by a national rep, Cleaver took the man out to a quiet bar, bought him a drink, then let him know that he knew he'd been had and asked quite calmly how the man had done it. The national rep, sweating lightly and high on a mixture of guilt and relief, proceeded to reveal a good deal of inside information to Cleaver. And so it went. Within months he was walking all over the media bitches, and in less than two years was a full buyer at $18,000 a year plus a substantial bonus. By 1980 the figure had tripled and the bonus with it, and the only way he could have been earning more was if one of the agency's rivals had offered him a job, which given his record of performance was a constant possibility.

It had not always been that way. He had married early, and their son, Sam, was conceived soon after that; when the boy was young they were poor, living in a rented apartment in Venice, and that had been both a bond between them and another spur to Cleaver to get ahead in his work. His wife, Laura, had been a nurse from Montana. They had been drawn together initially by her blond, outdoor good looks and Cleaver's magnetism, and then the recognition of a mutual toughness, good sense and laconic humor, leavened on her side by a quiet compassion that had helped him through the difficulties of adjusting to the loss of the 13 and to his very different life in the city.

Now they lived more than comfortably in the West Valley, Cleaver accepting the long drive to and from work every day as a trade-off with the quiet, better air, safer streets and private school for his children. But they were also up against suburban narcosis, the numb strangeness and apathy that endless blue skies, the pool and the Jacuzzi, a full freezer and a constant background of the kids' television and video games could induce. They tried to counter this; they took adventurous holidays, to the Caribbean, Europe, Mexico, and whenever possible camped and hiked in the hills together as a family. But increasingly the pressures of the job left Cleaver with little energy on the weekends.

The marriage too was now not altogether happy or unhappy but, like most, swam in stippled waters composed of subtle or not so subtle discontents and partial, though occasionally profound, happiness. Cleaver still loved Laura, but sometimes hot, gusting winds, an internal Santa Ana, would blow in his head from the old free life he had known. Then occasionally he would take an opportunity with one of the quite easily available women who surrounded him; knowing as he did so that he would find some relief, which was real, but probably little of that more complex reality, satisfaction.

He had met the woman in Merlin's, a quiet enough bar in Venice; for obscure reasons he sometimes went by the old neighborhood after work.

He was drinking and watching the characters and the muted pickup scene with some amusement, when he saw her. Alone and disdainful, she was overdressed for California; cocktail hats were just still around that year, but the fox fur stole, the shiny black slit skirt, the dark forties-style hair and glistening lips? Wrong bar, lady, he thought, wrong town, as he moved over and offered her a drink.

She turned black eyes wearily up to him and away again declining to reply. He sat down anyhow and lisped,

"Of all the gin-joints in all the towns in all the world . . . ," but she cut him off in irritation.

"Doing your very best Bogart? Come *on*. . . ."

"Okay, here's a proposition. Have a drink with me. All the time we're drinking, I don't do any old movies."

"If you put it like that," she yawned. When the frosted glasses came he raised his and toasted.

"*A la vôtre.*" He had carefully acquired a little French on their trip to Europe. Eyebrows raised, she looked at him with eyes that seemed to see all the way back to Hunter's Point.

"You're cute," she said, her painted lips enunciating carefully, and paused suggestively before finishing, "about as cute as a shithouse rat."

It rocked him for a second, and he racked up points for her as with a barely perceptible pause he continued his approach, for uncharacteristically he was finding her highhandedness and even her aggression perversely exciting. But several daiquiris later it was still uphill work; she repelled him at every turn and unfailingly was as rude as possible. It only increased his determination to have her; he sensed that she would not even bother talking with him if that was not a possibility.

It was after midnight when she went to leave and he followed, finding he was quite drunk. She walked haughtily across the street to an open Porsche, got in and accelerated away quickly, leaving him to scramble along in her wake as best he could, grateful that he had recently rewarded himself by trading in the gutless Eldorado for a Mercedes 280 SL.

After a ride full of incident, when she finally pulled into a wide driveway, it took him a while to realize where they were, outside one of the sensationally opulent houses on La Mesa Drive, one of the older ones as well. He pulled to a halt behind her car and strode over as she climbed out into the darkened driveway. She turned lazily, saying, "What, are you still . . . ," when he caught her arms and pulled her to him hard. She bit his lip but he pressed the point, forcing her against the car, and quickly felt her mouth become hungry and her body writhe against him. He pulled away as she said breathlessly, "Full of vitamins, aren't you?"

"Listen, will you stop fucking around for a minute and ask me in?"

He followed her again, in the darkness, with all around just the impression of a fragrant, spacious garden and the generous proportions of a dignified Spanish-style dwelling. When she let them in the front door still there were no lights. The heavy oak door thudded shut behind them. He was hard, and reaching for her again when he froze. A clicking sound on the polished tiles had told him they were not alone.

There were three of them, standing relaxed and attentive in the shadows. Silent dark silhouettes, small ears, lopped tails. Attack dogs, Dobermans. Ball biters. Her Dobermans.

"What's the matter, don't you like animals?" she taunted.

"Sometimes they don't like me," he muttered.

"Too bad. Because where we go, they go. Come on, if you're coming."

Still there were no lights. Dumbly he followed her across the sprawling living room and up a wide staircase. The dogs stayed at their heels. In the bedroom, in the slashed shafts of streetlight through the Venetian blinds, he saw the dogs squat on their haunches around the big satin-covered bed, dumb acolytes at some arcane ritual, as she fell back on the covers fully clothed. From there she grabbed at his crotch with her right hand, as her left one clawed up the slithering satin of her skirt, jerking it above her waist, then tugging down her panties over the suspender belt and off. He fell to his knees on the bed beside her, clawing at his clothes. He was pushing himself forward on her when she shouted.

"No! No fucking!"

As he hesitated he thought he saw the dog on his left tensing.

"Go down on me, you *bastard*," she growled thickly.

This is crazy, he thought, something in him mutely rebelling, but there was a drunken logic to it all, and dumbly he found himself about to obey. At the last moment he said, "I do it if you do."

She cursed, and he felt her body slithering round on top of the bed beneath him, and then her mouth reaching up to close hungrily over his cock, smearing the shaft with lipstick. In the dark his face lowered forward, and with her fish-net stockings rasping his ears, his tongue went in among the black musk of her curls and he began lapping at her, fast.

After he found what gave her most pleasure, there was little technique. The two of them sucked and bit, licked and gorged like wild animals with a kill. When she came the first time he nearly missed it as she simply stiffened, her legs stretching out straight rigidly. It happened again, more and more frequently. All the while he was aware of the dogs, of what they could see and hear, of what they were smelling. He found it excited him. When quite suddenly he came she took it all, gagging before she swallowed, gulping and then cursing him thickly when it was over, until her glistening mouth, the teeth just sheathed, closed over his half-hard cock again and, as he groaned, she went on.

In the end her stiffenings became less frequent, and then she jerked once more and rolled away, pulling herself from his mouth. Kneeling, Cleaver turned to look at her.

"Oh, get out," she said.

Rage flared in him, and then froze. He fumbled his clothes straight and stood. On the bed she pulled the soiled skirt down and curled up with her back to him. From the door he said softly, "Good night, ladies," but it didn't come out quite right. The dogs were around his feet; they followed him down to the hall, mute accomplices.

Out in the warm night air he stood by his car, trembling and wiping a hand repeatedly across his face. He feared the thing he was now becoming. For the first time in a long while he thought of the old days with the 13. Until, behind the wheel again, his mind turned to excuses for Laura. He felt terrible and swore to himself that this was the last time. But he knew he had made similar resolutions before.

When he got home his wife was asleep, well used to his working late and seeing clients. She was also very tired herself, as with their little girl in school, Laura had gone back to work part time at a nearby medical center.

Cleaver had not been sure how he felt about that, but had made no objections. The second week she had been there, another nurse had been shot and wounded in the parking lot by a junkie after hospital drugs. Laura told him that they all worked with the doors locked when they were alone, and that for the same reason she usually took her lunch with one or another of the doctors, most of whom were younger than Cleaver. He felt uneasy about all of it, but Laura insisted that at this point she needed to get out of the house.

Cleaver was still digesting this when he made a discovery of his own. Early one Sunday morning as he took the garbage out, he noticed a large number of Pam and Liquid Paper aerosols in one of the cans. With a shock he put this together with a TV program he had half-watched on young glue-sniffers, and with the way his son Sam had been acting lately. For long instants, out in the passageway that ran beside the house, Cleaver was paralyzed by conflicting emotions—anger, deep caring, but also a flash of guilty feeling, that he of all people was surely not the one to interfere if someone wanted to go to hell at his own speed. But Sam? At eleven? Cleaver experienced despair. A fresh wave of problems was rising to meet him, and already he felt he lacked the strength to handle them.

Numbly he let himself through from the passageway into the garage and got into the Mercedes and sat behind the wheel for a minute, staring sightlessly at the shrouded shape of a motorcycle under a cover in the corner. After a while, Cleaver knew in himself that his mental impotence would pass, and slowly thinking things out, his confidence grew that the feeling between him and Laura and the boy was strong enough to let them get to grips with the thing. He decided to watch and wait for a while, let himself calm down, and talk it over with Laura.

He left the garage feeling better. But later that morning, he lay in a lounger by the pool after exercising and swimming; and beneath the profound unvarying blue of the sky, the raucous cries of a flock of crows in the eucalyptus trees up on the hill behind the house once again seemed to mock his helplessness. He looked at Laura, blond and tanned, lying with her eyes closed beside him in the sunlight, smiling in the way she did when she dozed. Her slim belly was rising and falling gently, tiny golden hairs catching the light as it did so. He ached to speak to her, but insistent images from the previous night rose to intrude. She had remained only an icon of loveliness to him, distant, unreachable.

Though it had been the weekend, not unusually Cleaver had needed to go in to work that afternoon. When he had walked into his office, someone had been told he was coming and was waiting for him there. A garishly dressed bearded figure slouched in his deep leather armchair and sneered at him from behind black shades. Cannonball, a Louisiania ex-biker and the Judge's messenger, had come for Cleaver. The past flooded back to engulf him.

4

California, 1969

As the 13's third summer together drew to an end, within them and without them the brief sixties dream was fading, and the long sixties hangover had begun.

The best of their friends among the heads had already moved to the country, but only the Dude wanted that life. A rage seemed to grow in the others instead, and with it fear. They could not tell if the terrors looming just behind them as they rode, just behind everything, were only the shadows of themselves and other humans, or powers, forces. . . . Coincidence stalked them, messages seemed waiting for them, always just beyond the circle of their comprehension. And the same thin line between light and dark, luminous freedom and barking madness, they read in the faces of the people, the beautiful people of a few months previous.

Cleaver found it harder and harder to prevent their anger from venting itself among themselves. As *Sgt. Pepper* gave way to the *White Album* and the optimism of the early days was blocked at every turn, all he could fall back on was the knowledge that while they were moving, things were okay. But even that was becoming harder.

Sometimes their anger would be diverted onto a righteous target. They had burned out and run off one of the dealers pushing methedrine to mainline, a mind and body killer that produced the speed freaks who were tearing the underground communities apart. In the aftermath of acid, many heads, caught in the city, all laws and common sense blown away, rushed to speed and scag, frantic to stay high at any price.

But perhaps it was a drug for those days. Speed freaks, like the biker gangs, conformed neatly to the stereotyped notions of a society now running badly scared, so that the counterculture, tolerated before, began to be identified and treated as junkies, criminals and scapegoats for the nation's shame as the Asian war dragged its bloody way onward and downward. In straight minds and on the streets, the margin of freedom where bohemian figures like the 13 could operate was being eaten away to nothing.

Not only were the drugs ceasing to be a liberation and becoming a curse, but they began to know the tyranny of the road, sometimes even secretly began to wish the tarmac perpetually whirling beneath their wheels would let them off. Almost every penny they had that was not tied up with bail bonds went to maintaining their machines, which sometimes seemed no longer tools for freedom but hard masters. Most of them had gone down more than once; Cooch the Mexican limped now and always would, his left leg more than an inch shorter than his right after a horrific high-speed crash that had flung him over an eighteen-wheeler which had then come within inches of crushing him beneath its wheels.

Cleaver himself had spent time in the hospital with a broken collarbone. When the others had visited for the second time he had been moved from one bed to another in the same ward, but they pretended not to see him, with Levon and Leroy capering wildly around the empty bed yelling, "Whooee! He gone. He dead! That bad-ass Cleaver underground. Now we be the Man! Yass!"

But the laughs had gotten fewer as other pleasures had gone sour. It was the time of radical chic, and as underground legends, sometimes the 13 had an entrée to rich and fashionable L.A. parties, where more than once the sick rituals of bondage and abuse, often of very young girl and boy children, disgusted them despite their own free-wheeling ways. Outside on the boulevards, from the storm drains of the city late at night, they would hear the howling of engines as predatory women cruised high-powered machines in search of an anonymous sexual fix, the frustrated revving eerily like the snarl of wild animals in the dark time. It seemed a long way from some of the casual ecstatic fucking of the Human Be-ins and the Haight.

One day late in the summer of 1969 all of them were together in one room. Not sprawled about the well-appointed drawing room of Kemp's family mansion in Carmel, but crushed around the flimsy kitchen table of a crummy rented shack. The hut lay on the edge of the Mexican section of a small southern Californian town, where the sick-sweet smell from the tomato canneries permeated everywhere including the room, mingling there with the thick odor of stale beer and marijuana smoke hanging in the airless space.

They were lying low. Two nights before in a bar they had been using regularly up on Topanga Canyon, a man with Hollywood husband written all over him, and carrying a deer rifle, had walked in and demanded Baby Duane. There was a long moment's silence and then Six had waved with his left hand just before an automatic pistol appeared in his right and he loosed off one unaimed round, blasting the rifle out of the newcomer's hand. Unfortunately the man's trigger finger had gone with it.

They all took the dwarf's skill with a gun for granted by now, so opinion was divided on whether Six had fired too fast and made unnecessary trouble for them, or whether he had saved a life or two. But they did not stay to discuss it. There were several other problems outstanding involving the law, and Cleaver was not about to wait for them to arrive. They had come south and rented the shack from some incurious Mexicans Cooch knew there. The first day they rested up and tinkered with the bikes, but now it was halfway into the following afternoon and they sat in silence in the baking room, a rubble of scattered playing cards, cycle magazines, roaches, beer cans, empty Gallo wine bottles, and fast food containers scattered all around.

Finally Tor, with a Colonel Sanders bucket at his side and both his beard and the table littered with taco shrapnel, belched once and rumbled disgustedly,

"This place, it's a stone drag, man."

"Don't look at me, fatso," Six sneered. "If you're thinking it's down to me that we're stuck in this rat's asshole, forget it. If Romeo here," he said, jerking a thumb at Baby Duane, "had kept his dick in his pants . . ."

"Hey now, man," grinned Duane, "now tell the truth, would you have? I mean we're talking Barbara Blaine here. From now on, even if I live to be a hunnerd, every time a Barbara Blaine movie comes on th' TV, I can tell my grandchildren I *been* there. . . ."

"You fucked up, man," Six cut in. "You got caught, and now we're all of us stuck here in beaner heaven. . . ."

"Eh, hombre . . . ," began Cooch, but Six interrupted,

"Hey, the limping pepper-belly got something to say. But could you make that in English, amigo?" and then leapt back into a half-crouch, his chair crashing over as Cooch lunged across the table with a knife that ended less than six inches from the squat gunman's throat. But Six's right hand was already inside his jacket as he murmured breathlessly,

"How'd you like Mr. Smith and Mr. Wesson to give you a third eye, taco-head?"

"How'd you like me to take those things off you and ream you both new assholes?" Cleaver said loudly. "What is this shit? What are we, a bunch of kids? We don't need that right now. That's right, back off," he went on as the two of them subsided. "What's been done, we can't do nothing about. What we do now, that's what we got to get to."

"Haul ass out of this place, that's for sure," grumbled Tor.

"Listen," said Duane, "I ain't sayin' I done wrong, but I do feel a little bit responsible. So how about this. Why don't y'all do what I been telling you for like years now. Come on down to Badwater. It's a new scene, it'll get us away from the heat, and my people'll look after us real well."

"They look after *us*?" said Leroy ironically, eyes rolling whitely in his black face. "You putting me on. Me and Levon'll get to pick that cotton while you boys set on the porch sippin' them mint juleps. Lawdy, no suh, thank you, boss."

"C'mon, you boys, we're talking about Louisiana here, not 'Bama. You with me, y'all be fine as kind, I tell you," Duane said, his baby blue eyes roving around the table reassuringly. They all liked Duane.

"I did hear Southern cops are kind of spiteful and nasty," said Cleaver doubtfully. "Probably wouldn't take too kindly to us."

"Man, I must have told you about Badwater a thousand times. The whole county's run by one fella, that's Judge Lafayette. The po-lice, everybody, they're all in his pocket. Now he is one strange old party, but it just happens I'm asshole buddies with his second son, Jimmy. We were kids together, we run wild, hunting snakes and gigging frogs and everything. And his sister, Emily," Duane laughed modestly, "well, tell the truth, she's a little bit sweet on me. Now she's a lovely creature, and anything his kids want, and especially *her*, the old man makes sure she gets it. And she'll sure as hell want me and my friends around!" Duane finished, so enthusiastically that they couldn't keep from laughing.

Cleaver said, "But if it's so civilized, we're going to stand out bad." He gestured round the table, as the Dude lit a joint before returning to the paper he was doodling a sketch on. "A bunch of longhair dopers, dirty and degenerate, that's really got to bug them."

"Man, you think we got no bikers down there? Listen, right in Badwater there's a bike gang, and they are *heavy*. They call themselves the Mothertruckers, and I tell you even the cops walk soft around them. 'Cause just for one thing, their president is the Judge's eldest son, Cal Lafayette. He's—a little weird. But what I'm saying is, there's no way we gonna be the maximum social deviants down there—that position is already filled."

"Yeah, and if they bikers, maybe we can get to dragging for beers with 'em," said Bob the mechanic, "pick up a little change." Dance the ace rider nodded his agreement.

"Just so's you smile real polite while you're doing it," said Duane dubiously.

"Hell," said Krass, "we got the equipment. But it seems like we haven't been going anywhere with it for a while." A joint reached him and he took a heavy hit, and holding the smoke down, gasped out, "No . . . direction."

"Direction, my ass," growled Tor, emptying a can of Bud and crushing it in his fist. "Let's just get out there and do it. I'm for it."

"What do you think, Dude?" Cleaver asked.

The skeletal figure straightened, and wordlessly shoved the drawing he had been doing into the middle of the table. They saw he had sketched an elaborately ornamented old-fashioned carousel. But instead of wooden horses, motorcycles were fixed in place, with four or five of the 13 recognizably crouched astride them, as the wheel went round and round, going nowhere.

Surprisingly, it was Dance who took exception.

"Listen man, what's so special about you? You're stuck there, same as us. You do your thing with silver, you draw a little bit, you fool around with the fiddle, but what do you finish, man, what do you ever do for real?"

"*Real?*" said the Dude.

But Cleaver was looking at the drawing and nodding reluctantly.

"Maybe we have been going in circles a little bit," he said. And thought, but it can't go on much longer. They were falling apart—not only the rage in all of them just below the surface, Six and the Mexican scrapping, but Kemp silent and detached off to one side, paying more mind to dealing, and Dance with his professional riding. If Cleaver was going to stop the disintegration, he did need a direction, and maybe also a little pressure from outside. Suddenly he realized how fiercely he wanted them to be at least once more as they had been before, all together and going good, with him at the front.

"I dunno," Six was muttering, "it's an awful long way. Who needs the hassle?"

"Ever since you shot that dude's finger off we got hassles right here," said Cleaver harshly. "But you're right—it's always easier to be a big man on your own turf, isn't it? What do you say, Cooch, you up for a little freeway boogie?"

"*Embalao*," said the Mexican, showing white teeth as he grinned. "Like a bullet."

"Listen," said Six angrily as they laughed, "anything the beaner can do, I can do."

"So you're on," said Cleaver. "Everyone else?" He looked around and found no objections. "Okay then. It's me, Six and Duane they're looking for right now, so we'll put our scoots on Kemp's truck, which is clean, and go that way. The rest of you ride in twos and threes, and we'll meet up somewhere every night." He could see the enthusiasm growing in them at the prospect of the long ride to unfamiliar country. "Hell," he said, "it feels right, so let's do it."

But he turned once more to the end of the table and said, "Dude?"

The cadaverous figure shrugged once and after a silence said,

"Whatever goes down—it'll have gone down before."

There was a further minute's uneasy silence, and at that moment some of them felt the coincidences that stalked them coming closer, the forces behind them take a deep breath.

Then Krass broke it as he laughed.

"Hey man, you from another garage, you know that? Like Robert Johnson said, *Oh baby, Baby don't you want to go?* Chicago, Badwater, what the fuck. Let's get it on."

5

Badwater, Louisiana, 1969

Judge André Lafayette sat and watched the sun sink over his land. The fiery colors of the sunset, interrupted by a single mare's-tail of motionless smoke, deepened the green-black darkness across the river, where his fields merged into the bayou.

The fragrance of nearby wisteria came to him. Another man might have welcomed the relief that the September night, though still sweltering, would bring from the burning day. Or taken pride in the two-story colonnaded mansion behind him, the thousands of plantation acres stretching away from it on all sides, all his. But the old man had schooled himself to indifference to both his body and his material fortunes. His passions were less tangible. But they did reside in Badwater County.

He had come there from New Orleans in the twenties after his father had died, the younger son of a society family whose fortune increasingly failed to match their pretensions. He had inherited a small, run-down plantation in Badwater largely because no one else in the family wanted it.

A passionate Catholic in his youth, he had lost his faith early, but not its underlying assumptions of order and purpose in the scheme of things. It was not reason that had made him doubt God—indeed he bitterly distrusted the Enlightenment and all its works; but a sense of the degeneracy of the church, its absence of fervor. Then he came to Badwater and saw the brutalization of the backwater people's life, the poverty and cruel exploitation of poor whites and, in their turn, blacks, who still had to step off the sidewalk into the mud if a white man approached, and take their orders to the back door of the town's stores. His reaction had been neither a liberal's call to arms, an aesthete's revulsion nor a reactionary's secret satisfaction. Because when Lafayette saw pain and evil face to face as an everyday occurrence, he saw hierarchy and an ineffable purpose, and he believed that here he could begin to live, and, in contrast to the lazy city he was leaving behind, to become hard, joyfully hard. And at the bottom of his satisfaction was a profound and instinctive love, inherited perhaps from French forebears, a great love not of the southern way of life but deeper, of the rich earth itself.

A short, dark-complexioned, delicate youth, he had had many obstacles to overcome: the locals' suspicion and contempt for him as an outlander, his own commercial and agricultural inexperience, his squeamishness, his fear of horses, of women. He had single-mindedly schooled himself to surmount these things. Through long years in the traditional plantation office there at Beau Mont he had patiently learned cotton and rice, learned to oversee his acres effectively and to increase them judiciously when neighbors failed; had come to dance with grace, to ride hard and, when occasion called for it, to fight harder. For though it had been between the wars, once he had emerged successfully from a duel with pistols.

But he never lost his deep and well-concealed contempt for what he considered these archaic forms, however high the esteem which the mastering of them had brought him in the eyes of the local gentry. These proud ones were lost in the rural southern dream and its codes and principles, the conventions that the Judge perceived unwaveringly as shallow, sentimental, and ephemeral, though he honored the straight thinking and endurance that sometimes dwelt beneath them. To the poor people, as their landlord and, at length, their Judge, he was unvaryingly hard but fair, and thus never loved by them, but profoundly respected.

In only one instance did the Judge vary his silent contempt for the South, and that was in the person of his wife, Louisa, a fair-haired, high-spirited innocent; in her alone the sweetness of the land and its life worked their soft magic on him. It was true that marriage into her well-connected and influential family had consolidated his power in the county once and for all, and could have opened doors to much wider fields of achievement, on a state or even national level, had his ambition tended in those directions. It was as an alliance of this sort that the match was viewed by the watchful neighborhood, accustomed to Lafayette's indifference to the pleasures of both flesh and human society.

But they were in error. No ambitions wider than the mastery of Badwater disclosed themselves, though it was at this comparatively late stage that he took a new direction, pursuing studies in the state's unique and complex Roman-based law and rapidly qualifying as an attorney, the first step on the road to his ultimate position as Judge. It was as if his new love had released a fresh energy in him. For André at thirty-five, courting the twenty-year-old Louisa, winning her, living with her, was the fullness of life itself; almost in spite of himself he felt his heart unfold and his spirit expand, as he watched her gradually transform and soften the previously functional plantation homestead of Beau Mont, filling it with flowers from the formal gardens with their brick terraces that she had designed and commissioned to be laid out, and laying a cross of rowan wood over the threshold of the house, signifying a refuge. For he indulged Louisa's faith in the same silence with which he met his neighbor's ways but with none of the underlying contempt, though with no shred of concurrence on his part; it was one limitation of their intimacy that she was rarely privy to his mind.

The transformation of Beau Mont was completed by the arrival of their children, the two boys, Cal and James, after the end of the war, and then a late bloom, their daughter, Emily. Cal had been a difficult, near-fatal birth for Louisa, and there was a sense on all sides that the Judge, on an instinctive level, never forgave him for nearly killing his mother. James had presented no problems. But Louisa, always delicate, was in her mid-thirties when the girl was conceived. She was advised against having the child, but chose to ignore this, and was supported by the Judge in her decision; approaching fifty now, he keenly anticipated the new baby. In the event, only the little girl had survived.

The death of his wife had come as a hammer blow to the Judge, and he reacted at first by turning inward and isolating himself still further from the world. His eldest son, Cal, already a difficult, pale, nervous child, and now further unstrung by the loss of his mother, was dispatched immediately to a military academy, which proceeded to wreak final havoc on his character. James, the younger, was luckier. He was allowed to stay at Beau Mont, kept from his father's way in the care of two devoted retainers, the black steward, George Washington Brooks, and the housekeeper, a local widow with a son of James's age named Duane. The boys ran over the land together, and the Judge became accustomed to their presence on the periphery of his world, and so failed to implement his original intention of sending James away as soon as he was old enough. G.W. Brooks loved and guided both the lads, for the Judge's attention really centered on his little daughter, in whom as she grew he fancied he detected a thousand likenesses to her mother, and who, like Louisa, came to represent life itself to him in the midst of a barren desolation.

Yet even she did not touch that cold solitary chamber of his thought, which already had been kept apart from her mother. In business and in court, his dealings became capricious, sometimes savage, sometimes whimsical, but always with an internal logic that colleagues and competitors, court and prisoner alike, felt, sensed, even if they were unable to fathom it. The Judge's application of the law was so rigorous that it became a mockery of the law itself. At first sight apparently nihilism, it was in fact the opposite; a triumphant affirmation of self, as he felt himself become the channel for a deeper law.

This unpredictable directness, together with his power and solitude, made Judge Lafayette a much-feared figure. But to be held in awe, or even to feel the satisfaction in the effective exercise of power, was not his purpose. For after the death of his wife, he had begun increasingly to sense a greater test of the qualities he had developed, a test yet to come. Something was going to rise, as if from the flat metallic surface, dead and still, of the bayou itself. He never once doubted it would come.

A source of strength to him in these difficult years was Rampike, his Sheriff. Like the Judge, Harlan Rampike was an outsider. He had drifted into the county unobtrusively in the years just after the war, a short, spare man, seldom speaking, but when he did so, disclosing a soft Virginian drawl. Years later a story filtered into town, of moonshine business to the north, and a man left dead. But by then Rampike was part of Badwater, if never quite one of them. He had gone to work at the town's garage, and quickly shown outstanding skills both under the hood and behind the wheel of an auto. It was the start of the fifties, the time of the automobile explosion throughout the Southern poor. Soon news of the Virginian's skills spread, and he was able to set up on his own, taking the bulk of the old service station's custom with him and ultimately closing it out. His outstanding driving skills made some of the local boys suggest that he enter the auto races at the Shreveport fall state fair or even events for NASCAR, the premier Southern auto racing circuit. The way he promptly turned down the idea suggested to one or two of the brighter boys that if he had gone, he might have risked recognition from previous appearances in another life.

But there was ample exercise for his skills right there in Badwater, where every kind of mayhem and madness had taken to wheels, while the aging Sheriff's department was still geared to the pace of bloodhounds. The Judge was aware of the situation and he knew of Rampike's capabilities, as he knew of everything that came about in the county. It was he who suggested this unlikely new candidate for Sheriff (which in Badwater was tantamount to ensuring his election), and he who persuaded Rampike to accept. The Sheriff's dogs stayed, but took a back seat. And Rampike, lacking a home, a land and a family, quickly developed an unshakeable loyalty to the Judge.

This led him to carry out his new duties with rigor. In pursuit, he drove only one way, flat out, on blacktop, dirt, or gravel; fences, ditches, banks, even bodies of water provided no obstacle to him. Many of the country boys he was chasing drove the same way, but as he observed dryly on one of the few occasions he could be persuaded to speak about it, "All most of these fellers know is the steering wheel and the loud button," while Rampike, who built his own cars from the ground up, knew exactly what was involved every step of the way until the moment he ran his quarry into the ground. The sound of his rumbling Chevies became as familiar around the country as the sight of his battered old sweat-stained brown felt hat.

He never lost a man. And the uncompromising approach went beyond automobiles, though he was far from being foolish enough to believe he could dominate a rural county by strong-arm tactics. Mostly, wisely, he relied, like the Judge, on an awesome reputation, coupled with the widest personal knowledge and contacts—so that a word in the ear of a parent or friend would sometimes forestall a potential lawbreaker before anything had happened. But then one day in the heavy spring rains, a young fugitive in a stolen car held up the store in Badwater, shooting the storekeeper's wife. Less than an hour after Rampike had lit out after the kid's Buick, the people of the town saw the Sheriff's car return, with the bullet-riddled corpse of his quarry lashed face forward like a dead deer over the hood, his blood drying, hardened on the hot metal before the rain could wash it away. From then on, no one doubted that he could and would do what he had to do. To most it appeared that he lost no sleep over the killing; only the Judge, who talked him through it later, knew his Sheriff for the decent, troubled, far from simple man that he was.

As the sixties began, a new complication entered Rampike's life, for one of his regular duties now was arresting the Judge's son Cal. The latter, ejected from the military academy and then from college, had returned to run wild in the county, gathering a pack of lowlifes and motorcycle bums around him. Seldom at home, he often wound up in the town jail. While rich boys were no stranger to Rampike, who knew how to pedal soft with them (after which the Judge's sentences would often come as a surprise to them and their families), this was different. It was not just the personal involvement with his friend and patron, but the stories that were whispered about Cal—

bad stories, even for an area and a Sheriff well used to the violent, twisted results of hard-poor existence—stories to make you swallow hard, make your scalp crawl. But none of it could ever be proved. And the Judge did nothing.

On the porch the Judge looked up at the dust trail crossing the bridge before his gate, and the unmistakeable muted rumble of his Sheriff's automobile approaching. He saluted Rampike as he emerged, and the short Sheriff came up the steps to him, battered hat in hand.

"Drink, Harlan?" asked the Judge, and when the Sheriff ducked his head, with no further instruction a black servant poured bourbon and branch before retiring into the house, closing the porch doors behind him. Rampike was slightly surprised to notice that the Judge, also, a normally abstemious man, had a half-full cut glass tumbler of bourbon at his elbow.

"Thought I'd come by, Judge," said Rampike, after a sip and a satisfied sigh. "Probably nothing. But Duane Watts is home to his mother's with a bunch of boys on motorsickles, from California. . . ."

"I know," said the Judge. "My boy James has gone over there now with Emily to see Duane. Why, is there something wrong about that?"

"Nothing I know about," said Rampike. "Being they're friends of Duane's, I'd guess they're pretty much okay. But you know we got the Labor Day weekend coming up. And seems like these fellers are going to meet your boy Cal and his friends out to the Black bayou, and drag their sickles and party down, which I can't help but believe will mean some kind of trouble."

"And you want me to tell you to stop it?" queried the Judge, raising his glass and his eyebrows. "But you know, sadly, how little influence I have with Cal now."

Only you ain't really so sad about it, are you? thought Rampike. What is it? The kid acting out the old man's bad side for him? Or the kid pulling all this stuff just to get his daddy to look his way? That happens, I do know. Or what?

"I know that he spends his time with trash now—yes, *trash*," the Judge repeated, relishing the dismissive epithet. French having been his first tongue, he still occasionally enjoyed American turns of phrase, which resonated for him as a foreign language would. America the visceral, he thought, the language often so clumsy when it attempted logic and progression, nevertheless effortlessly conveying more basic truths.

"But because they are capable, Cal's friends, and yes, probably these other boys too, capable of all the bad things—that's precisely why I look for good from them! Or rather, for something else. Something more real. 'For all things have been blessed in the well of eternity, and are beyond good and evil.'"

Rampike's lips twitched fractionally, and thumbing the brim of his old hat slowly round and round, he muttered, "Hope you're right there, Judge. But can I ask you one question? If, like I've heard you say so many times, you think politics stink, and the law's a piece of dirt, and right and wrong jest tales to scare kids with—then how come you're up there anyhow, judging away?"

"How do I know it's right? Because it feels right. After all, I *am* the Judge. It's me being me," he chuckled. As he did so, Rampike had a flash of memory; under the harsh lights of the jail, Cal Lafayette, head lolling, the front of his white T-shirt covered in blood, mumbling, "Why did I do it? 'Cause it felt right, man. Like m'daddy always says—you got to live in the now. But I'm a bad boy—oh yes—I am a bad boy. . . ."

"No, Harlan," the Judge was saying, "I judge because— thus was it always so. Masters rule. The rooster in the yard, the boss in the fields, the man with the woman, the master in his house. When they begin to doubt their right to do so—it's the moment when things fall apart. And if all that sounds self-serving and cynical, you know me to be neither of those things. It is only when you recognize these kinds of truth that you can begin to look for an alternative to them, begin to consider becoming someone, some thing, in which your *contempt*"—he spat out the word—"for both modern mediocrity and the eternal pettiness of the majority can be absorbed. So when I judge, you see," he smiled, "I . . . finger forward . . . toward me.

"And if I am doing that, so I believe is my son Cal. So don't think in terms of his *going wrong*. Try to think of what he may be going *toward*. I feel it may be . . . something extraordinary.

"That's what it is with Badwater, with the country, d'you see, Harlan? Its secret, its magic—that it's so close to nature. And the penalty; that it's as unjust, in human terms, as nature herself. But there is a wild justice. . . ."

Rampike, nodding doubtfully, thought, you say it, but could you live with it, my friend? Suffer that injustice you talk about, yourself?

There they let it rest. But the question concerning his position had worried the Judge, or rather the fact of Rampike's asking it. For his secret fear had always been that his contempt would run in reverse, that men would see his own moral—pragmatism at least, possibly unsoundness—as clearly as he saw theirs.

How could I look for him to do something about Cal, thought Rampike, shaking his head. There is a man so tied up in himself, and his picture of himself, that he don't even rightly *see* his kids—just feels them, feels his love and need for them, every once in a while. Meantime, it's down to us chickens. As they spoke of other things, Rampike decided he'd better be there on Saturday, him and the Smuckers and maybe Otis, round that Black bayou, with their heads down and their eyes wide open. Just in case.

As he left, the Judge looked down at his slight figure climbing behind the wheel and felt a wave of concern and affection for the man. He worried about Rampike. He wished the Sheriff had got himself a woman. Didn't seem to have normal needs in that respect. Carburetors perhaps fulfilled that function for him. But then again, neither do I, thought the Judge. Except that I do. I have my princess, my Emily.

A few miles away, beneath the trees behind a crooked, weather-bleached wooden house, as evening fell, the 13 lay in the weedy late-summer grass of Baby Duane's yard and let the peace and stillness soak over them. They were bone tired from the run to the South, but it had been a trip, a right-on trip, unreal, exhilarating, full of insights, slightly scary, and in the end it had leapt them feeling good.

From the west Texas border they had been stopped, hassled, their long hair and bikes gawked and jeered at, had hurt their bellies with truck-stop cooking and coffee and their butts with being too long in the saddle, as they bored on through in small groups, taking care to follow Duane's instructions—stay out of this town, ride around that one! Over the border in Louisiana they had only been shot at once, a half-hearted ɹ .nk with a .22 that had still sobered them enough so that the next day they left the cheap motel early in the misty chill just after sunup, and all together for the last leg rode through, pulling to a halt at the little house that afternoon, where Duane had leapt off his machine, and as the porch door opened hesistantly, had run to scoop his mother up in his arms.

Now they lay around under the trees with a square bottle of bourbon slowly circulating. It was good to stop, but even better, they felt welcome. This was not just due to the cooking smells coming from the little house where Duane's mother was laboring on a feast for them. Soon after they had arrived, though their bikes were parked discreetly behind the house where the mechanics Bob and Ariel had started in on some adjustments and oil changes, people had begun to drop by— buddies of Duane's, and then a rider from the Truckers, Cal Lafayette's bad-ass club. Massive and bearded, he had given them the hard eye, particularly Levon and Leroy, and they stared back at him and his long chopped Harley Sportster with its hard-tail and six-inch overs at the kicked-out front end. "My meat," Dance the racer had muttered, but the guy had simply hailed Duane and asked them all over to party down for Labor Day at the weekend, before he rode away.

Then the Judge's black servant, George Washington Brooks, had arrived with his son, and Levon and Leroy, after five minutes playing the city slickers to these country bumpkins, unwound in relief and made new friends. And as the afternoon sun reddened and the sweltering day drew in, a long white Cadillac convertible pulled over and two good-looking young people emerged, both fair-haired, pale and cool-looking in light summer clothes. The blond-haired girl smiled hesitantly and blushed at their scrutiny, but Duane ran to the young man and they embraced, whooping. Then Duane intro-

duced his friend James, the Judge's younger son, and James's
sister, Emily.

The 13 were entranced by the girl, obviously shy, but
open, as she shook their hands, exchanging a soft word in a
low and delightfully Southern-accented voice with each of
them in turn. Only Six, sprawling obese and a little drunk next
to Tor on the porch swing, as Emily with her back to him bent
forward to smile with Cooch, groaned, "Oh baby, let's see what
you got," at which Tor, without looking, casually short-armed
him rather hard in the ribs and stared him down when he got
his wind back. By then Emily was strolling off under the trees
with Duane.

The guys weren't so sure about Jimmy, with his slight
plumpness and his fancy car and clothes, but he won them
round with a series of gently droll tales of him and Duane as
kids, backed up by G.W. Brooks. But mostly, as with the other
people they had met at Duane's, what they liked was the sense
that the man was pleased and interested to see them and hear
what they had to say and tell. When Tor, speaking of the trip
down and the way a long bike run made them feel, said, "The
land's right there at your elbows, rolling by,"

Jimmy replied, "Man, I know what you mean," and rich
boy or not, they believed that he did. From then on Jimmy and
Tor in fact established an unlikely rapport, sitting close
throughout the evening.

Then, as it grew dark, Duane's mother bustled out on the
porch and hollered, "You boys help get the trestles set up now.
James Lafayette, go hunt your sister and that son of mine for
supper."

"Did she say *supper?*" cried Krass, falling to his knees and
raising clasped hands to the dark sky. "Like, *food?* Holy Moley,
I don't believe what I just heard. My *stomach* can't believe it. My
stomach thinks my throat's been cut. Oh, let it not be nothing
but a beautiful dream. . . ."

"Come on, wise guy," said Cleaver, hauling him to his feet.
"You're tall, so get these lamps up in the trees." As the long
table was put together, Cleaver heard the Dude mutter,

"Our very own, genuine Last Supper. The real thing,
baby!"

Quickly they set out benches and sat, and the food began to arrive. Duane's mother had had some warning of their coming and had killed the fatted calf, almost literally, only the calf had been a hog and half a dozen fowl. There was gumbo and prawns, reed birds and a sugar-cured ham, fried chicken, ribs, redeye gravy, field peas and bacon, hash browns, collard greens, yams, corn bread, pecan pie, watermelon and sugar cane, washed down with liquor, either red (more bourbon) or white, Mason jars of corn, colorless and potent. The meal rambled on, their voices ringing in the night beneath the gently shifting shadows of the trees and the swaying lamps with their blurred frieze of insects, laughter rolling out to be lost in the dark silent fields all around.

When they had eaten, the last morsel of pie consumed and the last cup of fragrant coffee from the big pot drained, G.W. Brooks and his son Lester hesitantly produced a well-used guitar and banjo from old sacks. Seeing the instruments, the Dude whooped "'He carried his guitar in a gunnysack,'" and ran to unship his own twelve-string bottleneck as Lester picked up the cue and launched into a curiously lazy "Johnny B. Goode." The others subsided onto the porch swing or the long grass under the trees again as the vibrant music, hard as steel or soft as silk, rang out around the circle of the yard. The gleaming faces of the blacks, and the Dude's spare silhouette clad in black and white and hunched over his swelling instrument, were picked out by the light of the lamps and a small fire. The Dude rarely took his eyes off Emily Lafayette as she leaned comfortably against Duane. They fell to playing the Robert Johnson songs that the Dude had coached them to love, and the riders heard them as if for the first time there in the country that gave birth to them, heard them for the life-giving forms that they were, full of secret resonance, the brash rolling tunes with the beat of life like the fire itself keeping the encircling fear and loneliness from their tenuous ring, and the blues letting out the pain and misery, letting it return by mysterious filaments, root, stalk, spiderweb, to the dark earth surrounding them.

And more: in the music, they began to feel all the long roads that had wound to that place, that crossroads, that grove of trees, that night; the endlessly various passages of time and fortune that had pushed their forebears, miner, sailor, dirt farmer, cowboy, slave, all the trials and sorrows as their families had crossed and recrossed the vast web of woods and water, mountain range and plain and tarmac road that was America, and spun them together inside this fragile circle that the food and the fire and the friendship, the music and the stillness, so briefly created. And for the young ones there was something further: black and white, rich and poor, as the bright music flowed they felt part of a wave that was moving in the world, an idea whose time might still have come; they felt hope—that with their love, energy, music and humor they could beat back the darkness and yet still retain the best of the old, because the best of the old—this crooked wooden house, these trees, the fields around, this kind, tired woman—were the roots which they worked from.

Cleaver was lying next to Duane. Sometime after midnight, a three-quarter harvest moon rose above the trees, and as they listened to Dude teasing out the long mournful notes of "Love in Vain," the southern boy leaned over to Cleaver and said softly, "Now you see why I do get to feeling homesick once in a while?"

"Yeah," Cleaver murmured, "I can see how you might."

In the week that followed, with nothing said on either side, the 13 found themselves helping out around Duane's mother's place. They did chores and ran errands, repaired ailing farm machinery and pulled stumps; Tor chopped wood as the Dude and Kemp cut back her honeysuckle and roses, and even Six went hunting with Duane. The twins helped out in her few acres, and at the end of one long afternoon, Levon, stripped to the waist and glistening, sweating like a plow horse, straightened with a groan and sighed, "Oh, darkies, don't your heart grow weary?"

"I *knew* it end this way," Leroy commiserated. Cleaver and Kemp were passing and Cleaver called across the crop, "Why look at them laughing niggers. Don't fret boys, tomorrow's Saturday. We go fishing with Duane. . . ."

"And then go visit with them Mother fuckers and get a

little high . . . ," Kemp began, but then they all fell silent as along the road, bordering the patch, they heard the far-off rumble of a powerful engine and saw the Sheriff's '65 Super Sports pull steadily toward them, then slow and halt.

"Smile and comb your hair," muttered Krass.

As the road dust settled, the rear window lowered to reveal a short, elderly man in a linen jacket, with white hair, a trim gray mustache and penetrating dark eyes.

"Here come de judge?" muttered Leroy.

"Well, it ain't Colonel Sanders," Cleaver grunted, "and that cat with him's not the laughing gnome," as on the far side of the ditch, the Sheriff climbed out and gestured them over. Duane was indoors with his mother, but the others drifted toward the road in the dusty afternoon haze, as the older man spoke.

"You're Cleaver?"

Cleaver nodded once, unsurprised—Jimmy would have described him—and replied, "Sir."

The Judge stared at him for long moments, then went on in a level voice.

"And you and your friends are enjoying your stay with us here in Badwater?"

"I reckon," said Cleaver, and then he thought, what the hell, grinned and went on, gesturing, "'Course, most of us ain't used to field work. But the grub's real good."

The Sheriff, squinting from beneath his battered brown hat, now spoke up.

"Come Saturday, which of you boys are racing with them Truckers?"

Dance had wandered over, and half-raised his hand.

"You go on dirt much before?" said Rampike.

"Some," said Dance. Kemp started to say, "You bet he has—long-track, short-track . . . ," but a look from Cleaver silenced him at the same time as he realized that revealing the presence of a semi-pro, even one who raced under another name, would do nothing for the odds. The Sheriff had blinked once, as if his eyes were photographing the snippet of information. Speaking to Dance again, he said, "You like it? The dirt?"

"Love it. I've gone on everything, grass, road, circuits,

drag strips, but dirt's the one. It's always . . . different. Different from place to place, or the same place even but different weather or time of day. Plus it kind of keeps the assholes away."

Rampike ducked his head once, nodding.

"Sounds like how it was with the autos. Racing you used to have to do it all ways—dirt cars, stock cars, midgets, sprint cars, you name it. And they were about ten times heavier and harder to drive than now? You got to be stronger'n a mule to drive them old machines with the skinny tires. But you got a lot more feel of the machine, on the dirt."

Dance nodded; they understood each other. The Judge had been watching carefully. Now he said, a touch dryly, "Yes, in these parts, they have always appreciated a good race. Well, I wish you luck. Tell me, are you all planning to remain in Badwater for long after Labor Day?"

Cleaver stayed silent for long moments, until they had all noticed and began to feel uncomfortable. Then looking up deliberately to meet the Judge's eyes, he said,

"Might. Can't tell . . ."

The Sheriff began to speak in a low voice, close to a growl, "Now, boy . . . ," but the Judge cut him off with a wave of the hand.

"Harlan, Harlan, it's a free country. Is that not so, Cleaver?"

"Well—yeah. We're for freedom. And the people," Cleaver found himself saying.

"Rebels, eh?" said the Judge with a slight smile. "But you know, I have always agreed with the description of rebellion as merely the nobility of *slaves*. Yet in some terms, you consider yourself also an elite. The best riders. The fastest. Curious.

"But no—here especially, many have come from elsewhere and made their home. It has been home for Negroes," he said, nodding at Levon and Leroy, "for Acadians—the Cajuns, you know, further to the south—and also always for many of your *compadres*," he gestured to Cooch the Mexican. "Did you know that not far from here began and ended *el Camino Real*, the Aztec's royal road to Mexico City? Then of course there are the Creoles, my own ancestors, the French. So why should we not welcome strangers? As long, of course, as they are friends of our friends, like yourselves. And as long as they remain so."

With that, after a brief silence, as if with one accord the Judge's window went up and Rampike slid behind the wheel, wriggled once to accommodate his pistol holster, brought the engine to rumbling life and pulled away down the dusty road.

They stood in silence. It was awhile before Krass, standing at Cleaver's elbow, murmured, "Well. Now we been told."

"Yeah," said Cleaver. "But what?" He felt an inexplicable heaviness descending on him, and to shake it off turned to Dance and his mechanic, Bob, and said, "How about this race deal, anyhow? We come all this way, you better not fuck up now."

"No problem," said Bob. "Duane showed us where they run, and Dance's got it all up here," he grinned, tapping his forehead. They were all familiar with the racer's phenomenal memory, which together with exceptional eyesight made up a large part of his edge.

"We'll run my Harley hard-tail," Bob went on. "The tires'll do as they are—only thing to work on is the jetting and gearing." The red-haired mechanic grinned and put an arm round the taut-faced racer's shoulder. "Nothing to it."

Cleaver nodded and turned away. In the distance across the field, Duane was coming over the plow to call them home. Behind him in the west a fiery sun sank toward the rim of the hot earth, going under. Cleaver shivered once, and then started for the cabin.

6

Badwater, Louisiana, 1969

"You won't find that island on any chart."
—*King Kong* (1932)

"For I have sworn thee fair, and thought thee
    bright
Who art as black as hell, as dark as night."
—*Sonnet 147*, William Shakespeare

The noise was deafening. Out of the dark, from a dozen or more big speakers strung in the moss-draped trees, the Airplane screamed, "WE'RE VOLUNTEERS OF AMERICA, VOLUNTEERS OF AMERICAAA. . . ."

"Right . . . fuckin' . . . on . . . ," mumbled Kemp, weaving under the power of one of his own pills. He had handed them out to anyone who wanted them, which had meant some of the 13 but most of the Truckers.

Acrid smoke drifted over him. By firelight he focused on a group of riders clustered round the barbecue pit. The figures were all lit up weirdly, which could have been from the random colored lights and strobes mounted in the trees exploding continuously. Except that round each of their heads Kemp perceived a faintly luminous green wash, as if a child had smeared weak watercolor on a photograph. With all his drug experience, Kemp had only ever seen that one on record sleeves before.

"Strong fucking shit," thought Kemp.

The Truckers were stooping, hacking lumps off the half-cooked pig in the pit with hunting knives. They ignored two figures rolling around fiercely on the ground next to them, cutting at each other with the same big knives.

"Bad neighborhood," Kemp mumbled sagely to himself.

Lights and shadows from the trees shot at his eyes, washed over his body, stretching and elongating his own shadow weirdly in his own sight.

He was on an island in the bayou, over four hundred yards long but no more than about a hundred yards wide at its broadest point. Only a narrow dirt causeway stretching from the middle of the island connected it to the road, across the flat dark monochrome sheet of swamp water. No power or telephone lines ran along this causeway, and in gaps in the music, the thump of the generator that powered the speakers and the lights could be heard. On the surface of the bayou were reflected the winking lights of the deputies' cars drawn up along the road to Badwater.

"Pigs to the right of me, bad-asses to the left of me," Kemp caroled. He had hazy recollections of large numbers of the Truckers, at least forty, probably more like fifty, thundering over the causeway with them as dusk fell. There had been a few rough-looking women with them.

"Certified mean-looking dudes, them Truckers," he thought, more like river rats than a bike gang; an eye patch, missing digits, the flash of gold teeth and earrings, beads and tattoos, scarred faces and arms, some with striped seamen's sweaters under their colors, bandanas securing ratty tangled long hair, and always the big knives. Some had the swarthy features that Duane had told them indicated part Caddo Indian or Mexican blood, but as Levon and Leroy were acutely aware, there had been no blacks of either sex. Also many of them openly hauled pump guns and carbines in leather saddle-boots slung on their Harleys, as well as handguns in body harnesses under their colors. Of the 13, only Six was carrying.

And the Truckers' mood was uncertain, to say the least.

Dance had won the big race and taken a stack of folding money off them, and when one of them had tried to save face by bad-mouthing the 13's foreign bikes, the BSAs and Triumphs, the Dude had modestly suggested trying his twenty-year-old English Black Shadow against the guy's near new Sportster over a quarter of a mile of road, and proceeded to blow him into the weeds. More money had changed hands as Kemp whistled, "What made Milwaukee famous made a loser out of you," and none of it had done anything to sweeten the Truckers' mood.

Kemp looked around again. About fifty yards from him in the center of the island was the brightly lit clubhouse, a large hut of rotting timber with a moss-covered shingle roof, sur-rounded by a ten-foot-high chain-link storm fence topped by three strands of barbed wire, with a single gate set in the front of it. Fountains of light fanned from the cabin's door, from chinks in the walls and the crooked shutters; for Kemp the illumination, seen through the grid of the chain-link fence, was like slow-motion fireworks. "Fuckin' stuff," he muttered, shak-ing his head almost irritably, and focusing on the figure out-lined in the blaze of the doorway.

"Yeah, like, Lucifer," he thought. That Cal Lafayette.

The short, sturdy figure of Cal had been waiting for them at the clubhouse as the pack of Truckers and the 13 had thun-dered in, the Truckers flinging themselves off their machines and onto the cases of beer piled as high as a man, and the boxes of white liquor in plastic jugs. Cal had not come to the bike race, as if he had guessed the outcome and avoided being associated with the defeat.

Flanked by Cannonball, a massive limping lieutenant with a wide-brimmed leather hat and a heavy walking cane, Cal stared at the 13 as they climbed off and took in the scene, the tumbledown shack with a limp club flag up a hand-hewn pole, the darkening melancholy island dotted with moss-covered trees, with a cluster of decrepit sheds hung with nets and skin-ning frames off at one end, and the big noisy pack of angry bikers making ready to get mad drunk as the night came on.

The face of the Judge's son had seemed somehow twisted, the thick, curled lips echoed by the meanders of black hair that fell over his swarthy forehead and over thick eyebrows into the piercing dark eyes he shared with his father. He had taken them all in with a long, expressionless glance, then waited as Cleaver came toward him, and abruptly stepped forward and embraced him wordlessly, in a way that seemed to have as much violence as welcome about it. Then he had turned rapidly on his heel and, still without speaking, had strode rapidly back into the clubhouse with Cannonball at his side. Within seconds the weird light and deafening metal music flooded the island.

Now Kemp twitched as with a pulverizing heart-stopping crash the music lurched into the pile-driving marching beat of "Purple Haze." Yeah—*Purple Haze,* like the smeary light on their faces! Something about Hendrix's sinuous guitar coupled with the song's primal rhythm set a tickle and then an ache going in Kemp's crotch. Have to go hunt some pussy, he thought, nodding again, casting his head about, eyes jammed wide open. The mill of shouting riders by the fire was growing loud, loud enough to be heard above the music. He flashed on the roadblock, the weapons, how they were outnumbered. "A bad fucking neighborhood," he thought solemnly again, and giggled helplessly.

In the shifting orange light he made out some of the 13; Tor's massive bulk swaying gently with a beer can in each hand, the squat shape of Six poised in an ominous forward crouch—he'd done a tab of whatever it was Kemp had—and a little way off the taut silhouette of Cleaver, with Krass looming tall at his side. Number one and number fucking two, thought Kemp. My brothers. Well, maybe. Sometimes they even forgot about his folk's money. Sometimes he even did himself. But feeling the uncontrollable surge of his drug-soaked senses, he thought that when you got as close to the edge as this, you were always out on your own.

His balls still ached. He turned and crept, stooping through the shards of flashing lights toward the darkness at the back of the island, looking for a woman.

Rampike, frowning, gazed at the mad riot of flashing lights reflected in the dark water as the crash of hard rock rolled out over them. His Chevy and his deputy Otis's cruiser were drawn up nose by nose, a hundred yards to the right of where the causeway hit the road, standing between the bikers and the town of Badwater.

Beyond the artificial lights and clamor on the island, a nearly full moon, dark-flushed by the swamp vapors released from the bayou, rose ominously above the island. The Sheriff found himself remembering the Judge's dry voice talking of Cleaver. *"Unless I am in error, there is a young man who thinks like myself; that the secret of harvesting the most out of life is: to live dangerously."*

Bad moon on the rise, thought Rampike, and he pulled his hat down tighter.

Headlights flared from the Badwater road and then slowed as Otis's light flagged down the approaching car. Rampike stepped forward when he recognized the white Cadillac convertible and the two young faces inside.

"No trouble is there, Harlan?" asked James Lafayette with elaborately polite concern, gesturing at the roadblock.

"No," said Rampike slowly, taking in Emily sitting next to him, a magnet to the eye in a pale blue blouse and white slacks, her blond hair fastened loosely with a single yellow ribbon. "Just making sure none of those boys getting tanked up over yonder don't take it in their minds to ride on out and tear up the town some."

"Gracious, don't say that, Harlan," said the girl lightly. "We're on our way to visit with them."

"Well, I wouldn't advise that, Emily," said the Sheriff quickly. "It's pretty drunk in there now. . . ."

"Oh come now, Harlan," James cut in, "we'll be all right. Duane and his friends are okay. And no doubt my brother Cal will take care of us," he added with a mildly ironic expression, "if the worst should come to the worst."

"Does your daddy know you're out here?" asked Rampike levelly.

"Why sure he does! What's the matter, Sheriff? Aren't we free, white and twenty-one? Well, nearly twenty-one," he amended, chuckling, and Rampike realized that the young man, no, probably both of them, had had a drink or two. Not usual for them, and not too damn clever out here.

But there seemed to be a fever rising
helplessly, Rampike let it affect his judgm
Judge knew. . . . He gestured to Otis to me
let them through. Jimmy smiled and salut
turned, her eyes alive with pleasure and excite
great white car nosed forward toward the turn, the s
carrying away her words of thanks.

Rampike saw them cross the causeway. He heard a howl
up from the bikers. He shivered, though the sweat of the
humid night, and something else, was gathering on his face
already.

Animals, he thought, with a surge of hatred. Bastard animals.

He strode to the trunk of the Chevy, pulled a bulky package out onto the road, and carried it down to the water's edge.

"So we ran this pig on a hog off the road . . . ," said Bob, his
ruddy face shining in the firelight.

He, Ariel, Dance and Cooch were squatted by the parked
machines, talking bikes and swapping road stories with some
serious bikers among the Truckers.

"You better not try it with the law down this way," a lean
Trucker counseled, jerking his head at the flashing lights
across the water. "Don't fuck none with that Rampike."

"I don't know, dad," said Ariel with his perpetual grin
broadening. "On the way down, our pickup got pulled over by
some jerkwater Texas town cop, and he struts up to the
driver's side, and Duane just winds down the window and asks
him for two double cheeseburgers and a cherry coke."

There was a moment's disbelieving silence and then the
laughter exploded.

"It's true, it's true," insisted the moon-faced mechanic.
"The cat couldn't believe it. Told us to get on out of there
before we totally blew his mind."

One of the Truckers wiped his eyes and said, "Yeah, that
Duane, always was that way; like if bullshit was goose down,
Duane'd be a hunnerd dollar bag."

"Yeah," said Dance, "but also they can see we ain't no

eavies, no Hell's Angels, just a bunch of guys that like to
putt. . . ."

"Listen," said the rider he had beaten that afternoon,
grinning ruefully, "just tell me how you put that scoot together . . . ," but he was cut off by a deeper, sneering voice
from the shadows.

"Maybe tonight's where you guys do graduate; get to be a
real club," rumbled Cal's henchman, Cannonball. "If you make
the grades, that is."

In the firelight by the cooking pit, he and the massive Tor
of the 13 were eying each other almost lovingly. Now Tor ignored what Cannonball had said, and pointing to his cane and
stiff left leg asked, "How come you need that thing, man? You
lose it on the high side one time too many, or what?"

"'Nam," said Cannonball shortly. "Same place I got these,"
he sneered, brandishing a large circular key ring hung with
smaller objects. As Tor peered over at them uncomprehend-
ingly, Cannonball shook the ring and laughed.

"Ears, man. Gook ears. And other stuff, too."

"Them's just the man's table scraps," another rider
grinned from across the fire, watching Tor's face intently for a
reaction. "They don't call him Cann'ball for nothing."

Tor took a long pull from one of his beers, swallowed half,
spat the rest on to the fire with a hiss and rumbled, "I guess
that'd pass for class in the swamp."

"You don't like the bayou, man?" another Trucker
shouted, his eyes mad, looking ready to jump the fire and get
to it.

"Like it fine," called Tor. He waved up at the speakers,
pounding out Blind Faith's "Can't Find My Way Home." "And
the sounds sure beat that 'Louisiana Hayride.'"

"You don't like our music . . . ?" another rider started to
shout when a roar went up from behind them and they turned
to see the white Cadillac sweep in off the causeway, Jimmy waving ironically to the flood of riders that surrounded the
boatlike vehicle as he drew to a halt beside the parked motorcycles.

Smiling nervously, Jimmy and Emily walked to the fire
along an avenue of yelling, jeering bikers and a few of their

women, though no one laid a hand on their president's brother and sister. Jimmy's face brightened with relief when he saw Tor, Cleaver and Krass by the fire, and the couple went straight to them. Cannonball was limping away hurriedly toward the clubhouse.

"Seems like a hot time in the old town tonight," Jimmy cried, throwing a white-suited arm around Tor and Cleaver's shoulders. "And how are you, sir?" he asked Tor. "Still got that land at your elbows? And are they keeping that ol' Southern hospitality coming?"

"You could say," Tor smiled, and, keeping his eyes casually on the surly riders all around, resentful at the attention they were getting, turned to Emily and offered her a beer from the two depleted six-packs at his feet.

"Why thank you, I believe I will," said Emily, smiling as she took a sip from the can and then glanced around carefully.

"I think I'll go for something stronger," said her brother, and scooping up a half-empty plastic jug of white liquor, hefted it to the crook of his arm and poured some into his mouth. After a moment's breathlessness, he gasped,

"My, but this stuff don't die without a fight, does it?"

"Try one of these," said a voice at his elbow. Jimmy turned to see the squat figure of Six with his left hand extended. Peering down, he saw the small blue pill in Six's palm. "Go on, take it," said Six, "there's plenty more, Kemp's handing 'em out like they was candy. Guaranteed to liven you right up."

"Well, like my Daddy always says," Jimmy grinned, brushing a lock of fair hair from his eyes, "let's live dangerously," and without hesitating, plucked the pill from Six's hand and swallowed it, washing it down with another sip of white lightning. Tor began to protest but Jimmy waved him away amiably, saying with a smile, "No, I want to be like you people for once—do it all."

"Oh Jimmy," said Emily, shaking her head in mock despair. Then they all turned as the volume of the music died away, and with a commotion and more yelling from the Truckers, Cal emerged from the clubhouse and strode over to them, stopping on the far side of the fire to gaze piercingly at Jimmy with his arm round Tor again, and at his sister standing quietly by Cleaver and Krass. After long moments of silence, Cal, his dark eyes fixed gleaming on Emily, his bare chest beneath his cut-offs matted with damp dark hair, raised both hands to the height of his muscular shoulders.

"You come at last," he said loudly, "and you too, baby brother. *Bienvenue.* Welcome. *Bienvenue au royaume de Cal*—welcome to Cal's kingdom. Have you come slumming, eh? I hope you will not encounter anything that—disturbs you. . . ."

His twisted lips and dark eyes smiled at Emily, who quickly looked away. Emboldened by his words, one of the Trucker's cycle sluts shrieked out of the shadows, "Turn 'em out!" and then giggled once nervously in the heavy silence that followed, until Cal lowered his arms to his sides and said in measured tones, "If anyone, *anyone*, lays a hand on my brother or sister, they don't leave this place alive. You all know that is true." He paused, and then turning once again to Emily and Jimmy, went on, "Enjoy this place. But not the clubhouse; that's only for the club. Enjoy the night." He grinned wickedly once more and gestured with his left hand into the darkness at that end of the island. "And if you're looking for Duane Watts, I believe that he is out there somewhere."

Emily's spirit had returned now, and she straightened, tossed the beer can away from her, and without a glance to left or right, or a word to either of her brothers, stalked away from the fire in the direction Cal had indicated. Cal followed her with his eyes for long moments before turning away and, still flanked by Cannonball, walking back through the gate in the fence to the clubhouse.

Tor looked down at Jimmy and said quietly, "With family like that, I reckon you don't need no enemies."

Jimmy responded with a rising laugh; the drug had begun to jam his eyes open, wide and wondering. Now he said simply, "I'm all right with you around," and leaning forward swiftly, placed a kiss lightly on Tor's massive right bicep.

In the silence that followed, in the moment before the bikers who had seen them digested what had happened, the music rent the night again with a crash, the calliope cadences leading into "Light My Fire." Looking up at Tor's still, open-mouthed face, Jimmy grinned and yelled, "Well, isn't that what it's all about? Freedom? Do what you feel?" He laughed aloud joyously, and then yelling, "I better go look out for li'l Em," danced away chanting "The time to hesitate is through," in the direction his sister had taken.

Tor stood still in silence as Six shouted,

"Love your date!" and then nearly fell in the cooking pit from laughing. Lost in his guffaws was Tor's reply,

"I ain't no faggot."

And no one paid any heed as the big man stumbled off into the electric shadows of the light flashes, his rising curses lost in the shriek of the amplified music.

Out in the dark at the western end of the island, Levon and Leroy stood stock still, turned away from each other so that they faced outward, with Leroy's left shoulder just touching Levon's right one so that they could locate each other. The lights and the Doors music pulsed in the distance.

Around them in a loose circle stood four of the Truckers, and by the side of one of them, a young slovenly sag-breasted dyed blonde in a yellow tank top, with mean, mischievous dark eyes. The tallest rider, a gaunt figure with an eye patch over his empty right socket, spoke again.

"I said, what you doin' here, boy?"

Levon cleared his parched throat and muttered, "We just come away here to be, like, quiet."

"Naw, naw. I mean what for you bring your black asses to our island?"

"We come with our friends, Duane and them. . . ."

"Friends?" said the one-eyed rider, looking around exaggeratedly. "I don't see no friends. Looks to me like you out here all on your own." He let the silence sink in, then went on, "Oh, but I know, I got it now. You talking about the mean Teen gang, the fancy-ass foreign-looking Yankee queers that cheat us out of the race money today. . . ."

"We won that fair and square," Leroy muttered quickly.

"Say what?" shouted the eye patch. Neither of them answered, just stood completely tense, knowing anything they said would be wrong. The nightmare they had dreaded all along was coming down.

"Naw, we know them. And we know what you really want here, nigger."

"Hey, listen, man . . ."

"Don't you hey listen me, boy! Don't gimme none of that shuck and jive! Right? Am I right? Now what you *really* want is to stick one of them big ol' black things of yours in one of our women. Like Mary-Lou here," he said, indicating the blonde who rolled her eyes in mock horror, tense with excitement.

"Ain't so," Leroy croaked.

"Ain't so, you say. Well, we'll make it easy for you anyways. We're gonna cut the nasty things clean off you, then there won't be no problem, right?"

Leroy blinked at the sweat running into his eyes; through his left shoulder he could feel the tremor as Levon's right hand began to slide toward the back pocket of his jeans and the switch-blade there.

The men were circling now, and the big knives coming out, when someone stepped out from the trees to their left and a voice sang out,

"Levon, Leroy! How you doing?"

It was Duane, a slim elegant figure in Texan heels, tight, dark bottle-green trousers and a faded blue denim shirt with pearl-snap buttons embroidered with silver studs and rhinestones, his long blond sideburns glistening with drops of sweat, and a bottle of Southern Comfort hanging loosely from his left hand. He came up to the brothers, glanced at the others casually with baby blue eyes and said, "Spider, Bubber, Mary-Lou, what's goin' down?"

Spider, the rider with the eye patch, had drawn back a pace. He spat and gestured at Levon and Leroy.

"They been lookin' wrong at our women."

"At Mary-Lou?" Duane threw back his head and laughed aloud. "Mary-Lou? That gal's the most in-tee-grated female this side of the Mason-Dixon line. Since she turned twelve years of age she been putting out, God bless her, without fear or favor, for anything in pants and in range, black, white or khaki." He laughed again, and then lowering his voice and fixing first Spider and then the other riders one by one with his mild blue eyes, said softly, "And you guys know that it's so."

There was a long ominous silence, finally broken by the girl's strident voice crying, "You going to let him get away, talking that trash about me?" and when the silence simply lengthened she screamed, "I'm going to get me some *real* men! Fuck you, Duane Watts!" before stumbling off into the trees.

"Already been done, darlin', don't you got no memory? Love you too!" laughed Duane as the girl disappeared and he turned back lazily to the four Truckers and extended his bottle. "Drink, you guys?"

But the one-eyed man was too pumped up to let it go. His hand returned to the brass-bound handle of his knife as he growled, "Them's ours, Duane. Get out of our road or we'll run right over you."

"Aw *come* on Spider," said Duane casually, "I *know* you, we was at school together, remember?" With a sudden movement he tossed the liquor bottle from his left hand to catch it by the neck in his right, so fast that the riders flinched instinctively. "And you other guys too." He grinned and murmured quietly, "So don't let your mouth get you into nothing your ass can't handle."

Memories of Duane's wildness before he went away, and the sight of him now, relaxed and confident, flanked by the two tall and motionless blacks, had its effect. In a little while, one by one, the riders began to back away, until Spider, feeling isolated, turned too, only flinging behind him a last, "Later for you guys."

"Yeah, catch you later. *Laisser les bons temps rouler,*" called Duane. "That's French for 'do it to it,'" he turned and explained seriously to Levon and Leroy, who began to laugh hysterically in nervous release.

"Jesus, Duane," Levon gasped, "don't *nothin'* ever get to you?"

"Not much that's bad. Life's too short, you know?"

"You saved our asses," said Leroy flatly.

"Shit, t'aint nothin' to it. You'll do the same for me one day, I know. I 'pologize for that one-eyed son of a bitch and them other assholes. Liquored up. Pilled up most likely, too. You guys do any of Kemp's new shit? No, me either. Don't need all that to have a good time, do we?"

"A good time," said Levon in a hollow voice.

"Sure," said Duane easily. "Say, you try any of that pig-meat yet? Jes melts in the mouth. Let's come on to the fire and grab some. I seen Cleaver and Krass and some of the other guys up there too."

So they began to make their way through the moss-hung trees, toward the flashing lights and the music, the Stones "Gimme Shelter," and the flickering fire in the distance. But as they walked, Leroy felt, rising from the fear that had drenched him, a choking, unquenchable hatred growing inside him; a hatred of whites, of everything white, which he knew was burning in his brother's heart now as it did in his own.

They were halfway there when abruptly darkness and a momentary silence, followed by a chorus of groans and curses, dropped around them, as the generator at the clubhouse shuddered to a halt.

Deep in the drug, his long, black-clad legs stretched out up on the high curved bough of a tree, the Dude sat propped against the top of the trunk, gazing unblinkingly at the moon that hung framed in foliage in the night sky directly before him, seeming so close that he felt he could reach out and touch it.

He sensed the luminous queen's vibrations through his chest, felt the lunar power pulsing in the planet's arteries and in his own, and finally came to hear the disembodied ethereal voice, sacred and confidential to his innermost ear alone. The voice unfolded a pattern before him with great clarity, but it was a pattern of which he too was a part. He could question and even dispute the voice, but truly he knew that it never erred.

He saw now why there were 13 of them, how this connected with the thirteen lunar months and with the thing he had encountered in his occult studies, the universal pattern of change. Of change and of sacrifice. One must go down. And then a second one, and the pattern was complete and could begin again. As it was beginning now; he felt the earth turning and the changes flow, and heard what the pale Goddess above told him. Him alone. He saw it all.

He stirred, feeling the muscles rippling like snakes beneath his skin. He realized the lights and music around him had ceased. Yes, he thought, of course. Soundlessly he slipped from the long branch and dropped silently to earth, to go into the night and play his predestined part in the pattern of things.

The night grew madder. With the lights and the electric music gone, the bestiary of the crazed bikers could be heard in full cry, and snatches of scenes by firelight or moonlight suggested more than a light could show. Cries and howls, grunts and groans, the crack of a whip and then screaming rose as bodies fought and coupled, bled, vomited and even burned, when first with a foul smell of smoldering bone the carcass of the pig, and then a drunken Trucker, fell into the fire pit, to lie there unaided until he woke with screams of agony to find his jeans ablaze and other Truckers howling with laughter, with only one or two helping by urinating on the burning limbs.

For some time Tor, back by the fire with Cleaver and the others, had wanted badly to take a piss, but with the prevailing chaos had been reluctant to do so. Finally muttering, "Got to drain the radiator," he walked off into the trees.

A minute later he was buttoning up his Levis when a man's voice from the shadows under the trees said, "Outstanding looking piece of equipment you got there, man. Want to come on down here and get some?"

Tor walked forward and peered into the shadows, where several figures stood and knelt around bodies down in the dirt. A rider, his jeans around his knees, was humping a girl on the ground beneath him, holding her wrists, grunting and growling as he thrust, using his body like a weapon to club and smack the ample quivering flesh beneath him. The woman was naked, with torn clothes scattered around her, except for a black bra wrenched down around her waist, with her breasts tumbling either side of her body. There was a confusion of limbs around her and after a moment Tor realized that there was another body beneath her, hanging onto her hips and penetrating her from the rear. A third figure squatted by one of her arms, forcing her head round into his crotch, pumping himself into her face. She was mute but for a continuous groaning, impaled, her hair in the mud, the skinny bodies scaling all over her and two or three standing around with their pants open, rubbing themselves slowly, waiting their turn.

"Yeah," the one at her head grunted again, "you got a big dick, and I hear you guys from California are all randy as boar coons. Come on and get a piece of Mary-Lou."

Tor stood there for a long moment before rumbling, "I never had to fight a chick for it, or pay a chick for it, and I ain't about to stand in line for it now." He was feeling a sick fascination and had to concentrate to keep his voice steady. "Besides, with you boys behind me, I'd have to be watching my ass every minute of the time," he finished.

Turning on his heel he walked away to howls of derision from the Truckers clustered around the girl. As he turned to look back once at the grunting, thrusting shapes down in the dirt, one voice yelled, "Maybe that Jimmy Lafayette's more your speed, big boy!"

Tor walked on. About halfway to the fire he almost knocked down Six as the squat gunman stumbled into him in the dark, shouting,

"Who the fuck's that? Tor! My man! Listen man, I seen them!"

"You seen who?"

"Them, man! I seen the fucking frogs!"

"What you talking?"

"You don't remember? The first time we did acid and Duane saw them frogs on the road? Well every time we got stoned since then, I looked for them. Nothing. Till tonight, that is. They're all around here! They came out of the swamp, man. They're red, green, everything. And listen man—I think they're *trying to talk to me.* . . ."

"It'll all grow back, man," said Tor placatingly. "But I wouldn't go down in the woods that way. Them Trucker pigs are making some poor chick pull a train."

"Yeah?" said Six casually. "Terrible thing, terrible thing." But already he was stumbling off in that direction.

At the fire Krass and Cleaver were nowhere in sight. A rider sat crouched astride his howling machine, stock still, revving insanely. Tor scooped up two fresh beers, wincing, as nearby a deranged biker hacked screaming at his own long hair with a hunting knife, the matted locks falling in the fire, where their stench mingled with the marijuana fumes and the acrid smoke from the pit. Inside Tor a massive wave of bad feeling was building. He began to curse. Across the fire a knot of muttering Truckers shot mean glances at him. Instinctively he moved slowly around the pit to put the chain-link fence at his back. Normally placid and easygoing, now he longed for the punks to make a move, nodding, a rhythm building, feeling his muscles tense in anticipation.

When something brushed his back he whirled, his massive right arm cocked, but then flinched away. From inside the chain-link fence, a bearded figure, his pale naked body crisscrossed with phantom chains, the fence's reflection as the firelight shifted through it, his chest blood-streaked, scarred with deep diagonal slashes, was straining his fingers through the mesh, reaching out to Tor, fixing him with haunted, unblinking eyes. He was whispering something. Despite himself, Tor bent closer to catch the words.

"Who am I?" the man was breathing. "Please. Can you tell me? Who the fuck am I?"

They stared at each other in silence for a long minute. Then Tor backed away and turning, stumbled into the dark.

"Out," said Krass. "We gotta get out of here."

Cleaver nodded mutely. They had come to the island because they had always taken risks, priding themselves on doing things and going places where others could not. But in spite of all the tight spots in their past, the frenzy all around now was too palpable to ignore, a mood of violence they both knew had to break around the 13, the outsiders, before much longer.

Without words they made their way away from the fire and the bikes, toward the eastern end of the island, on a sweep to gather their own. It was long past midnight, the moon was riding high, the lights from the cop cars still blinked over the black water, and disaster lurked in every luminous glade, in all the dappled shadows under the trees. They paced quickly toward the end of the island, casting around for their friends. As they left the clubhouse and the fire, the sounds of the howling bikers and the shrieking machine receded. For the last hundred yards, as the island narrowed, there was no one to be seen.

They were approaching the dilapidated huts at that end of the island when both stiffened at the sound of a long whimpering moan. They froze like animals, casting around to trace the direction of the sound. Off in the shadows at the back of the island they sensed movement, circling them. The moaning came again, and something made the hair rise on the nape of their neck. Both reached behind them for the buck knives they carried in leather cases on their belts, but Cleaver's hand came away empty. The flap of his case was undone and the knife gone.

They moved forward, spreading out, passing each side of the ramshackle shed. So it was Cleaver, moving to the right, who first saw what lay behind it.

His pale clothes shining in the moonlight, Jimmy Lafayette, his trousers round his ankles, sat with his legs stuck straight out in front of him, his body tied with rope against a skinning frame, his head slumped forward. He was motionless. Cleaver took a step forward, and then another, as if feeling his way in a pitch dark room, for the air felt to have thickened around his head. Something was glistening around the seated figure's belly and lap. Cleaver stopped stock still when he saw the knife hilt sticking low down in Jimmy's left-hand side. But beneath was worse, the shining where the boy's guts were spilling disemboweled from the belly, and the seemingly endless reservoir of blood from the mutilation below.

He heard a hiss of breath from Krass to his left at the moment when they both realized there was something more. Beyond Jimmy, huddled on the ground completely motionless, was a figure with her knees drawn up to her chest, her hands up to her face. It was Emily. She was naked from the waist down. Only the whimpering moan betrayed that she was conscious or even alive, so still did she lie.

"Oh, no," Krass muttered, but Cleaver had crossed to her quickly and dropped to one knee. Ignoring the smears and stains of blood and semen on her clothes, face and thighs, he felt for her pulse. It was there, though uneven. There was no reaction to his touch; she continued to lie as heavy and unresponsive as stone.

Cleaver rose quickly and crossed to the figure by the post. He pulled a cloth gag from Jimmy's mouth and felt for the pulse in the boy's neck. The flesh under his fingers was warm to the touch. After a minute he said quietly without looking back at Krass, "Go get the others. Just them. All of them. Do it quiet. Now move it!"

As Krass faded back into the shadows without a word, Cleaver reached up and closed Jimmy's eyes. As he did so his gaze went to the knife in the southerner's ribs. With a chill, he made out brass letters tapped into the wooden handle, and bending closer, saw the curly JC. It was his own initials, his own missing knife.

For long moments he stared at the blade and the dark ooze staining Jimmy's light-colored shirt-front. Then quickly he reached out and, grasping the hilt, slid the blade free. Straightening, he walked quickly to the water's edge at the rear of the island, and drawing back his arm, flung the blade as high and as hard as he could, and long seconds later heard the far-off splash as it hit and sank to the swamp mud below.

He knelt and dabbled his fingers in the water till the blood from the blade was gone, then hurried back to crouch by the side of the motionless girl. He pulled off his jacket and covered her nakedness, then touched her shoulder gently and began to talk to her softly, quietly reassuring her. But after a minute with no response, he contented himself with patting her shoulder, and devoted all his mind to the 13's next moves. For he knew now that they must and would run.

He stiffened at the sound of soft footfalls, but it was Krass returning with the massive bulk of Tor at his side.

"Dance, Bob, Ariel and Cooch were still with those guys talking bikes—I gave them the word and they're on their way. We ran into Kemp and he's fetching Duane. I can't . . ."

But he got no further. Out from the shadows of the trees close by stepped Cal Lafayette and Cannonball.

"What is this?" Cal cried, his eyes fixed on the prone bodies of his brother and sister. His hand was whipping to the

the shoulder holster under his colors as he screamed, "You murdering bastards . . . ," but the words died in his throat as Tor stepped in and swung on him with full force, his hamlike right fist connecting on the point of the shorter man's jaw, the power of the blow lifting Cal clean off his feet before he crumpled on the dirt.

But Cannonball had stepped back and already had his weapon halfway clear, when like a black wind Levon and Leroy jumped him out of nowhere, dragging him down in a soundless rush and, punching alternately, hammered him into unconsciousness. A switch-blade appeared in Levon's hand, but even faster Cleaver lashed out and kicked it away.

"That's enough," he said grimly, scooping up Cannonball's Magnum. "Now we have to get out."

The others were nodding, when Duane stumbled from the trees, with Kemp behind him. Duane ran to where Jimmy lay and fell on his knees beside him.

"What have they done to you? Oh Christ, Jesus, what happened?" He cradled the dead boy's body, looking from one to the other of them. "He was my best friend, we were kids together. . . ."

"We don't know what went down," said Cleaver. "But we have to get out of here."

Now Duane became aware of the girl lying motionless by his side.

"But . . . Emily! Oh Jesus God, you too?"

"She's alive, but she's been stomped and raped and she's in some kind of shock. We can't help her and she can't help us. They'll put it all on us. Now come on."

"No. No, John, no. She'll come round, she'll tell them what happened. We can't leave it this way. We can't leave her."

"By the time she comes round, if she does, these guys will have cut our nuts off and fed us to the swamp. You heard what Cal said about touching these two? Now, how do we get out of here? From the way we came in, I know if you turn left after the causeway and carry on, a couple of miles down the road there's a crossroad that goes three ways. Where to?"

Under the lash of Cleaver's quiet voice, Duane spoke, haltingly, reluctantly.

"Right takes you north to Shreveport, left goes south to Lake Charles. Straight on's the quickest way to the Texas border." Then he was turning away to Emily again when Cleaver shot one more question.

"How many ways out of those towns are there? There'll be buses. But airfields?"

"Yeah, there's airports at both of them."

Then they heard movement coming through the trees and tensed again. But it was Dance and the other three from the bikes. The racer's taut face revealed little as he took in the scene and then spoke direct to Cleaver.

"Krass told us. We've fixed the Truckers' bikes; gas lines, tires. And we're ready to roll."

"Okay. We all head left at the end of the causeway. You four, when we get to the first crossroads, carry right on. The border's around fifty miles. Soon as you can in Texas, park the bikes, split up and hop a train or a bus. Tor, Levon, Leroy, Kemp, you guys go north to Shreveport, same thing, take a bus or a plane out. Me, Duane and Six in the truck, and the others—shit, where's the Dude?—we go south to Lake Charles."

He reached into his pants pocket and handed a fat wad of bills to Krass.

"Here's the race winnings. Split it even among the guys. Cab fare."

"And the law?" said Dance, jerking a thumb at the lights across the water. "You want me to draw off that Sheriff? I'll carry him back to the country, you say so."

Cleaver shook his head.

"No! It's night, they say he's shit hot, and he knows the roads. Six—are you straight enough to shoot?"

"Shoot the eye out of a frog at fifty paces. Only I wouldn't," the short figure solemnly assured them, "'cause they're my little buddies, and they know a lot of stuff. . . ."

"Oh, Jesus," said Cleaver, "we better just hope our shit's better than their best. You get in the flatbed, Six. When we've crossed the causeway and turned left, I'll pull up. Then you've got five seconds to take out the front tires on the Sheriff's car and the cruiser. Only don't for Christ's sake hit any of them, even if they return fire."

"I hit what I aim for," said Six soberly.

"But the bikes, man?" said Bob. "We really got to dump our machines?"

"Which you rather lose, your scoot or your ass? Don't sell them, garage them if you can, maybe truck back for them later if the heat goes off. But for now this is the big one, man. Rape. Murder one. Local people, well liked, well connected. We'd be lucky if it even got as far as a trial."

"I ain't pulling time in no southern slammer," said Levon softly, Leroy nodding behind him.

"*Oye,* Cleaver, where we going to meet up again?" Cooch asked diffidently.

"We don't. Ever," Cleaver shot back. "That's all she wrote for the 13, end of the road. Down here they don't know who we are, just street names. I'm sorry it has to end this way, but if there's no 13 any more, we got a chance they'll never find us. . . ."

"I'm not going along," said a voice. They turned to see Duane standing over Emily. "I can't leave here this way. It's my home, these here, Emily and Jimmy, are, were, my friends. You people go. But I can't."

As he spoke, Cleaver had gone up to him. Now he simply nodded and turned away, but as Duane stared down again at Emily, Cleaver abruptly swung back and carefully cold-cocked him over the head with the Magnum, Krass catching the southerner as he fell and swinging his inert body over his broad shoulders.

"He'll see it my way later," Cleaver ground out. "Put him in the truck with us," he went on, glancing round now with increasing tension. At that moment a tall figure detached itself from one of the encircling trees, and the Dude's laconic voice said softly,

"That Cannonball said maybe we'd graduate tonight. I guess this is Graduation, then. Don't sweat it," he said, holding up his hands as Cleaver began to talk. "I've heard enough. Saw enough, too," he added, looking Cleaver straight in the eye. "Just thought you'd better know there's some guys coming this way, looking for these dudes," he said, indicating the unconscious bodies of Cal and Cannonball. "If we're going to get it on, it had better be now."

With no further hesitation, they all moved together, turning from the sheds without a backward glance at the motionless forms they left lying there. They ran together in a half-crouch back toward their bikes.

They were only halfway there when there came a series of faltering thumps, and then a blinding flash of light and a deafening crash as the generator revived and the lamps and music burst into life again, still playing "Gimme Shelter."

Rampike and the deputies jumped as the sound and lights started up again, but they had relaxed once more when there came a rending of metal closer to them. They spun round to see a red pickup truck at the island end of the causeway knock aside two or three bikes that had been left across the track there and shoot out onto the narrow strip. With a deafening roar that the music had masked, a pack of unlit bikers now thundered behind and beside it.

The deputy, Otis, dived into the cruiser to unship his pumpgun, but the truck had already reached the end of the causeway and screamed round to the left onto the road on two wheels, then slammed to a halt forty yards from them, with bikes slithering and snaking around it on both sides, accelerating away from the roadblock into the night.

Rampike watched open-mouthed as a squat figure, laughing insanely in the back of the pickup, popped to his feet like a jack-in-the-box and threw down on them two-handed with a large automatic pistol. The Sheriff was still fumbling with the hammer strap on his holster when Six, sighting down the vee of his two arms, opened fire. Rampike flinched at four double concussions, the slam of the automatic and the explosion of the tires coming so fast they blurred into one another. In the moment's ringing silence that followed, Rampike met the gunman's eyes as he stood, still laughing hard, the big gun held loosely but half-raised and pointing at the lawman.

But at that moment the truck dumped cork and the short man was pitched, yelling, half out of the flatbed, clinging on with one arm, the echo of his curses mingling with the squeal of tires as the unlit truck vanished into the night before Rampike or the deputies could get off a single round.

In the truck Cleaver ignored Six's abuse, hitting the switch that Bob had rigged for them months before to work the headlights while the taillights remained extinguished. Next to him, Duane swayed limply in his seatbelt, still unconscious.

In all the confused emotions Cleaver was feeling—the shock and horror of what someone had done to Emily and Jimmy, the exhilaration of escape, the cold calculation necessary to keep them all free—one thing swamped the rest; self-disgust, that on his decision the 13 were running, splitting apart like a bunch of cowards in the night; that even if they got away, this was how it would end. And Cleaver would live the rest of his life uncertain about his motives. After he had found and thrown away his knife, he could never know whether simple self-preservation had come into play to influence his decision that they cut and run, not stay and find the truth.

Grinding his teeth, Cleaver drove on, barely slowing as the crossroads loomed out of the darkness and he hurled the truck on two wheels onto the left-hand road.

Three hours later, in a gentle dawn of pearl and rose, a doctor emerged from a single-story brick structure built down by the river where it ran behind the Judge's mansion.

The building was the old cook's house, which, when the Judge's wife had been alive, she had converted into a pleasant guest bungalow. That night, on the Judge's orders, Emily had been carried there from the island.

Two guards with shotguns cradled in their arms straightened from the wall as Doctor Gritz emerged. He ignored them and walked quickly to the bank of the stream, where the Judge stood motionless, his hands clasped behind his back. He did not turn as the doctor came up and began to speak.

"She'll be all right, André. Physically, that is. She's in profound shock, something approaching catatonia—she still hasn't moved or spoken yet. Some of the physical injuries are nasty—she'll lose one of her teeth—but there are no broken bones. . . ." Gritz continued with a hurry that was somehow reluctant.

"And the sexual assault?" the Judge cut in flatly.

"She was attacked—in every way," the Doctor muttered hurriedly. "I had them run the semen tests at my clinic right away as you requested. There were at least two perpetrators, perhaps more. André," he hurried on, "I know how you must feel, how anxious you must be after this not to expose poor Emily to any more than is absolutely necessary, but I have to urge you to get her to a hospital, to Shreveport. In view of her state of mind—entirely understandable, after what she's been through, after seeing her brother . . . André, I'm just a country quack, there they have specialists, proper treatment," the Doctor babbled on, excruciatingly aware of the tension between his Hippocratic oath and the things that the Judge knew about him, previous incidents from his professional life, secrets that constituted an unbreakable tie between Lafayette and himself.

The Judge turned and cut off the flow of words with an abrupt chopping motion of his hand.

"She stays here."

"But the police, André, the trial when they catch these boys . . . ?"

"The Sheriff's taking care of it," said the Judge, with a ghastly smile up at the nervous medical man. "Nothing goes any further. We find them, we bring them back, we have a trial, with myself presiding. *None* of this goes any further. You understand that well, I hope." After a pause he went on, "And we'll take care of our own."

He gestured across the river to the spot beneath a beautiful live oak tree, where in the first light, a gang of men toiled to dig his son's grave.

"Emily, too, stays here," he went on, "where she will be truly cared for—with your help, of course, my friend—until she is well again."

But Emily did not recover. The total immobility diminished as the weeks drew into months, but she wore her silence and listlessness like a protective cloak. For convenience, and the isolation it afforded, she remained lodged in the cook's house. It was found that she became violently agitated in the presence of men, whether it was the doctor, her father, her brother or the servant G.W. Brooks, so soon only Brooks's wife and daughters waited on her; Duane's mother no longer felt she could work for the Judge, though Lafayette had made it clear that he held her in no way responsible for what had happened. Mercifully, Emily did not become pregnant.

One day Brooks had been picking at his guitar out at the back of the mansion, and his wife noticed the pleasure that this gave the sick girl. Unobtrusively he began to play nearer the cook's house, and more regularly, until soon every evening the music, gentle and profound, would roll out over the fields and resonate softly in her room. If Emily was alone then, sometimes fragments of expression would come and go on her face, as if she were reliving moments from her past, often evidently happy and animated times. Then the voice of the Judge would sound from his office at the rear of the mansion, or Cal would call to someone across the yard, and the blank frozen mask would descend on Emily's face again.

Cal was to be found at the mansion less and less. After that night the Truckers had dispersed, in some cases being forcibly encouraged to leave the county by Rampike. Cal himself almost immediately volunteered for officer training, was posted after training to a predominantly southern infantry unit and in less than a year shipped out for Vietnam, where he served in the dispirited and chaotic last days of the war, and came back with medals. When he returned he quickly immersed himself in the oil and gas business, a burgeoning facet of the New South, and visited Beau Mont little more, though certainly no less, than duty required. He and his father seemed reconciled in some way. It was true that he stayed loosely in touch with the hard core of the Truckers, like the one-eyed Spider and his henchman Cannonball. He saw the latter on business, as Cannonball now worked a small helicopter charter service to the offshore rigs in the Gulf. The big man was one of the few of them who still rode a motorcycle, on the weekends.

On the other side of the country, the 13 had done as Cleaver said and dispersed quickly and effectively. Several of them also had ended up in Vietnam. Bob, Six, and the twins, Levon and

Leroy, were drafted, the latter as marines, extending once and then again, and making their lives as gunnery sergeants and twenty-year men. Only one, Kemp, had volunteered; with the 13 gone, he had finally broken from home by joining the air force, qualifying as a transport pilot and, after a tour of duty, transferring to one of the civilian airlines in Cambodia, by then transparent covers for the CIA, and remaining in Southeast Asia flying clandestine operations until well after the fall of Saigon.

Duane had joined the merchant marine, shipping out of the West Coast, reluctantly staying away from the South. Tor moved up to San Francisco. Cooch had immediately and prudently taken his share of the winning stakes and gone back to a country town south of the border, where he set up a motorcycle repair shop and got married. Ariel remained at his old field and eventually started a free-fall parachute and hang-gliding school there. The Dude settled in New Mexico, where he devoted himself to his music, playing the bars and clubs of the Southwest. After a while he made a somber but soulful one-man concept album titled *Swamp Oak,* in style somewhere in Ry Cooder, Doug Kershaw and Leon Russell territory; it made him serious money, but there was no follow-up. Dance continued to race under his professional name and, as well as becoming a champion on the dirt, was one of the front-runners of the successful American challenge to the previously European-dominated road racing.

Finally there were Krass and Cleaver. Despite Cleaver's strictures to the others, the two friends continued to meet occasionally for about a year after what they always echoed the Dude in calling Graduation. But Krass had re-enrolled at Berkeley, while Cleaver was hanging out three hundred and fifty miles south in L.A. And soon Krass began to date Karen, a sociology and social welfare graduate student and an incipient New Woman, of the kind who mistake bluntness for honesty. After a first question and answer session, Cleaver cordially loathed her. It was mutual, but he knew Krass was pursuing her with intensity, seeing her in the way that Cleaver himself saw his work, as a means to reorder his life. After Krass had completed his Ph.D. the couple married quickly (Cleaver, though disliking himself for it, had invented a trip elsewhere to coincide with the date), and moved to take up academic appointments in a small Midwestern state university, leaving Cleaver to follow his upwardly mobile way in downtown Los Angeles.

They had all got away clean, it seemed. In fact, there had been little pursuit. A combination of Rampike's and the Judge's influence had kept the incident from police or federal records. There was little enough to go on; the Sheriff had not thought it necessary to log their bikes' plates, so there were only a few names, their reputation as the 13. But nothing was done until too late, and soon the 13, always hazy figures, were genuinely dispersed.

Then Cal finally prevailed upon his father to hire a New Orleans private investigator to look for the 13 in California. The gumshoe, venal and obese, opted to go west personally, where he ate and drank well and frequently, still padding his expenses, and finally returned with a costly blank that had somehow been expected.

The Judge was not dismayed, for he had always felt certain that the thing would resolve itself, in time. Every evening as darkness fell, he would stand by the river behind Beau Mont, and scarcely an evening passed without his remembering the night when he had first heard of the outrage, and how his habitual self-inquisition had not been able to ignore something in him, a fierce flash, a "Yes!" as they had told him, something that recognized the event which he had anticipated, formlessly, for so long. It had been only seconds before simultaneously the sorrow hit and self-loathing descended in a black mass, but he recalled the moment constantly, and it fed his faith in the inevitability of what they were enduring.

Though the seasons came and went, and the South changed, Badwater changed less than most, and both the Judge and his county seemed frozen in a patient, brooding dream. Every evening as the sun sank and the water before him darkened, the Judge would look across the stream to the mound of his son's grave, then turn to the brick house that held his daughter; and he would shiver, not from the chill night air, but because he felt again nature working her way within himself, and knew that he was an instrument, self-forged and ready, of something terrible to come.

None of the 13 forgot. For all of them, even against the massive mindless violence of war, the incident at Badwater, perhaps because of the brief time of happiness and tranquillity that the South had offered them before it, stood as a granite landmark in their lives, an extremity of horror.

7

California, 1982, Sunday

Back in Los Angeles later that evening, Cleaver chose to eat at Big Dean's Muscle Inn, a noisy coast bar with beer, loud rock and excellent cheeseburgers. He wondered idly whether opting for the youth bit was some unconscious attempt on his part to get them back in the groove. But to Krass he rationalized.

"In joints like Musso's or the Rose, we might run into someone I know. Or we could have gone to one of the places I go for work, but even on the weekend there's guys there spending as much time with their tongue up their guest's ass-holes as on their food. Not very appetizing."

"It's fine here," said Krass, who was moving in a daze—from seeing Cleaver again, and from the news he had brought, from the flight west, and the trip in Cleaver's Mercedes from L.A.X. airport down the coast to Ascot raceway, where Krass had known that the racer Dance was riding professionally that Sunday; and from what they had found when they got there.

Under the circumstances, the Coast, seen from the car window in the last light of the early summer evening, had seemed entirely appropriate, a vague dreamlike scene of surf haze and sandpipers, though somehow smaller than he remembered. Like always, I guess, thought Krass. The crowd in Big Dean's, with their outfits, their perfect tans, their good-humored chatter, seemed like friendly aliens to him after the years in the Midwest. The only thing he could think of that didn't seem either strange or less was Cleaver, and at that moment, as their food arrived, he realized vaguely that from the minute he had met his friend again, it had never crossed his mind to do anything but go with him, wherever the thing was leading.

They ate hungrily, in silence, draining what was left of their beers and ordering up coffee. Only then did Cleaver lean back and say, "How did Karen take it when you called? Your coming away like this?" The big man made a face. "Not too good, huh?"

"But nothing is, right now, to tell you the truth, John. I . . . aah, you can't talk about it. . . ."

"How's work?"

"Okay—no more than that. I was set for tenure at the last place, but then we moved and now I'm back to square one. Things were bad between us even then, you see, and we thought a change might . . . But I don't know, I'm afraid it's been much the same. Karen's heavily into her women's group, all of that."

"Any kids?"

Krass shook his head.

"We had an agreement always that if we did, it would be a mutual decision. Up till now, Karen hasn't felt that she wanted to. Now she feels she might be ready," he shrugged helplessly. "But I find that I'm not too sure. . . ."

He wanted to talk, evidently, so Cleaver got to the bottom line.

"How's the sex?" he asked.

"How's your memory?" Krass came back, and sadly they laughed. Cleaver knew it was time to start building up his friend; he had to get him up and firing on all four, because this thing was going down fast, he thought, faster than you could possibly imagine, faster than a fucking speeding bullet. And like he always had, he would need Krass.

"Hell, which of us is married, hasn't got problems?" he said. "Laura, my old lady, just started work again, and I'm worried about my boy, I think he may be on something, sniffing that glue. So when it isn't a tug of war it's a mine field."

"Yes, but what we just saw down there," said Krass soberly,

jerking a thumb south, back toward Ascot, "rather puts our problems in perspective."

It had been less than a forty-five-minute drive from the airport. Down where the Harbor and San Diego Freeways intersected, as dusk fell they had taken the exit for Gardena. Instantly they were down the grimy vacant lots, with the raceway only a couple of turns away, huddled next to the endless checkered yellow expanse of a municipal school bus depot.

They circled the track's outside wall of hinged, sagging, dirty-white panels, suggesting the biggest chicken shack in the world, and went in as regular customers. The races were already under way, and they stepped from the car into the dusty blare of the P.A. fuzzily relaying a local station until announcements of the next race cut in. They walked through the crowd toward the grandstand, unremarkable figures, Cleaver still in the STP jacket and Krass wearing the old clothes in which he had driven to the hill climb, and the red No. 2 jersey against the evening chill. They wandered through the strangeness of the dark-white light thrown by the halogen lamps on their poles around the track.

The lamp poles, the few rotting palm trees, the telephone posts, all two-dimensional under the light, the smell of fried onions and burnt engine oil, the weird silhouettes of the heavy vintage tractors that harrowed the brown dirt from which all of this rose, the dirt that had already begun to clog their noses, that streaked every billboard and surface around, these were all unchanged, just as Cleaver remembered from the time when Ascot was his local circuit. But he hadn't been down there in years, and it was a long, long way from that downtown L.A. he now thought of as normal.

He had also stopped following the sport, and Krass had been bringing him up to date on Dance's successes and his status, high in the second rank, below the greats like Mamola and Roberts, but only just below. Looking around now, Cleaver couldn't help thinking that Dance might indeed be a prince of the tracks, but what kind of a place was his kingdom?

No soft one, Cleaver did know. On the dirt you raced at speeds of over 100 mph on the straights, with no front brake, and then on the curves hurled the wheels out of alignment so that the twisting, bucking machines slowed fractionally, enough to be wrestled sliding through the turn and straightened up to slam the power back on. You did all this elbow to elbow and wheel to wheel with hard-ass, cold-eyed riders as equally determined to win as you were, in a blurred maze of noise and a blinding shower of dirt loaded with stones that could fly up and hit you like bullets, cutting through your leathers and the L.A. *Times* that Cleaver remembered Dance wadding up beneath them. All this with the solid, three foot wooden perimeter wall never far, sometimes only inches away, waiting for the slightest slip. Injuries were commonplace; Dance had broken most of the bones in his body, as well as his back. Fatalities were not unknown.

Yes, Ascot was a hard, gladiatorial arena, the kind of place you might reasonably expect to leave behind as your racing stature grew. But like the King, Kenny Roberts, like all of them who came up through dirt racing and had it in their blood, Dance, Krass had said, came back, if not by choice, at least with relish, not only for the Grand National points, but for the face-out, the winning, among like minds, on the mercurial dirt. Real racers. And the crowd, truckers and urban cowboys, Okies and Valley boys, greasers and losers, knew this, and it produced a fierce affection for the ones they felt were their own.

As Krass and Cleaver reached the base of the grandstand, the P.A. and the crowd's roar were swamped as a deafening crackle of motors rose to a crescendo and they were just in time to see the machines leap from the start, a wall of dirt half as high as the grandstand shooting up from their spinning rear wheels and still in the air as almost immediately the whole howling pack were slewing all the way from the far outside across into the apex of the first corner, left feet going down to skim the dirt. In an instant, Cleaver recognized Dance, his spinning front wheel and flexed, tensed arms sculptured by the dark light, on a scarlet Harley XR 750 among the lead riders.

Then they were round, accelerating from the pall of dust very fast and deafening for a few seconds, and Cleaver felt the old pull of the race, the concentration and the thrill as the pack flashed between light stanchions from a colored mass to a shadowed one, and yes, it came flooding back, the speed of Ascot racing because so many top riders raced there so often, and the wide-open quality, because . . . but then the bikes were thundering by them again and they stood transfixed by the speed of the slides and the tough, graceful arabesques that the bodies of the riders became, weight far back to force the rear end down but arms bowed to absorb the beating from the lumpy ground, and torso moving in a range from minimal adjustments to extreme arcs, as jostling each other, they wrestled the pivotted handlebars, wriggling like fish, through the turn to the vital drive-out point. Cleaver found himself bellowing with the crowd, choking in the dust, outshouting the commentator, urging Dance on.

By the last lap, the two leaders were clear and the race had resolved itself into a titanic struggle for third place, with three riders in it, one of them Dance. Coming up to the first bend for the last time, he and the rider lying fourth were strung out in line behind the man in third place; Cleaver could see they were drafting, using the vacuum at the center of the turbulence created by the leading man to be sucked along and then, as Cleaver watched, from a perfect position catapulted out and ahead as the leading rider shut off a fraction too early before the turn. But both Dance's Harley and the Yamaha V-twin ahead of him got through with their positions unchanged.

As they came to the last bend, the crowd was on its feet for the two riders in third and fourth, total icons of concentration, evidently evenly matched. Cleaver, tense with excitement, knew there was something, just one thing about Ascot that might give Dance a possibility of getting through. It came to him in a flash as, leading the pack, the two hurtled up the last straight. Ascot had been a cushion track. Not by day; in the heat of the day it was a groove track, the nature of the dirt dictating that your racing line followed the groove, the fastest way round, a quickly worn path on the track. But by night it used to be possible to ride the cushion; to go round the outside of corners, closer in to the fence, out on the untracked dirt that formed a cushion there, and if your nerve and judgment held, to drive through and ahead. But even as the thought flashed, Cleaver remembered that the days of the real cushion were said to be gone now, killed by modern tires and the power of engines that piled the dirt against the fence, destroying the usable cushion.

Then he was shouting in true panic, for Dance had entered the last left-hander and now had lost it, evidently straining that fraction too hard, his machine skidding far out from the apex of the corner, too far, too fast, barrelling straight for the perimeter wall as Dance, his every sinew tensed, seemed to wrestle to regain control. And then the cry of panic turned in Cleaver's throat to a howl of exultation as he realized, with a thousand others, that before their eyes Dance was doing the impossible, running an outrage on accepted physical forces, as with a combination of brute strength and exquisite control, at the head of a tall rooster-tail of dirt, he rode around the outside, around what there was of the cushion and, in a way that he now made seem inevitable, slipped around the Yamaha to blast out of the corner far on the outside and storm home third.

Krass and Cleaver turned to each other, their delighted yelling lost as the crowd roared its approval of a local boy on American iron coming good.

As the races finished, Cleaver got a message through to the pits, and while the crowd drifted away, pale washed-out figures under the lights leaving only a scatter of litter and a haze of dust, a guard let them in through the wooden double doors to the inner ring where the bikes now stood, facing forward from a low concrete wall, surrounded by paraphernalia and mechanics. Cleaver spotted Dance's scarlet Harley with three figures clustered around it, one of them familiar.

They strode over. The machine stood on an old piece of carpet at the center of a semicircle of components, carefully arranged tools, a stack of tires and another of shining spiked sprockets stuck like horseshoes on a wooden pole. At a distance there were folding chairs, styrofoam cups of cold coffee, crushed beer cans; for a sport at national level, it was a low-rent scene. But there was nothing casual about the three mechanics working swiftly in prayerlike attitudes around the bike, stripping it. None looked up as they approached. Cleaver said, "Hello, Bob, long time no see."

The red-haired Tennesseean raised his head and looked in their direction. He wore an old olive drab fatigue cap with white tide marks of sweat etched into it, and heavy black-rimmed sunglasses. His face was alert but otherwise expressionless. After a long pause, still on his knees, he said, "Cleaver?"

"What's the matter? Did we change that much? Don't you recognize Krass either?"

There was a curious pause; something was wrong, Cleaver knew, without knowing what. The other two mechanics, younger men, never looked up from their work. At last Bob moved, still on his knees, his right hand went out in a practiced sweep to the concrete wall, and they watched it there close surely around a long white cane.

A voice at their elbow said, "Bob lost the use of his eyes on the Mekong Delta. But he's still the number one guy around with a wrench."

They turned from the speechless flooding embarrassment of the moment to find Dance at their elbow. The upper part of his colored one-piece leathers was pulled down off a T-shirt soaked dark with sweat, and the arms knotted around his waist. His left foot looked lopsided, still encased in the heavy metal skid shoe strapped over his boot for negotiating the dirt. His features, streaked with dust and sweat, seemed drawn taut over his skull beneath damp hair plastered down from his helmet.

They turned and began to congratulate him on the race, but his pale blue eyes never blinked and they stopped talking as he said softly, "The two of you together after all this time— tells me that this isn't just a social call. You'd better fill me in, John. Krass, why don't you get reacquainted with Bob?"

Cleaver and Dance walked away a short distance, and noise from the pits masked their words. Krass turned back to the machine where Bob was already crouched again, his scarred and calloused hands flying over the nuts and bolts of the still-hot engine. Krass watched the economical movements in fascination until the silence had held for too long.

"Well, Bob," he said carefully, "how's it going?"

Beneath the dark glasses Bob's mouth twisted into a smile. He said nothing.

"The main thing is, treat him normal," said Dance quietly. "He doesn't think being blind is some kind of badge, says he's got the right to be treated special, so I don't lay it on him."

The racer had arrived later at Dean's in his motor home

with Bob. Cleaned up and changed, Dance's spare features were emphasized, the blow-dried longish hair like a wig on his taut skull. Now Krass had taken Bob to the men's room and Dance took the opportunity to speak.

"Another thing," he continued, "when you speak to him, call him by name or he may not know you're talking to him. Tell him who you are, he may not always recognize your voice. And did you see how Krass got him by the arm? It's better to let him take yours. Walk a little way in front of him. And do what he says; he'll usually know what he needs better than you will."

"You've helped him a lot," said Cleaver.

"Listen," the racer came back quickly, "I'm not doing him any favors. It works for me. You got any idea how hard it is to keep your team pumped up the way it should be, in our line? Well not with him around. Here's a blind guy doing their job better than they can. It keeps everyone sharp."

They watched the couple coming back across the restaurant, Bob's long cane sweeping ahead of him carefully. As they approached and Krass helped Bob seat himself, Dance asked casually, "OK there, B.B.?"

"B.B.?" Krass queried.

"Blind Bob," said Bob crisply, bringing a spread hand down onto the top of his beer glass to locate it, then raising and draining it carefully. "That's me."

"Is that your Merc out front, Cleaver?" asked Dance. "Yeah? Well whatever it is you're doing now, you must be doing all right."

"You know the three great Californian lies?" said Cleaver, "Like, 'yes, the Mercedes is paid for, and yes, the mortage on the house is assumable, and yes, those are only cold sores.'"

They laughed, but Dance pressed him and Cleaver found himself explaining a little about his work at the agency.

"But it's not all grins," he finished. "I told you we handle a lot of movies. Now if you go to a picture, you see the picture."

He realized too late what he was saying but guessed it was worse for Bob if he backtracked.

"But I'm seeing the grossing potential," he went on, "the potential audience, the target audience. I'm wondering will it have legs, and if it's a summer picture, will it do business in the soft-tops, that's the drive-ins, and that means the kids." He shrugged. "Stuff like that. It makes it hard to just sit back and enjoy the movie.

"Sounds like grown-up business to me, Bob," laughed Dance. "And you say that Trucker Cannonball showed up at your office downtown? He must have gone down there like a turd in a punch bowl, unless he's changed a whole lot."

"The fucker hasn't changed too much," said Cleaver quietly, remembering the numbing moment when he had walked into his inner sanctum, knowing only that there was someone waiting there who had upset his P.A., and caught sight of the hulking biker's figure slouched in a corner chair, wearing a loud leisure suit but still bearded and in shades, and carrying the heavy black walking cane.

"What exactly did he say?" Dance asked.

"Just said he had something for me," said Cleaver, looking around casually as he fished in his jacket pocket and pulled out a plastic bag, unfolded the handkerchief inside it and held it out to Dance, concluding, "It was this."

About two inches long, the stiffened, wizened white object with a metal band around the thicker end for long moments made no sense to the racer, until with a rush of revulsion, he recognized the 13 emblem on the metal, identical to the silver ring he still wore himself.

No one spoke or moved, until Bob half-whispered urgently, "What is it? Tell me."

Dance cleared his throat and rasped, "It's Duane's pinkie. With his 13 ring on it. The bastards must have cut it off."

Cleaver nodded.

"To show they weren't fucking around, Cannonball said. And he went one better. Told me how the end was ragged? Said that Duane had good taste. Or at least that he tasted good."

Then he lived again the moment of blind fury when he had lunged forward like lightning at the ape-like figure, seizing the heavy cane, snatching it from Cannonball's hands and holding it poised over the big man's head as the Trucker cowered back in his chair. Then bringing the cane swiftly down and in one movement cracking it in two over his own knee and hurling the pieces in Cannonball's face.

"Give us the whole story," said Dance flatly.

"Duane's mother died this month," said Cleaver, relieved to talk. "Duane took his wife and their little girl back there to bury her. He also meant to go to the Judge and try to make it up. But Cannonball and Cal Lafayette guessed he'd show and laid for him at the cemetery. They hustled them off to that clubhouse and threatened the woman and his kid until Duane spilled all he knew about the rest of us. Which turned out to be where I worked; I'd run into him one time years, ago, just after I started with the agency.

"So they cut off his finger, but before anything worse went down, Cannonball said, the Judge showed up and made them lay off. It was the Judge who set the terms. We have to go down there and face the music for killing his son and interfering with his daughter. The way we cut and run has him sure it was some of us that did it."

There was a long moment's silence as each of them, but Cleaver most of all, remembered whose decision it had been that they run. And also felt a darker fear surface, something which had preyed on them all during the intervening years; that what the Judge believed might actually be true, that some of the 13 might have done it.

"Anyhow," Cleaver continued, "he says we'll get a fair shake—he'll let Duane's family go as soon as we arrive, there'll be some kind of trial, and only the guilty ones will get their wrists slapped. But if we don't show by next Sunday noon, he says he'll turn Duane and his family over to what's left of the Truckers. He says if we go to the regular law, he'll know about it just as soon as we do, and Duane and Mrs. Duane and the kid will just vanish. And Cannonball seems to believe that the old guy means it."

There was silence again, a ringing silence in their heads that excluded the loud rock music and carefree chatter all around. At length Cleaver said, "How I see it is we have three ways to go. We can leave Duane and his family down there, do nothing and try to stay underground. Or we can get as many of us together as we can and take the Judge up on his offer, go down there and let him put us on trial."

"If it got that far," said Krass.

"And number three?" said Dance.

"We can go in and try to get Duane and his people out."

"You mean fighting?" said Dance.

"Sneaking in, fighting, running, whatever it takes," said Cleaver shortly.

"They'll be waiting for that," Dance stated.

Cleaver just nodded, but he was remembering Cannonball's parting shot—"I hope you Yankee faggots do try something. Cause we'll be ready." Cleaver smiled slightly, remembering how he'd stared the big man down, before replying, "You can die," nodding once for emphasis, as if agreeing with himself, and then concluding, "Now get out of here before I slap your fucking face off," in a voice so coldly furious that Cannonball had left the room and the building without another word. Cheap thrills, thought Cleaver now somberly.

After a longish pause, Dance said, "What do you think, John? What do you and Krass favor?"

"We were sort of partial," said Cleaver slowly, "to number three."

"Bob?" asked the racer.

"I'll go with whatever you say."

Dance thought unhurriedly for a long minute, then, unsmiling, lifted his pale eyes to meet Cleaver's and said,

"Doesn't seem any other way. We'll go along."

Cleaver's face showed none of his flooding relief. He simply said,

"Good. Now where the hell is everyone?"

8

San Francisco, Monday, 1:30 A.M.

It was a modest bar, standing on the corner of San Francisco's Mission district closest to the Bay, by no means smart but not too sleazy either. A green and red neon sign blinked on and off with just one word: TOR'S.

It was all that Dance could give them, but he was sure that the big man had information on several of the others. One of the racer's crew had arrived at Dean's to pick up the motor home and take Bob back to Dance's home in the Valley, and then Cleaver had driven the three of them back to the airport where they had caught a shuttle up to San Francisco.

Cleaver paid off their taxi and the three of them walked across the street to the bar and went in. It seemed a pleasant, unexceptional place, low-key and spacious, the soft thud of taped music matching the soft tubes of neon light around the bar. It was after one in the morning, but the place was quite busy and animated, and they secured the last free table. A young waiter in a white shirt came to serve them, and after he had taken their orders, Cleaver asked if the owner was around. When the kid said he thought so, Cleaver sent a message that they had arrived; Dance had already phoned ahead and explained things briefly to Tor.

They watched as the waiter went behind the bar and

talked to a tall, handsome woman with angular features and reddish-blond hair cut short in a swooping bob, who gestured upward and sent the waiter away.

"Do you think that's his old lady?" said Krass.

"If he's got that and he's got this place, he's doing all right," said Dance.

"You married?" Cleaver asked the racer.

"Oh yes. But she's used to me being away a little bit."

They sat and drank their whiskey quietly. After a while, Krass tuned in to the fairly strident conversation between two men at the next table. One, with a carefully trimmed goatee beard and a double earring, wearing a tight-fitting white nylon cap-sleeved T-shirt, was leaning forward to his friend and saying, " . . . so I went to the clinic and the doctor did the tests and told me I had it, and he asked me how I thought I came by it. So I told him, and he asked very calmly, mucho professional, you know," and here the narrator's drawl took on a deeper tone, "Was your role in the, ah, encounter, active, passive or oral. . . ."

"My God," breathed his friend, but the narrator rushed on, " . . . so I simply said, 'Doctor, all three—*but not necessarily in that order,*'" and the couple dissolved into gales of laughter.

Krass grinned at Cleaver and Dance, who had caught the end of the story. He was just registering that apart from the two women behind the bar, the congregation in the place was all male, when he caught sight of Tor striding between the tables toward them.

But Tor had changed. No longer was this the obese, heavy-gutted figure they remembered. He had shed perhaps fifty pounds. A black T-shirt with the bar's logo revealed rippling biceps in perfect tone, and a jutting torso which tapered to a trim waist and muscular stomach. He still wore tinted aviator shades, and his lustrous black hair was still long, but now it was swept straight back from his forehead to fall in a single sculptured wave to his shoulders, and his full black beard was carefully trimmed. The old shambling walk was gone, as, followed by a younger fair-haired man, he picked his way lithely between the tables, inclining his head slightly to customers he knew. But looking up at Tor as the tall figure loomed over their table, Cleaver thought that, though sleek and muscular now, there was still something bear-like and benign, comforting even, about the big man.

Tor looked from one to the other of them, and, grinning broadly, raised his arms to encompass both the bar and his new physical profile.

"I told you," he said, "one day I'd be thin, and I'd be rich. . . ."

"And we're not sorry," said Cleaver, laughing and rising to pump his massive hand. "Good to see you looking good, man."

"This is a friend of mine, Billy," said Tor, introducing his companion.

"How you doing, Bill?" said Krass as the pair put their drinks on the table and sat down. "You really have a nice place here, Tor," he went on; then leaning closer and lowering his voice, "and I guess wall-to-wall gays kind of goes with the territory in this town." He smiled and took a drink.

When there was no reply, he looked over at Tor. Both the muscular giant and the boy next to him were staring at him impassively. After long seconds had passed Krass for the second time that evening felt the hot blood of embarrassment flooding into his face.

Cleaver started to say something, but Tor rumbled quietly,

"Billy, could you be kind and get us another drink all round?"

When the boy had gone, Krass blurted out, "Look, I'm really sorry, there's days I can't seem to do anything but live up to my name. . . ."

Tor removed his shades, and looking round at them slowly said,

"Now we'd better have it out front right now. From the little Dance told me on the phone I can just about guess what's going down. But what I have to know also is how you guys feel about getting into this with," and here he tapped his chest, "a two-hundred-and-twenty-pound fruit."

Cleaver looked at the mortified Krass and at Dance, who shrugged once. Finally Cleaver said, "It's late in the century. We're all grown up. And it's your life. . . ."

"That's right," Tor cut in quietly, "it definitely is. And I found out who I am. Can you guys say the same thing?"

San Francisco, Monday, 11:30 A.M.

"A blind guy, a college professor and a faggot!" Six snorted. "Great team!"

"You forgot to mention a three-time loser thief, which is what you are," Cleaver came back at him. "With the other guys, I'm *asking* if they want in or not. But you, fuck-pig, either you're with us or your ass goes back in the slammer so fast your feet don't touch the ground. . . ."

"Okay, okay, I'm widja, I'm widja," muttered the squat gunman, hands nervously loosening the knot of his loud wide tie.

Tor had proved a valuable source of information; since five years previously when he had got his own bar, people had kept in touch. He knew where the Dude's New Mexican spread was located, he knew where their rich friend Kemp could be reached, he knew the marine base where Levon and Leroy were currently posted, he knew the name of Ariel's airfield; and he knew that Six was currently inside San Quentin, awaiting trial on a charge of illegally dealing in automatic weapons. His buyers had revealed themselves as undercover federal agents at the moment that they busted him, and his bail was set way beyond anything he could meet or even Cleaver could contemplate.

The night before, at Tor's suggestion, late as it was, the big man had called Kemp, who currently resided on the southern Florida coast just outside Miami. When Tor had filled him in, Kemp had gone along with Cleaver's thinking without hesitation, and things began to happen. By the time the banks were open, a substantial sum of money had arrived for them to deploy, the very best legal advice was pulled off all other work, and Six had been rapidly sprung.

"Who *is* Kemp now?" Cleaver had asked Tor when it became clear what was happening. "How does he run these numbers? His old man wasn't *that* rich."

"This is his own bread," said Tor quietly. "Down in Miami he does what he did in the old days, only a little more so. You know what they say; the dopers down there don't rob banks, they own them."

The result of Kemp's money and influence was standing before them in Tor's apartment, dressed in the bookie's suit in which he had been busted. There just seemed to be more of the same old Six—more paunch, more sleaze, and more foulmouthed truculence. But now he diminished before Cleaver's anger.

"Now listen up, turkey," Cleaver grated, "we're still short one Mexican, Cooch. You heard anything of him?"

"Yeah, yeah," Six mumbled, "happens I have. 'Cause he's in the same situation I was, couple hours ago." When they looked puzzled, he said, "The crossbar hotel. The joint. He's in his local slammer, some piss-ant beaner town north of Guadalajara. I heard about it inside. Seems somebody said something he didn't like to his old lady. So Cooch cuts the cat a little and sends him on his way. Only the guy's the chief of police's brother-in-law. So Cooch gets flung in the hole, which, being it's south of the border, ain't exactly the Hotel California, plus also the *jefe de policia* drops by and whales on him every once in a while. Hard times for Cooch."

Cleaver turned to Tor.

"Get on to Kemp and tell him," he said. "See what he can suggest." He turned back to Six, who was muttering, "Listen, I been inside a couple of months now, I need to grab a couple of drinks, loosen up a little, you know what I mean?"

Cleaver ignored him and spoke directly to Krass.

"You take this piece of shit out of here and get him working. We need some hardware that can't be traced, and that's one thing he's good for. A dozen handguns, a dozen pumpguns, half a dozen M16s, two hundred rounds for each piece." He held up a hand to quell Six's objections. "When he's done that, take him up to North Beach, get him drunk, get him laid, but before the night's through, get him on the truck you're going to hire and haul him and the guns out to the Dude's ranch by Santa Fe. If he's any trouble, if he even looks like he's going to make a run, call the court and the feds and tell them his bail's been withdrawn. Okay?"

"Yeah," said Krass reluctantly, "but . . ."

"What is it?"

"Well, are the guns really . . ."

"What do you think, they're going to say sorry like good boys and just hand Duane back if we ask real nice? Listen," he went on in a quieter tone, "of course, we're going to do everything we can not to use the damn things. But they have to be there."

"I guess so," said Krass slowly. "Now how about you? Where will you be?"

"I'm flying back to L.A. now, going home and picking up my bike, and then Laura and I will ride down to Santa Fe."

"What's with the bike?" said Tor. "You don't mean we're going in there the same way as last time?"

"I think maybe some of us are," said Cleaver.

"Nah, but how come your old lady's going along?" Six sniggered.

"They know where I work, they'll know where I live. Laura's sent the kids to her parents, but she'll be safer with us." When silence greeted this, he went on brusquely, "Hell, she's insisted on coming. And she's a trained nurse. It could be useful."

Six was leaving the room, still muttering,

"Jesus, what a team. Even the boss is pussy-whipped. . . ."

"Krass, give him a peanut and get him out of here," said Cleaver wearily. When they had gone and he was alone with Tor, he went on,

"Will you call the Dude again and let him know we're on our way?" As the big man nodded, Cleaver was drumming a pencil worriedly on the desk top.

"What's up?" said Tor.

Cleaver stroked his mustache slowly and then said, "Well, it looks like we're getting the guys together all right. And Kemp's bread is a real break; we don't have any worries about things we may need. But if we're going to do this right, we want accurate information—about the clubhouse and about every part of the ground down there. It won't do us any good to rely on thirteen-year-old memories. But any of us hanging out there would stand out like a´rabbi at high mass. And the clock's running; we've got less than five days."

"I think it'll be all right," said Tor. "I think the Dude's got an inside end down there."

"What?" said Cleaver.

"It was real weird," said Tor. "When I called the Dude and began to lay it out for him, you know what he said? He said, 'At last.' Just that. 'At last.'

"When I asked him what he meant, he said the whole thing had been on his mind since day one. That maybe goes the same for some of the rest of us, but the Dude did something about it. He wanted to know how the girl, Emily, had made out, so after we'd got away he called the Judge's servant, you remember, that old black guy, G. W. Brooks? The Dude says he's stayed with it, they've gone on calling each other from time to time."

"But he's the Judge's faithful retainer and all, isn't he?" said Cleaver. "Surely he wouldn't do anything to cross Lafayette?"

Tor tugged his beard uncertainly, but said, "Well, the Dude is sure the old guy will help us, cause he raised Baby Duane, he never did believe him or his friends did what was done at Woodstock South there, and he won't sit by and watch while they off Duane and his family."

"But the clubhouse . . . ," Cleaver began.

"He can get in there with the Judge," said Tor. "The old man visits every day. To make sure Cal and them stay in line. . . ."

9

Louisiana, Monday, 12:00 A.M.

Duane sat propped against one wall of the cabin, watching Cannonball and Spider closely, without seeming to do it. One trouble was the furnace heat inside the airless shack; sweat streamed from him, running in rivulets even over the headband Mary had twisted for him from the sleeve torn from his shirt. So he had to move sometimes, wiping the stinging drops from his eyes with his right hand. Once in a while this caught their eye.

He was careful not to use his left hand, because that made him think of where his finger was gone, and he had found it better not to do that. Not even to look at the inflamed wound, the ugly red puffiness spreading up his hand. At least the cuts on his face where they'd beaten him the first time were healing up. And the Judge had seen that he was bandaged right. But beyond that there was nothing to do, so it was best he didn't think about it.

Instead he looked down at Mary and then at little Annie, dozing in the noonday heat with her head resting lightly on his thigh, the fine fair hair sadly matted despite her mother's combing. They wouldn't let them wash.

Just seven years old. She shouldn't have been through all this, any of this. Seeing him when they cut him. Listening to the scuttle of the swamp rats in the cold damp nights, or to Spider talking trash, what he was going to do to the little girl and her mother when the Judge turned them over to him and his friends. Duane squeezed his eyes tight shut, suddenly tortured for the thousandth time by the guilt at having brought them both to Badwater county, exposed them to all this.

But if their presence was a torture to him, he was also often grateful for it, being too busy looking out for them to have time to worry much about himself. The pain when they suffered was sometimes balanced by the ring of warmth and love which the three of them created among themselves.

He looked carefully across the room again. At the front the only two windows were shuttered, but shafts of light let in from the rotting joists and shingles of the roof fell across the trash-strewn stamped-earth floor of the long room to the decrepit table where Spider sat lethargically playing out another hand of poker with Cannonball. The latter's eyes were shaded by the peak of a black baseball hat carrying the emblem of his helicopter service.

Duane remembered the big tub of lard arriving back from California. He was gloating at having tracked down Cleaver, but something about the vicious, angry way he talked let Duane know that Cleaver had rattled him. Right on, John! he thought again, feeling a surge of hope course through him. Cleaver wouldn't let them down. But quickly he damped the feeling down. Everything had to be rationed, it seemed like, including hope. He had found things went better that way.

And mostly he did wish that Cleaver wouldn't try anything. There were never fewer than two men in the cabin with them at all times, and there were scatterguns propped by the table, which would be turned on all three of them, as Spider had explained gloatingly, at the first sign of trouble. And that was only the tip of the iceberg. Not just what was left of the Truckers, but much of Badwater had rallied to the Judge on this one, seeing it as doing right by his dead son and his poor crazy daughter. Hell, Duane could understand. He'd kill whoever had done it himself if he caught them. From the talk on the hut's CB, he knew that there were local men in boats sealing up the bayou at the back, and shifts of guys at the far end of the causeway, and then again at the crossroads to the west, as well as the approaches to town to the east. It was hard to see what could be done

Duane's attention came back to the here and now, as with a curse Spider threw down another losing hand and jerked upright, upsetting his chair. The crash woke Annie; the child jumped, and the movement caught Spider's good eye. Still cursing, the spindly biker stamped across to near them, where the bucket that was their only toilet stood by the wall. Ripping open his Levis, Spider urinated into the bucket, sneering, "See anything you like, little girl? Cause I jest love bald pussy. I surely do."

But Annie was looking into her father's face for reassurance, and this helped Duane keep calm. He thought about asking Spider in a civil way to do his business outside, but remembered the days they would still have to get through, and so said nothing. He kept his eyes away from the Trucker, letting all his anger center on a single thought: if I live, he dies.

Then he forced himself to concentrate on Annie. As Spider turned away, Duane brushed a matted lock of damp fair hair off the child's soft forehead and asked quietly, "Are you hungry, hon?" And when the girl nodded, wide-eyed, he went on, "Me too. Won't be long now. Wonder what the old gentleman will bring us today?"

For the past two days the Judge, accompanied by Rampike, had come at midday with food for them from the town. They had learned to eat everything they could get down while he was still there, for when he left the Truckers took anything that remained and ate it or threw it out, from meanness. His visits were their only guarantee of safety.

Duane had been struck not by the external changes in the two older men—Rampike's grizzled hair when he removed his wreck of a hat, the Judge's slow gait, and the way his head now sat on his shoulders like a turtle's; but by the way both of them, but especially the Judge, seemed not so much to have changed with the passing years as to have been compressed, solidified into the essence of themselves—sparing of speech, patient, deliberate, emanating an aura of profound will and a kind of wisdom that everyone instinctively deferred to.

Only trouble was, you couldn't get through to them.

But the visits were really marred by the presence of Cal, who came with his father, and by his business dress and the new refinement in his manner made it clear that he now stood with the old man rather than his former friends. But sometimes his narrow and overshadowed dark eyes would fix on Duane and his family, and Duane would remember how Cal had been when they had cut off his finger. But he knew what he knew about the Judge's son, and as long as the old man kept coming round, Duane had to guess it was a trade-off, that Cal would stay backed off to make sure that Duane kept his mouth shut.

There were no guarantees, though; anything could happen to them at any time, and once again to Duane the answer seemed to be narrowing the focus, getting by on living from day to day, hour to hour even, not thinking, hoping or fearing too far ahead, just staying calm and very watchful. Sometimes when things were quiet and the women were asleep he did let himself drift away into memories and visions, which with him always seemed to be moments of movement; bright windy mornings shipping out from the Bay, with gulls circling and high overhead the great red bridge sliding by, or earlier, summer days riding the coast road below Carmel with the 13. These mental journeys would come to seem vividly real to him, and it was a painful wrench to return to the reality of the sweltering, squalid cabin.

He wondered if it was the same for everyone who was shut away from freedom. He knew that he had been easygoing, had never really thought what it was like for prisoners, and he hoped that if they ever got out of this, he would not forget all the people, all over the world, who were living in this same hell.

10

Mexico, Monday, 8:30 P.M.

Emiliano Hernandez, on tiptoe on his uneven legs, watched through the tiny window of his first floor cell as the light faded from the street below and the hills beyond.

It reminded him of a thing his grandfather used to say, back in the southern California shantytown after a day's back-breaking work, peach-picking. As the darkness fell and coolness came, the old man would smile through his fatigue and murmur,

"Ah, in the night, there are no mountains."

Correct, thought his grandson now, turning from the window and lowering himself with a slight rueful smile onto the floor. But maybe still a few little hills.

Emiliano Hernandez, whom the 13 knew as Cooch, found the one-finger push-ups hard for a number of reasons.

The most obvious were his two ribs that *el jefe* had broken in that first, terrible beating. Then there was the problem of the guards; always he had to listen for them, because he must remain with the appearance of feebleness, and some feeble-mindedness also, to keep everyone unwary, and above all to keep them from working over his hands. He smiled tightly as he held his breath, pushing and lowering with all the weight on just his two forefingers, remembering the guard's laughter as they found him with his bowl full of sand he had accumulated from the floor, pushing his fingers into it rhythmically. When the sand had gone in favor of pebbles, the *pendejos*, laughing like mares, had even tossed him some through the bars.

Then there was the pain in his eyes. But his grandfather had warned him of that. The old man, recognizing his aptitude early, had been the one who had taught him the knife; not just the short-fight tricks and the whirling fighting forms, but a thorough working knowledge of anatomy too, both his own and opponents'. For *el abuelo* had been a famous man in his day, an artist in matches in the old days south of the border. And when the government of Mexico in its wisdom had clamped down on knife-fighting with its savage ordinances of 1938, *el viejo* had gone down the route he himself was forced to travel now, discarding his old weapon but forging new ones. And had found, as Emiliano was finding, that the strengthening of the hands led in some mysterious way to weakness of the eyes. Grandfather had had a medicine for that, but, Emiliano smiled to himself, as he shifted to a fresh round of twenty on his middle finger, in this hotel he did not think room service would oblige with a bottle of it.

He knew his chances were not so good now. But it had been a good life. For the most part, he amended, biting his lip hard as a lance of pain stabbed at his ribs. The wild free days with his *yanqui* friends, then the coming home, to Mexico, *Mexico lindo*, the getting of his own place, his business. And then Rosa, who had done him the honor of choosing him despite her family's wishes, and in their marriage brought to him his first knowledge of true happiness, and borne their three fine children. And was beautiful still, beautiful enough to attract the attentions of that *hijo de la gran puta*, that *hijo de la puta reputada*, *el jefe*'s brother-in-law—the scarred one, now.

Yes, but life was good. And if sometimes it threw strange things at a man without warning—well, had anyone ever said it would be different?

For most of it was gone now. Rosa, thanks to God, had got away with the children, and he had heard that they were all safe with her family in the country. But shortly after they had put him in jail, the shop had been broken into, all his stock of machines and tools stolen, and his workplace wrecked. *Mysteriously*, the police had no leads on who did it. And now *el jefe*, *chinga su madre*, had persuaded the landlord from whom he had rented the place to terminate the lease on the grounds of his absence.

So they kept him here, isolated so nothing could be passed to him, here with no bedspring, no metal fork or spoon to sharpen, for they knew something of his reputation; kept him here awaiting *el jefe*'s drunken pleasure. For the man was a drunkard, *un borrachón* who got loaded and came here to beat him, to try and break him, for pleasure. It was Emiliano's greatest fear. A few drinks too many one evening, a little too much force, and before his opportunity had come, Emiliano would be dead, officially "while attempting to escape," and *el jefe* would be free. And they both knew it. It was a matter of mood with *el jefe*, and for Emiliano, of timing. Ay, but the man knew how to hate. *Pos pues*, Emiliano might still surprise him one time, a little, in that department.

In the middle of an upward push he stiffened, and then in one motion rolled over and slid back onto the filthy cotton bedding in the corner. Far off down the corridor he had heard the sound of heavy footsteps on the stairs. Let it be for someone else, he found himself praying. But the footsteps were approaching inexorably. They were coming for him again. He steadied his breathing and his pounding heart. And to compose his mind, told himself once more that soon it would pass, and it would be night. And that in the night, he knew, there were no mountains.

11

Florida, Tuesday, 7:00 A.M.

Kemp's eyes snapped open and he was awake again. But he lay rigidly, unmoving, jaws clenched, his body clogged, heavy as lead, with no power of the slightest movement, in the slatted light of the Levolor blinds, in the aftermath of the dream. Dimly his ears were aware of the faint rustle of palms outside his window, the susurration of the surf on the beach below. But most of him still resided in the dream.

It had been a gunship over Vietnam. A lone figure had been running in a lane between the green, green paddies below. The gunner had fired a single shot. The pilot had landed, waiting apprehensively. The gunner, somber, had gone and confirmed the kill. Kemp was the gunner.

The scene had shifted back to the flyer's camp, low green open-sided tents in a mud-soaked compound. The pilot was there, revealed to be fat, drinking from a bottle, loudly wishing he had made the kill, praising the gunner. The pilot's wife, a woman with pig-like features, also drunk, very, also overweight and showing it in an ornate black lace bedroom outfit, echoed his praise. She worked her way on her knees through the mud separating the two tents, and when she reached the gunner's bed, leaned forward and began to suck his cock noisily. But the gunner remained limp and unexcited, protesting quietly that he had a wife of his own at home.

The scene changed again. The gunner and his wife, a

pretty girl with dark curly hair, were back stateside, walking at night toward a very brightly lit glass and metal service station. A huddle of figures were standing under the harsh white light; one of them was the fat pilot, who owned the station. When he caught sight of the couple, he made a big noise over the gunner and his wife, making the gunner uneasy with his effusiveness, the "my old buddy" talk to which the others hanging out there, sullen, did not respond.

The pilot produced white plastic-wrapped parcels, presents, for the two of them. "Do you want it?" he said, over and over again, until uneasily they took the parcels, but still he kept on asking the question. They felt some complicity being set up. Then a customer, tall, crew-cut, smartly dressed but brutal-looking, came in and began to explain. He could ask them to do anything now and they must do it, for anyone who was part of it (and it was all across the nation) had to. The gunner's wife must suck the guy's cock if he said so, or anything else. Because under the harsh white light they had taken the parcels, because they knew about "Do you want it?" And there was no reversing the fact that they knew, no way back.

Kemp blinked and stirred slightly in the bed, coming out of it. Crazy, he thought. He was a pilot, not a gunner. He had never been in a gunship, and they certainly hadn't slept in any bloody tents. He didn't know where the hell the pilot and his wife had popped into his head from. He thought he had known the brutal man, though he wasn't sure; he thought the fellow had been a friend of his father's. He knew the gunner's wife because he was in fact married to her. And he knew the white-wrapped parcels all too well.

He shifted slightly again to look at the fair-haired woman asleep beside him. The sheet had slipped from her, revealing a breast, soft and pink in the shadows of the room, the nipple circled by a big aureole. It was not his wife, Jessica. She had left him two years before when she realized how deep he was in dealing. She'd liked adventure, she had said when she went, but drew the line at commerce.

The blond girl with the elegantly bobbed hair breathing softly next to him was called Bonnie. She'd been with him for a few months now. He liked her. Women had been the earliest of the many ways he had found to take his mind off feeling bad, and they were still the best. But particularly he liked Bonnie's distance. Even when they were fucking there was something detached, disengaged, even a little world-weary about her, a certain lack of attention to proceedings, he grinned wryly, so that when he did succeed in moving her, she would exhibit an air of surprise at the tender indignity she came upon herself taking part in. He remembered a phrase out of somewhere— "She's from another garage." She was, yes. And he liked that.

It was not coldness, for she was friendly enough in a cock-eyed sort of way. The way she free-based his best stuff didn't hurt, of course. But whatever, it was distance. And he needed that, since Jessica had gone, and since the pressure kept on mounting; from the feds, the DEA, the Special Task Group, from his own fellow major stockholders, from the Colombians in the background, and from the competition and their feral Cuban gunmen. And now on top of everything, after so long, this thing with Duane and the others. All this, from that one night. So long ago. In a way it was gratifying; ironically, the guys finally needed him, and his bread. Also unusual, lucky even—to be able to put a finger on a turning point in their lives, and to go back and do something about it. He smiled secretly. How many people could say exactly where the slide in their lives had started?

He looked down at Bonnie again and shook his head. Who knew where it would end, any of it. But he did like her distance. He imagined it was the same for her.

Abiding by that, he swung his slim body silently from the bed now and padded into the adjoining ornate bathroom, to pull on a few clothes and his Lucchese cowboy boots, lift a Colt Woodsman automatic from its place in the medicine cabinet and stick it in his belt before clopping downstairs to the sunken garage.

All the while he was thinking hard, going over the plans he had hammered out in his head the night before after Cleaver had called him from California. He knew he was going to have to go round the outside of his corporation on this one. They would never sit still for the risk to the organization, with its computerized accounts department, its retirement and pension plans. These days, Kemp grinned to himself, sometimes he thought the guys had seriously lost touch with their roots.

By the same token, he knew he would have to fly this one himself, and as he slid behind the wheel, not of the Ferrari but of one of their more anonymous fleet of Fords, automatically fixing the long-barreled pistol to the clips beneath the dash, Kemp felt the tightening lift at the prospect. There might be opposition on the ground down South, but equally deadly would be any intervention by Customs planes; because even if he was clean, the corporation would get to hear of it and he would be finished, which in the volatile doper world meant only one thing. The feeling was the same one he would get in the Khmera cafe on Monivong Street in Phnom Penh during the last days in Cambodia, when word of another shaky run to Battambang or Kampot came through for him and the other pilots. Shit, he thought, even the planes were the same, the ancient DC3s they had out there, and now the C-47s he had picked up as a side deal and consequently had earmarked for this one.

Kemp winced as the big garage doors tilted up automatically and the light hit his eyes. Although it was the beginning of the day he felt curiously fatigued, tired and weightless, as if a breath of air would blow him away. Crazy life, he thought, cruising the Ford slowly out into the driveway and then the street, not bothering to check for surveillance, knowing it was all too likely since one of their snitches inside had let them know they had been priority target by the presidential narcotics Special Task Group. So he began his long haphazard ride around town, which would be interspersed with brief stops at random public pay phones to set up the plane for Saturday. And to confirm the clearance for Mexico tomorrow, thought Kemp. But the rest was down to Cleaver, getting them out on the ground. For an instant, as he thought of fugitives, Kemp flashed back to his dream, the figure running in the paddies. Distanced now, it was simply bewildering. What had that been all about?

Emil Mintz was not well liked by his colleagues at Operation Greenback.

His diminutive stature, tight-lipped and prissy demeanor, and the fact that he indulged in neither alcohol nor tobacco contributed to their attitude. It was reinforced by the way in which he worked, the remorselessly long hours and painstaking procedures. Though Greenback was the financial side of the Special Task Group, and presidential priority automatically meant regularly working their tails off, Mintz's colleagues, correctly, as it happened, identified his zeal as fueled by lethal ambition, the principal clue being his kiss-ass ways with their Director.

But the main reason they loathed Mintz was the realization that his close-cropped beard, his quiet, dry, overprecise way of speaking, the wide-eyed unsmiling way in which he delivered his demands and his little bombshells of information—that all of this, even his thin, gold-rimmed spectacles, which some of the younger guys swore were plain glass, all was in imitation of a movie actor, who, after starting out playing a Frenchman's assistant in a famous science fiction flick, had gone on to play in short order not one but two snotty DA's men in two other movies. Now the business of cops imitating movie cops was far from unknown; among the DEA men and the south Florida police you would find your quota of laconic Clints and boyishly grinning Burts. But that the little prick should be imitating *another* little prick was too much for his colleagues.

"Emmy's got the trots again," muttered one of them to another that morning as Mintz, clutching a straggling printout, was seen to proceed with short, fast, precise steps across the cluttered open-plan to the door of the Director's office, where he waited deferentially before disappearing within.

The Director looked up unwillingly. Mintz was standing there in that tense, overcontrolled way that meant he had something for you. Like a baby with a full diaper, the Director thought sourly.

"It's a possible break with GIMLET, sir," said Mintz, using Greenback's coding for Kemp's corporation. "Or at least their vice-president, William Kemp."

The Director nodded at the mention of the name. Kemp was an oddity, an Anglo high up in the coke trade, conspicuous and vulnerable.

"As you know, I've been on the audit trail with them for several weeks. And I believe that I have, that I *may* have, come up with something."

"Yes," said the Director, shifting in his seat.

"Most of their narcotics cash ends up in the usual tax havens, in their case a Netherlands Antilles corporation. But first, of course, it has to be laundered through the various dummy corporations they have rotating here, principally involved in real estate. One of these concerns itself with apartment and condo rentals, and I have found that for the past years it has been renting *en bloc* to Southern Sights Inc., a travel agency specializing in Florida holidays. This caught my eye, so I checked back." Mintz paused for effect, the Director groaning inwardly. "The travel agents are getting the leases for virtually nothing."

"Yes," said the Director.

"Because last year, presumably in return for highly favorable terms of this sort, Southern Sights quietly acquired a new majority stockholder. This was a minor corporation with a number of interests in California—a car dealership, a small chain of male boutiques, and so on." Again he paused. "Its name was Kemal Inc."

"Yes?" said the Director. Mintz was now caught between his ever-present desire to flatter the Director, and his narrative's implication, which was that his boss should have known what he was talking about. Opting eventually for a more-in-sorrow-than-in-anger demeanor, he continued, "Kemal Inc., as you will remember we discovered earlier in the GIMLET investigation, is the repository for William Kemp's own not inconsiderable personal inherited fortune."

"Yes," said the Director curtly, in a tone that implied this had been obvious to him all along. Mintz's mouth pursed, but then he plunged on.

"I consequently checked out any and every aspect of Southern Sights' activities since then. And came up with this." At which point, with a gesture as delicate as a courtier's bow, he laid the printout on the desk of the Director.

But the latter ignored it, simply repeating patiently,

"Yes?"

"In Arizona, in September of last year, three USAF C-47-Bs were sold at auction. All three were bid for and purchased. By a representative of Southern Sights."

"*Yes,*" said the Director, so that somehow when Mintz now summed up it was as if the Director was doing it himself.

"The planes were flown to southern Florida for extensive refurbishing, ostensibly with a view to extending Southern Sights' operations south of the border. So we now have three airworthy twin-engined aircraft owned by a major stockholder in what is unquestionably a doper corporation, ready for service in an area through which passes, as you know, two-thirds of all illegal narcotics smuggled into our country. I would therefore urge immediate and intensive surveillance of the three aircraft."

"Maybe," said the Director nastily, snatching the printout from Mintz and stuffing it into a drawer of his desk. He didn't like the little prick, either.

12

After the long ride down Cleaver felt unreal, slightly insane even, because it didn't seem credible at his age to still know such joy on wheels.

His bike, a three-cylinder Triumph T160 Trident, had spent most of its time unobstrusively under wraps in a corner of Cleaver's garage. He had traded in the Bonneville for it after he started pulling down serious money at the agency, but then with a young family, the new machine had seen little use.

Cleaver did not neglect it, however, sometimes resorting to the Trident as an area of his life untouched by either business worries or his domestic existence. Because he was a good and caring husband and father in so many respects, Laura had indulged the hours that he spent at night in the garage, finetuning both the motor and cycle parts to his own satisfaction, and fitting the flow of performance parts and the big-bore conversion that he sent for from England. But there had been little room in their lives for actually riding it. Sometimes if the car was in the shop, he would use it to get to work, or in the summer if the kids were away, he and Laura would take a run to the beach. But the thing was really a buyer's dream, a pampered obsolete minor classic with all its potential intact, a seven-year-old, low-mileage 140-mph projectile.

Cleaver had moved fast, and by Monday night he and Laura were clear of the city in an anonymous motel close to the Arizona border. Crossing the high desert, Cleaver had felt a righteous lift at the sight of the silver air force fighters going fast after each other to the north, sporting over the desert, exhaust smoke coming when they went down low.

In their room that night, Laura, slim in jeans and T-shirt, read or watched quietly as Cleaver, preoccupied, puzzled at the notes he was constantly making or spent time on the phone to Ariel, to Kemp and to the Dude. Laura was still absorbing the situation, could see the tension in Cleaver and feel the force of his organizing brain and of his willpower. She knew that there was nothing she could contribute yet, so she stayed out of it. But that night in bed they came together with an unaccustomed fierce wordless passion, and slept deeply afterward.

The next day was magic. They made a chill start just after sunup and ate a big breakfast later at a desert truck stop whose water tower legend

EAT
GAS

they had found irresistible. Then they rode on into the muted desert colors, under cloud, gray sky and yellow light on the horizon, the colors of the rumpled brown land muted, but the light clearer than it would be in the bright relentless blue to come. They ceased to notice the shreds of black rubber from disintegrated truck tires all along the highway, and sailed past scattered shacks and wire-fenced trailers, drinking in the sense of emptiness and dry space, the grandness of it.

Over the border into Arizona, Cleaver began to tighten up the rubber band and let the bike run on, abandoning the sixty to seventy miles per hour compromise that most traffic adopted with the blanket fifty-five limit, but keeping below ninety-five, as he knew this meant statutory imprisonment. Outside Kingman, the driver of a Mack eighteen-wheeler flipped them a wave as they blasted through his slipstream. At first Cleaver monitored the sound and feel of the Trident carefully, grateful for the oil cooler as the temperature rose, but though the motor sucked down juice like a sailor on a three-day liberty, the bike ran tirelessly and handled the changes of altitude well as they climbed into the San Francisco mountains. Before midday they were through Flagstaff and had laughed at a sign announcing TEN THOUSAND NICE PEOPLE WELCOME YOU TO WINSLOW. As Cleaver drove the Triumph across the Little Colorado River, he found himself singing at the top of his voice, "*I'm a steady rolling man,*" one of the Dude's old Robert Johnson tunes that he hadn't thought of in years. He only stopped when Laura leaned forward and shouted, reminding him of the time years ago under similarly exuberant circumstances when a bee had flown into his mouth.

He laughed, relieved; at first he had also worried how his wife would handle the run, but the Trident was a big, comfortable bike, fairly smooth for a Brit too, and Laura, light and fit, had always loved the long roads, in the days when the Bonneville had been their primary transportation. When they pulled in for a late lunch at a truck stop beyond Holbrook, with the fantastic shapes of the petrified forest in a heat haze off to their right, all Cleaver had to do to the bike was adjust the big rear drive chain.

Through the heat of the afternoon they raced on to Gallup, and over the mountains again to Albuquerque, with the sun beginning to sink, throwing shadows on the red, flat, telegraph-poled land. There they turned north for the last leg to Santa Fe and beyond, fatigue biting deep at them now, but a good tiredness, with the intended end in sight, and Cleaver thought he felt better than he had in years, his mind wiped clear of all the nagging worries by the concentratrion on the road and the fusion with his machine. As they approached Santa Fe across the sagebrush plains, Laura looked to her left, where the shapes of the mountains were outlined pearl-gray through the sunset haze, an eye of yellow light staring flawed through the indentation in them. She leaned her head against Cleaver's broad leather-jacketed back as they wheeled around the city and headed north again, through country which Cleaver thought he recognized from the 13's visit there in the sixties. They crossed the Rio Grande, and as the piñon-covered slopes of the Sangre de Cristo foothills appeared in the distance, Cleaver, following the directions given him, turned on to a dirt track and bumped down it for a mile in the soft evening light until they entered a perimeter fence of brushwood stick and wire, and finally drew to a halt before the raised gallery of a lovely, low, rambling one-story structure of wood and adobe, the Dude's place.

A pack of good-natured sandy-colored dogs surrounded them, and as Cleaver and Laura climbed off stiffly, their barking brought people out to them. As Laura raised her dusty visor and pulled off her helmet so that her fair hair cascaded free, she was greeted enthusiastically by a smiling, cadaverous figure crying,

"Welcome! Welcome! *Mi casa es su casa!*"

He was dressed in green aviator's coveralls, with a fringe of long hair round a bald tonsure which made him look something like a circus clown, or the butler in that *Rocky Horror* movie the kids went to over and over. When he turned to embrace Cleaver, on the back of his coveralls Laura saw a top and bottom rocker embroidered in red Victorian capitals with the legend

DOC
DUDE

Laura's attention was now on the figures standing on the gallery. The tall, burly smiling one with the cowlick of fair hair and an expression that managed to be both careworn and boyish, she recognized as Krass; they had met once in the early days. The benign, bearded one with the Herculean figure now displayed to good advantage in a purple singlet she knew must be Tor. And the shambling, overweight, aging runt with the mean eyes and, crisscrossed with leather straps, a grubby white T-shirt that read

CRIME WOULDN'T PAY—
IF THE GOVERNMENT RAN IT

That had to be Six, she thought, noting with alarm that a big automatic pistol casually dangled butt-down from the harness under his left arm. She thought vaguely that though they were all Cleaver's age, he alone seemed to have that finished, assured quality she would call manly.

The Dude was making the introductions when, like a whirlwind, the porch door burst open again and a stunning-looking very young girl wearing nothing but a long red-and-black-striped rugger shirt, with flowing dark brown hair, a dancer's nubile body and an aura of overwhelming sexuality, flung her arms round Cleaver and glued her full lips to his.

"Too much!" she breathed, still clinging to him when he extricated himself. "I mean—totally vicious! You're Cleaver, and you're like, totally, toe-dully . . ."

"Dude," said Cleaver politely, "who is this person?"

"That's Cherry," said the Dude. "She's—my mother. My daughter. We're, like, best friends. She's also the cook tonight."

"Cook?" Cherry exclaimed. "Shine cooking. With all these killer guys showing up? Cooking? I mean—snore on!"

"She did spend some time in the Valley," the Dude explained dolefully.

"Well, listen, Cherry," Laura cut in, smiling, "I'm Mrs. Vicious, and I just rode clear from Tinseltown to cactus country, and if you'll show me where I can take a shower, I'll be your second-best friend. After that I'm so hungry, I'll not only willingly cook and eat a horse, I'll also shoot the creature first if I have to. Okay?"

"Okay," said Cherry placidly, and after Laura had unstrapped the saddlebags from their machine, led her inside.

Cleaver watched the back of the rugger shirt until it disappeared, then shook his head and said without inflection, "She jail-bait?"

"Not since last month," said the Dude quickly.

Cleaver pointed at the lanky singer's coveralls.

"What's with the Doc tag, anyhow?"

"I practice a little, ah, alternative medicine, for the crazies hereabouts, counseling and such, as it were, straightening out their heads. . . ."

"Yeah, he's real good with the head," sang Cherry from outside.

"Who else is here?" asked Cleaver.

"Dance, he's lying down resting right now; him and Bob came in with the big transporter truck and some bikes awhile before you did. And Levon and Leroy flew in to Santa Fe this morning." The Dude's sunken face darkened with worry. "They're in their room," he went on, gesturing to the right of the house where an extension ran back like the long arm of an L, with doors dotted along it.

"Yeah, the ghetto is at the end," muttered Six. "Bad news. Bad fucking news," and he slouched away.

Cleaver was busying himself with his machine. The Dude told him where the garage was and then went in with Tor to see how Laura was doing. Left alone with Krass, Cleaver said, "That Cherry—you think she's going to stir things up with the guys?"

"Hell, I don't think so," Krass grinned almost shyly. "She's pretty nice." He chuckled. "When Bob met her it was weird; he asked if he could touch her face, to get some idea of what she looked like. And it was something—to see his hands running all over her features in silence, as if he was sculpting her. In the end he told her she was pretty. But he said he hoped she was nice, too, because one thing you learned when you were the way he was is that what people looked like didn't matter. It's what they are that counts. And Cherry just said, 'I believe that too.' It sounded strange enough, coming from those lips. But it seemed like the two of them understood each other, somehow."

Cleaver grunted.

"Sounds okay. But she just reminds me of that Hollywood story, the two studio guys talking about the star. One asks, 'Is she a nymphomaniac?' and the other one says he thinks she would be, if they could just get her quieted down a little . . .'"

They laughed and wheeled the Triumph around to the left of the house, where a cavernous barn had been fitted out as the Dude's garage. In its musty recesses, Cleaver made out stalls for animals, as well as a number of vehicles; a pickup truck, a Willies Jeep, a partially restored '52 Hudson Commodore, a stack of Spanish and Japanese trail bikes. But the portion at the far end stood in stark contrast to the rest. Under bright unblinking neon lights, a big area of spotless concrete was flanked by a fully equipped shop with workbenches, hoists and battenboard on the walls hung with tools. In the center knelt Bob, working on a black bike, which Cleaver realized with a shock of recognition was the Dude's old Vincent Shadow. His mind made another adjustment when he saw that the blind man was holding an open book, a tattered workshop manual for the Vincent.

"Bob, it's Cleaver," Krass told him, "he just rode in from California on a three-pot Triumph with a boss-lookin' old lady." Bob grunted acknowledgment but remained concentrated on his task. Cleaver saw that he was scanning the pages of the manual with what looked like a tiny camera in his right hand, while his left forefinger rested on a small finger plate. Krass saw him looking and explained.

"That's an Optacon Bob's using. You move the camera device over the pages, and it translates the letters and numbers into clusters of pins that vibrate your fingers. Tricky stuff, huh? Bob can read pretty much anything."

Cleaver felt wonder. He thought he would stick around for a while and decided to change the Trident's oil before he washed up. He parked the bike well clear of Bob's area and found a drain can. He spotted a wrench he needed lying by the Shadow and was reaching for it when Bob's voice came very sharply,

"Don't be touching my tools, please."

Cleaver realized then that everything was arranged in exactly the same way it had been at Ascot raceway. Like a Bedouin in the desert, for Bob, wherever the old carpet was spread, everything had to be where it always was.

"I'm sorry, but I get real bothered if my stuff isn't where I'm used to it," Bob explained gruffly. Cleaver took tools from the benches and quietly went to work, quickly growing accustomed to the mutter of Bob's voice as he used a minicassette to record into, the sight of him making measurements with a Braille micrometer, and the subdued squawk of the synthetic speed outputs from his calculator, from another precision measuring instrument and from his wristwatch.

"That's all pretty magic stuff," he said to Krass as they stood outside later, watching the last of the evening light fade, the animal smells from the barn mingling with the smell of piñon smoke that wafted to them from the house behind.

"Yeah, you just don't think how new technology can work for different sorts of people," Krass agreed.

"Hell, the old technology did the job on me again. That run down here was something. Do you have to be a bit crazy to be happy? It seems like it sometimes. After all the riding we've done, I'd still forgotten how good it can make you feel."

"But are we really going in down there on the bikes?" said Krass.

"Some of us," said Cleaver, and he laid out the outline of his plan.

"But there's another thing," he concluded, "and you and I had better talk about it now. You've heard the plan, you see how we'll depend on one another. Especially on Levon and Leroy, maybe on Dance, definitely on Kemp . . ."

"Just like in the old days," said Krass.

"Yeah," said Cleaver, "but the old days was before that Graduation. Now let's bite the bullet. Supposing one or more of the guys did have something to do with what happened to the Judge's kids . . ." and as Krass began to protest, Cleaver overrode him with, "No, I'm just saying *if* they did? Now you can figure that the guy or guys might decide to dump on the rest of us; it would satisfy the Judge and the others, and it would stop any one of us comparing stories and catching them out. So if any one of us did do it, for that reason if for no other, we have to know first.

"Dance and Bob and Cooch and Ariel were together by the fire all the time. You and me likewise. But that leaves seven guys. We need to know what they were doing, who can vouch for whom, what their stories are so we can check them against each other and what we do know for sure. Kemp and Dance aren't available, but that leaves the twins, Six, Tor and the Dude. You take the last two, I'll talk to Levon and Leroy and the poisoned dwarf. We'll compare notes about it Thursday morning when we get back from Mexico. We do need to know."

"Whatever you say," said Krass. "You know me—not much of a leader, but a good follower."

"Which there's too few of around," said Cleaver, clapping an arm round his shoulders, and Krass grinned once before walking off toward the house.

Cleaver stood for a moment in the gathering darkness. Wind soughed through the brush; Cleaver felt grit blow in his face and shivered once, suddenly feeling his tiredness after the long ride, and at the prospect of all that was to come. But in a moment he shook himself and walked along to the last of the guest bunkhouses.

As Cleaver approached there was a loud thump from inside the door of the end room. He paused a moment, knocked, and then entered. As the door opened inward something blurred by his right eye with a loud thud into the jamb, less than a foot from his face. Cleaver saw a bayonet quivering there and turned back into the room to confront the flat, unsmiling faces of Levon and Leroy, looking up at him from where they lay on the two beds in each far corner of the room. An open fifth of Wild Turkey sat on the table between them.

"Why it's Cleaver the man," said Leroy.

"Don't he know enough to wait till he get asked in?" said Levon.

Both were in uniform, but stripped to Marine Airborne T-shirts with gold recon wings. Beneath, each of their bodies was solid muscle and sinew. Their hair was cropped close and there were many small scars on their arms and their scowling faces.

Cleaver felt the blatant hostility in the room and quickly checked the anger he felt rising in response. He closed the door, which was festooned with other knives and bayonets, smiled, and said,

"How are you both? It's good to see you. Thanks for coming—I know it can't have been easy. . . ."

"Wasn't easy," said Leroy.

"And let's cut the happy reunion crap," said Levon. "We only come here for one thing, and it wasn't to see no shit-eating grin."

"We came 'cause Duane's in trouble," continued Leroy. "We don't like him no better than we like the rest of you folks, but he got us out of a hole down in redneck country that time, and we pay our dues."

"What do you mean, got you out of a hole?" Cleaver cut in.

Grudgingly, Levon told the story of Duane's coming to help them with the Truckers. When he concluded, Cleaver said intently, "Okay, you walked off with Duane and then the lights went out. What happened after that?"

"You want to check it out, ask Baby Duane, when we get him. We stayed real close to him, till Krass came and told us the bad news," said Leroy sourly.

"Yeah, we was acting humble and small," Levon spat in disgust. "Like we was Amos and Andy. But not since then, not never no more."

"We're black gunnies, lifers, and that's about as mean and nasty as you can get to be," said Leroy with satisfaction. "We love to teach those cracker assholes come to the corps. . . ."

"We eat 'em up," said Levon.

"And spit 'em out," chimed in Leroy.

"Okay," said Cleaver sharply, "how you feel about it's your business, just so you'll do it. Because you'll be at the cutting edge. You know the plan. Ariel's flying in for you tomorrow morning at dawn. When you get to his place in California you train all day tomorrow and Thursday with his partners; Ariel will be fetching and carrying us and Cooch from Mexico. Thursday night he flies you back up here and we'll all meet up to go over the thing one last time. . . ."

"*If* you come back from Mexico in one piece," said Levon, for the first time cracking a brief, mean grin.

"After that," Cleaver continued evenly, "on Friday Ariel drives the three of you into position, and you do the thing Saturday morning. If it goes right, long before midday we down, we gone, bye-bye."

"Still a smooth talker, ain't he?" sneered Leroy. "So we only get to spend one more night here? You want to keep us away from the white women, boss?"

"That be cool with us," said Levon. "We got our own women—and I'm talking about women, not little girls."

"Well I'm real glad to hear it," said Cleaver, putting an edge to his voice that made them stiffen. "From what I've seen,

I don't think I'm going to like what you've become any better than you seem to like us now. But I don't need you to pucker up to us; it's enough that you'll do what you say you'll do. And do it exactly right. Close is no good with this one."

"Yeah," said Leroy somberly, "close is only good enough for horseshoes."

"And hand grenades," added Levon.

"Right," said Cleaver, "I'll see you guys later."

After he had left, Levon reached over, drank, and passed the bottle to Leroy. The brothers toasted each other, grinning wickedly in silence.

Cleaver was talking about Mexico.

"In the prison, Kemp's people have fixed it so that Cooch has been transferred to the infirmary. That's a separate, single-story building just inside the prison compound, and the guards will be looking the other way when me and Krass go over the wall and bring him out. Kemp's also bought us the border clearance for the plane both ways."

"Pity he can't buy the fuckin' Judge off," said Six.

"Oh no, man," said the Dude, "don't you see that's the beauty of the Judge? He can't be bought. He's a good enemy."

"'Opposition is true friendship?'" asked Krass.

"Something like that," said the Dude.

It was after supper. They were all sitting round an open fire of aromatic pine logs, in the fine main room with its log ceiling and polished wooden floor covered with the beautiful geometric designs of Navajo rugs in red, gray and black. During the preparation of the meal, Laura and Cherry had made friends, and they sat together on one side of the fire; on the other, Bob was ensconced in the arms of an old deep leather armchair, following the conversation intently, with Dance sitting by him, quietly refilling his glass with the Dude's pisco punch when necessary. The mood in the room was curious, muted; the men all knew one another well but were still feeling out the changes since they had last met.

"Because," the Dude went on, turning to Cleaver, "this thing isn't just about us playing GI Joe to spring Duane and his folks, is it?"

"What then?" said Krass.

"Why the truth, man, the truth!" said the Dude, his fringe of long hair quivering comically with intensity, his sunken eyes shining in the firelight. "What's been did and what's been hid. Because if we don't find out what really happened down there at Graduation, what will it all have meant? Us being blown apart and now coming together again? It'll just be one more load of action without consequences—very twentieth century. There'll be no pattern; we'll have wasted our emotions and lost our history. Unless we find out what really went down that night. Don't you see it, man?" he appealed.

But Cleaver only grunted noncommittally.

"Because the only way we turn this from being something like revenge on those guys down there, who maybe don't exactly deserve it," he went on carefully, keeping his eyes on Cleaver, "turn it from that to something creative, maybe even help that poor girl Emily, is to get to the truth. . . ."

Six had quickly lost interest in the Dude's rap and turned back to Levon and Leroy, who seemed to have mellowed imperceptibly with the food and drink, to talk guns. On the floor in front of the two marines lay a kit bag, which clanked ominously when their feet touched it.

"Assault guns, huh?" said Six. "Small, light, fully automatic? Lemme guess. Uzi?"

Leroy shook his head no.

"Ingram?"

"Nope."

"Then they're CAR-15s, the specials, the MX?"

"Uh-uh," Levon shook his head emphatically. "You ever use one of those things? Sure they're only sixteen inches long, but it's still really just an M16, which means you're blinded by the fucking flash and deafened by the noise of a five-fifty-six mill round that never was a real stopper for combat anyhow. No sir, none of that for us."

"Me, I always thought a riot scattergun was best close in," said Six.

"Fine, man—if you're happy with an outside range of fifty meters. But who says that's going to be enough? Naw, all around what you need is one of these."

He withdrew from the olive drab bag a curious looking weapon, a snub-nosed tube barely eighteen inches long, with a pistol grip and trigger group unusually close to its nose. With the grip in Levon's big black right fist, a perforated yoke fitted easily into the crook of his elbow.

"Only one hand, see?" he said. "Easy."

"Where's the mag go?" asked Six.

"Here," said Levon, withdrawing a straight metal magazine from the bag, checking it was empty and snapping it into place in a receiver behind the trigger group, so that it protruded to the left of the weapon.

"Yeah, like a Sten or a Sterling—so what else is new?" said Six.

"This," said Leroy, and, gripping the magazine, swiveled it up and around the tube of the barrel like the hand of a clock until it now protruded from the opposite side of the weapon.

"It goes through three hundred sixty degrees and stops anywhere. That way you get to fire round the far side of something without exposing yourself."

"And you can use it left-handed," said Levon, taking the weapon and demonstrating. "Still one hand, see. It's only around six pounds all up weight. Aims real good, too. You point with the index finger, like a derringer."

Six took the weapon and examined it.

"Where's the switch to go to rock and roll?" he said.

"Automatic? There ain't one—it's a progressive trigger, single shot or full auto just by trigger control. A kid could use it."

"What's it fire?"

"That's the kick, man—pistol ammo, which has just got to be more controllable than a rifle round. But .45 ACP, so it's still got stomp. Or you can reverse the bolt, replace the mag and barrel and use nine-millimeter Parabellum."

"Well the .45 is nothing but good, man," said Six. "'Cause in case the fellers in the hut or wherever are wearing flak jackets or body armor, we have the technology."

He fished in a pocket and came out with a handful of stubby green-nosed bullets.

"Forty-five KTW rounds," he went on. "They're Teflon-coated, like your best fry pan, and they penetrate a heavy-weight vest. What's the rpm on that thing?"

"Twelve hundred rounds a minute. And it'll take a silencer, too. They call it the Sidewinder."

"I think I love it," said Six. "Where did you guys pick these up?"

"They send them to us—evaluation, like that. And other stuff," said Leroy, tapping the bag with his foot. Six carefully looked inside and drawing back, said quietly, "RPGs?" and when Levon nodded, "Run what you brung, huh? Tanks or birds?"

"Either one. It's foreign ordnance. Figured we'd like a little edge down there," he grinned.

"Listen," said Six, "when this shit is over, could you guys maybe get me some of this wonderful stuff? I'd go top dollar. . . ."

"No way, hard-on," grated Leroy, his face turning to a mask of contempt in an instant. "So you can sell them to your white supremacist buddies in the joint, or some tin-pot foreign colonel or terrorist group that turns them right back on us? No way, *thief*," he sneered.

Across the room, Laura had felt a sick numbness at the sight, inside the comfortable room, of the men handling guns. She shivered, and Cherry said, "Hey, you okay, Laura?"

"I guess so," she sighed. "It's just those guys coming on so hard, and that . . . Six. . . ."

"That skanky little zod? Don't let him bother you. I mean—shine Six!" she said with a toss of her magnificent dark hair.

Laura shook her head and sighed.

"No, it's all of them—even that Dance. He's polite enough, but so distant and pent up. . . ."

"Oh, no," Cherry exclaimed, "he's truly vicious, and I'm not just kicking off here. After they came, I got him to take me for a ride up into the hills on one of his bikes. Now the Dude knows the hills, and his Shadow is pretty fast, but this was something else. It wasn't just twice as quick—it was the way Dance threaded it all together, the curves and the straights, all of it, so that the whole road became, like, another thing. Yeah, like—a dance," she giggled. "When we got back, my legs were so weak and I felt so . . . I mean, I grabbed the Dude and we ran to our room and . . ."

Her voice fell to a gurgling whisper and her eyes rolled comically, so that Laura found she was smiling in spite of herself. Then the raised voices of Leroy and Six's quarrel jerked her back, and something snapped inside her. Squeezing Cherry's arm she stood up and said in a voice sharp enough to silence the room,

"I'll leave you boys with your toys. But I'd like to say that I think you'd do better along the lines that the Dude's suggesting."

In the silence she walked across the wooden floor and out into the night. After a moment, Cleaver rose and said, "I'll turn in, too. I'll see you all tomorrow at seven. We've got a lot to do. Goodnight."

"Hey boss," came Levon's voice mockingly, "ain'cha gonna tell us all what we do, come Saturday? Or don't you know that yet?"

"Yes, I have a plan," said Cleaver with a slight smile. "But it can wait till we're all here, when I get back from Mexico," and with that, he turned and left the room. Levon shouted after him,

"*If* you get back, remember?"

Krass said, "Why don't you knock off that stuff? Or have you been led from behind for so long that you've forgotten what he's like?"

Six scowled at Krass, drained his glass and shook his head.

"*El* fucking *segundo* speaks. Listen, Krass, there's one thing been bothering me. You know last night, all that stuff about your old lady and her dykey women's groups?"

Krass felt his face flooding with embarrassment. Drinking with Six in North Beach he had found himself pouring out the details of his troubled marriage. He had hoped the vicious little scuzz-bag had been too drunk to remember.

"Well my question is this, professor," Six went on. "When she goes to bed with one of them fag hags—do you get to watch?"

Cleaver heard the roar of laughter rise from inside the house as he finally spotted Laura. She was leaning against a corral fence behind the house, watching the still forms of a mare and foal standing motionless there under a crescent moon. She did not turn as Cleaver walked up behind her and gently put his arms around her waist.

They stood in silence for a while. It had showered briefly earlier, and in the dark, the breeze brought them the smell of wet hay and sage. At length Cleaver felt her body relax against his and heard her say quietly,

"I'm sorry, but suddenly it seemed like so much kids' stuff, with them brandishing the guns and bragging that way. . . . That Six . . ."

"I know," said Cleaver. "He's not exactly a nice person. But in a bad place, a bad man may not be such a bad thing. I know what you mean, I know how it looked, and I know how unbelievable it seems, the whole thing. But I'm afraid it's for real. I've seen what can happen down there, seen a man with his guts cut out. There's a woman and child under that kind of threat now. Maybe it's not such a bad thing we're trying to do: looking after them, and finding out the truth."

But Laura had heard how the last phrase had come reluctantly.

"What is it, John?"

"It's just . . . in the old days, things could get hairy, maybe more than we care to remember. And all we had to count on was ourselves. It went deep; we relied on one another and we accepted one another. And it makes me reluctant to face the fact, because I have to tell you this is a possibility, that one or more of us could have been sick or crazy enough to do the thing down there, the rape and that hideous murder. And I particularly don't like it when we're just about to enter a situation where our lives will be in each others' hands again."

As Laura saw this new dimension, instinctively she turned and held Cleaver to her with strong arms, yearning to fill him with her love and resolution.

"There's one more thing," Cleaver said with an effort.

"Nothing to do with any of this. It's the kid, Sam. I think he's got a problem. I was going to . . ."

"I know," said Laura. "It's okay, I know. We can talk about it later. You've got enough on your plate right now. Just don't forget that you have a life to come back to after this thing. That other people need you too."

Cleaver kissed her gratefully and under the moonlight held her close. In her arms he tasted the sweetness of life almost unbearably, now that once again, with the trip to Mexico on the next day, his life stood under the possibility of violent withdrawal.

So he did not tell her of his own lingering guilt at how taking the decision to run had seemed to dismantle the 13's invincibility. Or about his present fears, the mounting sense of foreboding he was finding impossible to shake now.

13

Mexico, Wednesday, 11:30 P.M.

It was all happening too fast for Cleaver.

Since Cannonball had arrived in his office and set the roller coaster in motion he had felt alive again, with the exhilaration of the group coming together and, yes, of feeling them going to his will once more; he'd got high on it. But now it felt as if everything was going too fast.

They had made the dreamlike flight down over the border in Ariel's Piper Aztec, a leased-back plane with bladder tanks fitted to handle the extra range inside Mexico. Ariel's moon face, his crew cut and his childlike air of happy enthusiasm were unaltered by the years as he took the little plane along the Sierra Madre mountains into the sunset. Cleaver had felt light, diffuse, and beneath the unreal calm there was a fluttering, constant and growing, of foreboding. In the last of the evening, Ariel had brought them down in a freshening headwind on a plateau some miles outside the town in the foothills where Cooch was imprisoned.

Now, like a vacationer, Cleaver watched numbly as beyond the dusty windows of their rented dinosaur of a fifties Cadillac, in the lazy warmth of the Mexican light the town unwound, making light of its own squalor. Kemp's man had been waiting with the car, and they had left him there with Ariel to refuel and watch over the plane. Krass was at the wheel; Cleaver had noted how he seemed liberated by their move into action, the occupation with simple tasks. Cleaver wished that he felt the same; he was careful that none of them should realize that he didn't.

The Cadillac crashed into another chuckhole and Cleaver winced as the .45 in a holster slipped inside his waistband dug into his back again. The joint of his right thumb also ached from the morning spent at practice with the big automatics and the little gunman. On the range that they had improvised against a dry bank behind the ranch, Six was transformed; highly skilled, precise, even articulate as he explained the mild customizing jobs he had done on their weapons, the Bomar Combat sights, the choice of bulkier Pachmayr neoprene Signature grips to cushion and control the big guns' recoil, or see-through Lexan grips so they could monitor the cartridges used.

"Otherwise they're your straight M-1911A1s," he told them. "Good, solid, combat-proved ordnance—the weight just takes a little getting used to, is all. And forget all that shit about never trust a woman or an automatic pistol. Don't know about the women, but the vast majority of automatic malfunctions were down to unsuitable or plain defective surplus ammunition. I'm here to see you get the best. Now let's shoot."

Cleaver and Krass had slipped on the earmuffs he provided and, crouching slightly, steadied the heavy pistols with both hands and sighted waveringly on the target yards away on the bank. Then the sound of the first shots had gone slamming out over the desert.

"That's good, Krass," Six had approved after they'd fired a full magazine. "See, a good group."

"But low," said Krass self-deprecatingly.

"It's okay, .45s do that, pull a little low. You'll soon learn to compensate. Look, clear the magazine this way, just one hand, let it drop and feed a fresh one in with the other hand, quick. Cleaver, you're shooting some good, some way off. It's early yet, but try to concentrate, huh? What's on your mind?"

"Just one thing; I'm hoping we don't have to use these," said Cleaver, staring at the cartridge hulls, scattered where his pistol had ejected them, shining on the rocky dirt.

"Hey, hey, man," Six chuckled gutturally, "you forgotten the creed? Do unto others and then split. Where you're going tonight, that ain't Cancun down there. . . ."

Goddamn right, thought Cleaver now, gazing through the dust-streaked window at the flat alien faces, scrawny dogs and transistors, neon and dung heaps, burros and Hondas, the straw hats, serapes and plastic sandals, fiery young exuberant women and withered black-clad crones as old as death itself. All life, thought Cleaver, and the other thing too, as they slid past two hulking khaki-clad cops standing scowling on a raised corner, caps, sunglasses, bristling mustaches and hand-tooled leather latticework holsters. The rank, rich smell of the town seemed to permeate the old car and clutch at his throat, and he longed to tell Krass to stop awhile, for a coffee, a piss stop, anything that would keep them from their appointment. But his habit of self-command again prevented any of this showing, and this in turn helped him handle the urges. Then they had eased out of the narrow street into a large plaza, darkened and nearly empty, and rising from its far end, like some crumbling Gothic cathedral, lay the dark bulk of the prison.

As they approached, Cleaver could make out, huddled against the walls or crouched around tiny flickering cooking fires on the steps below, wretched blanket-clad figures whom he guessed to be the wives and families of prisoners. The outrage this sight kindled fired him, and he stirred in his seat as Krass drove slow and wide around to the right of the main structure and bumped down a broad, formless track before turning left into another plaza, smaller and darker, whose near side was bounded by the rear wall of the prison compound.

Krass pulled the big car to a halt in the shadows some sixty or seventy yards across from the twelve-foot-high prison wall. They could just make out the tiled roof of a single-story structure showing above the wall. In the silence after Krass cut the engine, from somewhere across the town, Cleaver heard a church clock strike twelve, with a dead sound on the final stroke. It was time. Down in his lap, Cleaver checked the automatic, jacked a round into the chamber, eased the hammer forward and holstered it, and then almost gratefully said, "Let's do it," and stepped from the Cadillac into the humid night.

Quietly they pushed the doors to, and with cool, quick glances to the corners of the deserted plaza, ignoring the slum dwellings behind them, in dark clothes they crossed the blackened square at a steady pace. As they reached the wall, without a word spoken, both men unrolled the black silk balaclavas that had lain around their necks like scarves and pulled them up over their heads, both camouflage and a mask. Again wordlessly, Krass then faced the wall and dropped to his knees, and when Cleaver's rubber-soled shoes had found his broad shoulders, stood up in one smooth movement that raised Cleaver's head level with the top of the wall, and the jagged glass embedded in it. Steadying himself with one hand, with the other Cleaver reached inside his jacket for the dark sacking wadded there and spread it over the broken glass. He still felt its muffled bite as he pulled himself up to lie flat along the top of the wall and then scanned the feebly lit compound, the illuminated rear of the main prison, and the small darkened single-story building to his right, lit up by only one outside lamp attached to a corner. This was the infirmary.

After a moment, Cleaver reached down with his right hand, and getting the best grip he could on the uneven adobe with his left, grasped Krass's upraised wrist and took the strain as the big man launched himself upward and scrambled up the wall and then, with no pause, straight over the top to lower himself and drop silently down into the compound. He crouched there, motionless, as Cleaver thudded down into the dust beside him.

For long moments they waited in complete silence and concentration at this, the moment of maximum vulnerability if something had gone bad with Kemp's fix. Gradually their hearts steadied and their eyes grew accustomed to the compound's gloom, and began to quarter it methodically.

Then it happened. A hundred yards away at the rear of the prison a door smashed open. Cleaver, half-upright, froze. A bulky figure came out into the night, apparently staring straight at them. As his hands went to his waist, Cleaver and Krass too reached behind them. But then they saw the guard was simply fumbling with his fly, and soon the sibilance of copious urination came to them on the night air. After the door had banged shut behind him, Cleaver and Krass exchanged one look and then rose in unison and padded toward the infirmary.

They circled the building once, away from the lamp, and then without hesitation, their handguns out now and held down by their sides, they turned the last corner into the light and, opening the unlocked door, slid swiftly inside.

By the door to their left, a rabbit-toothed orderly in a dirty white coat rose as they entered, his chair toppling backward with a loud crash as his hands reached for the ceiling. His nervous grin let them know that their arrival was not unexpected. Cleaver stared at him, and without a word the man jerked his head in the direction of the main room.

While Krass sat the orderly back down on the chair and began to secure him to it, Cleaver padded down the short aisle between the two rows of empty beds and approached the only one covered with mosquito netting. There was a soft lamp burning over it, obscuring what lay within the net.

Cleaver paused, listening, then took a deep breath and, lifting the netting, carefully pulled down his balaclava, reached in and went to touch the man inside. But what he saw there made him freeze.

It was Cooch. But so emaciated that Cleaver could barely recognize him. He was stripped to the waist, a thick strip of soiled bandage encircling him to tape his ribs, above which big bruises still told of a terrible series of beatings. The Mexican's hair, once a glossy brilliant black, was now grizzled and unkempt, and a week's graying stubble covered his austere features, the flesh stretched taut on them briefly conjuring the El Greco saints Cleaver had seen once on a trip to Spain.

As Cleaver's hand hovered over him, the Mexican's eyes opened. The blood-veined whites showed all around the dark pupils. Quite calmly, smiling slightly, he gazed at Cleaver serenely for long moments, until he blinked once and then his eyes went wide as he fully awoke and took in what he was seeing. As his mouth opened Cleaver briefly registered the missing teeth.

"Cleaver?" he hissed, and then louder, "*Ay carajo*— Cleaver?" so that the American gestured urgently for silence, but Cooch, though quieter, went on, "You have come! Yes! And it was you," he pronounced the syllable *"djoo,"* "you who get me out of that hell-hole, into here."

"Right, amigo, and now we haul ass for real, eh?" smiled Cleaver.

"Sí, sí," Cooch breathed eagerly, then groaned and fell back as he tried to heave himself upright and off the bed. Cleaver called with quiet urgency to Krass, who was by his side in a few quick paces. Together effortlessly they raised the pathetically skinny Mexican, supporting him gently between them as he apologized continuously; it had been so long since he had walked, they must understand also that his ribs were still a little troublesome. . . . Cleaver noticed distractedly how Cooch's hands too seemed damaged, calloused and knobbly. Without words, Cleaver and Krass began to walk their limping friend up and down the length of the beds, supported between them.

Long minutes passed, but gradually they felt Cooch begin to support himself. They were both experiencing a surge of angry affection for the Mexican. But minutes were ticking away, and after one last length of the aisle, they exchanged a nod, turned, and under the wide eyes of the bound and gagged orderly, made for the door.

They were within three paces of it when a sound from outside made them freeze. Then rapid footsteps came close, and before they could move, the door swung open violently and the whole of its frame was filled by a mountainous figure in the uniform of the Chief of Police.

"Emiliano, amigo, que se . . ." the man was bellowing in mock concern, and then he caught sight of them.

For a long second nobody moved. Then with a convulsive jerk backward, the Chief's hand swept toward his holster. Krass's right arm was supporting Cooch, but Cleaver's was free. Yet in the split seconds available he found himself frozen, not moving.

But quicker than any of them, Cooch struck. His wiry arms snaked from around their necks and like a jaguar he launched himself forward and up at the bulk of his opponent, with both hands, fingers stiffened and extended, slashing ahead of him like knives. A single, chilling cry was released as he struck, his

132

left hand spearing over and downward into the side of the *jefe's* throat, while simultaneously his right, palm upward, came inward and up, with the whole force of Cooch's shoulder behind it, up beneath the left side of the big man's ribs, the iron-hard blade of his strengthened fingers corkscrewing in almost to the wrist, bursting and rupturing the organs within.

It was a single lightning strike, and as Cooch swayed back, the big man went down soundlessly, to reveal a second agent behind him clawing ineffectively at a holster strap, who now turned and ran away yelling across the compound toward the prison.

At their feet, the three men looked down at *el jefe's* face, the eyes too surprised to even form a question before they glazed over in death.

Cooch stepped forward and spat down into his face.

"None of that," growled Cleaver, "let's go."

They were halfway to the wall when an alarm went off tinnily, and a hundred yards away, the first guard came out from the back of the prison. At the foot of the wall Cooch stumbled as a shot rang out, and then another, gouging big chunks of dust and flying splinters from the adobe wall beside them. Krass went on his knees and Cleaver ran up his back and leapt for the top where the sacking was, steadying himself and grasping both Cooch's arms as Krass virtually hurled him aloft, and with the strength of desperation, Cleaver lifted the pitifully light figure nearly clear over the wall and dropped him over on the far side. As Krass came up a carbine crackled and the round ricocheted on the short section of wall just between the two of them; Krass flinched sideways and cut his left hand on the glass before they both dropped to the far side. Cleaver, winded, got an arm round Cooch's bare shoulders and gasped to Krass, "Get the car, we'll stop here."

Lights sprang on overhead before Krass was halfway across the plaza, and as he wrenched open the solid door and dove behind the wheel, a carbine round kicked up dust beside the rear tire. In the tenements, dogs were barking hysterically. When the shot came, Cleaver, beneath the shelter of the wall, momentarily ducked down instinctively, then looking up, located the wavering barrel of the weapon coming over the top of the wall. Keeping an arm around Cooch, he raised his .45, thumbed the hammer back and the safety off, and aiming up one-handed, squeezed off a shot that raised dust inches below the carbine muzzle. Correcting, he emptied the magazine methodically at the top of the wall, the Colt slamming satisfyingly in his fist as across the square the Cadillac roared and squealed into life. Cleaver was smacking in a fresh magazine as the car leapt forward in a screeching arc toward them, not stopping as the two offside doors flew open and they hurled themselves in, immediately slammed backward into the upholstery as Krass floored it.

They were nearly to the far edge of the square and around the corner when there was a noise like an electrical short-out, and the rear window collapsed around their ears.

"You okay?" yelled Cleaver at Cooch as the unlit Cadillac careered along the flank of the jail. Down on the floor, the Mexican was shaking uncontrollably, and it was only after long moments that Cleaver realized he was convulsed with soundless laughter.

"Sí, sí, perdón, perdón, I'm sorry but I don't have too much fun this last little while. Ay, but did you see the look on the face of that pig when he go down? And thank you, amigos, for leaving him to me. El hijo de la gran puta, he was the one who took my business, my liberty, my teeth and my ribs. He even come after me in the infirmary! Oye, I been getting ready for that one for many months. God is good!"

"Maybe so," shouted Krass, wrenching the balaclava off his head as he swung the car fast back the way they had come, "but dead cops are always bad news, and they're not part of our deal." But his voice sounded excited rather than panicked, even as he yelled.

"And here're a couple of live ones!"

The two officers they had passed earlier were pounding up either side of the road toward them, pistols out and held high. At the sight of the fast-moving, unlit Cadillac they steadied themselves to fire. Krass gave the wheel a half-turn and stamped on the brake, sending the long car skidding half-broadside fast toward them both. The two policemen leapt for

134

the gutters as Krass corrected the skid with panache and rocketed onward, pistol shots banging out behind them and a siren
starting up as they slammed on to dirt road and shot past the
last houses of the town.

"*Arriba tigres!*" yelled Cooch delightedly. "*Andale muchachos!*
Go, Krass, go!"

14

New Mexico, Thursday, 6:00 P.M.

"Like, tell me everything at once," cried Cherry for the hundredth time as Cleaver came in.

She and Laura were sitting in the Dude's comfortable tiled kitchen as Laura redressed Krass's cut hand. Laura had already looked after Cooch as best she could, retaping his ribs, seeing to his other wounds, feeding him and watching as he slept deeply after their return early that morning. But she had been unable to keep him resting during the afternoon; Cooch had declared himself fully restored, and once the situation had been explained to him, eager to help his old friends. He had spent the afternoon checking out the nearly new black Triumph Bonneville which the Dude had provided for him, and ended up riding into town to buy some things, most of which Cleaver guessed would be metal, sharp and pointed.

Krass was smiling and blushing, embarrassed but obviously not unhappy at Cherry's extravagant attention. With her exuberant body crammed into a minimal scarlet tank top, startlingly short stone-washed cutoffs and rainbow-colored leg warmers, Cherry had been a big distraction to them all that day, but one even Cleaver found it hard to object to.

"I told you already," said Krass, "we drove out of town with no lights . . ."

"*You* drove, you mean," Cherry corrected.

"All right, *I* drove, we reached the plane before them, and Ariel got us out of there and brought us back here. No big deal," he concluded insincerely, all too aware, as well as Cherry's big dark eyes eating him up, of Laura's gently ironical look as her skillful fingers finished their work on his hand. With relief Krass saw Cleaver come in and cried, "Hey, John, how are you?"

"Fine as kind," grinned Cleaver, though Laura noted the dark circles under his eyes; she was tired herself, but she knew he had had little time to rest since their return. A courier from the South had arrived with detailed maps and plans that Cleaver had requested and that Kemp, across in Florida, had expedited. Cleaver had also continued to monitor the Gulf weather and correlate it with this and other matters gleaned from a long telephone call with G. W. Brooks, the Judge's black servant. There were various vehicles to organize, flight plans and routes south and east to agree, and weapons and communications equipment to check out. It had been a long day for Cleaver.

"I'm looking for Six," he said. "You know where he's at?"

"He was in the garage, working on his Harley," said Krass.

"That doesn't sound like the man," Cleaver grinned, "fixing his own machine when Bob's there to do it for him."

"Probably something evil on his own hook, I guess," said Krass. "You remember the way he talked about those green-nosed bullets? 'Like, a significant increase in lethality. . . .'"

"Oh, I love a fancy talker," laughed Cleaver. "I'll go look for him out there."

"John, don't forget supper's at seven,' Laura reminded him. "Big eats for the boys. Good stuff."

"Yes, ma'am," said Cleaver, throwing her a mock salute. Then, as he was going through the door, he turned to Krass and added,

"Oh, by the way, professor, I happen to think the young lady's right, you know. You did real good down there last night." Then he left quickly.

"See," Cherry said, "now how about it. . . ."

"Uh, let's maybe talk about it later," said Krass, getting up hastily, blushing beneath Laura's arching eyebrows. "Catch you guys at supper," he muttered, and slipped hastily from the room.

Out in the hall on the way to his bunk room he heard a soft voice, and, looking into the main room saw the big shape of Tor, turned away from the door, and speaking quietly into the phone. As Krass hurried past he heard the rumbling voice say, "Billy . . ."

Krass could not ignore the feeling that the single word expressed, and the soft laugh that followed. As he walked on, Krass felt the slight strangeness of it, that the big man seemed to have a more tender and loving scene with his boyfriend than he, the straight college professor, had ever had with his wife.

But right at this moment it was Cherry rather than Karen who filled his thoughts. The lovely girl's sexuality was awesome indeed, but she was so friendly that somehow it didn't intimidate him. And he realized that despite his unhappy past and the highly uncertain immediate future, even despite not really knowing if he had gone with Cleaver to run from his situation or to help his friends—still and all, he was feeling pretty good.

Cleaver heard the crash of metal as he rounded the corner of the barn. He increased his pace as another smash came, and the sound of wild cursing.

He stepped inside and stopped dead. Six was nowhere to be seen, but at the far end under the stark neon lights, Blind Bob was performing a dervish dance of helpless rage, spinning as he hurled tools and components in every direction, a stream of obscenity ripping from his lips. As Cleaver closed on him, one of Bob's flailing hands struck a rack of files and blood sprang from it. It came to Cleaver that someone had described blindness as objects holding their breath before hitting you, and then he was talking quietly, announcing himself before he touched Bob, and the slight figure collapsed into his arms.

Minutes later they sat together on a bench; Bob, his left hand wrapped in a rag, was drawing deeply on a cigarette.

"Sorry, sorry," he muttered at last, "I guess I blew my stack. Okay now."

"You want to talk about it?' said Cleaver. "Fine by me if not. . . ."

"You was always a one to listen, in the old days," said the Tennessean, a slight smile on his gaunt face beneath the sunglasses. "Yeah," he went on, "if it don't turn you off, right now I could stand to do some talking."

He took another shaky drag and paused again for long moments before he said,

"You know something—when I could see, I never did sleep too well. Any little light would keep me awake. But there's none now. No light at all.

"I ought to get me a ten-percenter patch—less than one in ten of us blind folk are completely in the dark. It's also sort of easier if you're born that way; gives you time to get acquainted with the idea, and adjusted to the fact.

"The first few months was bad. I was right out on my own, and I didn't want to move. My mind was wrong. I still kidded myself that I was going to get better, somehow. And I didn't know who the hell I was; this wasn't me, Bob, good man with an engine, but Blind Bob, scarred-up, crippled. So ashamed. Worse when anyone tried to help me. I gave Dance a hard time those first months, I tell you. Long months, they was. I was still cursing fate, and everything else, the doctors, the army, my family. 'Cause it was just so unfair. Like, why me? I think deep down I thought it *was* me—I used to rerun that last day on the Mekong just endlessly in my head, to see how if I'd done different, I might still have my sight.

"I was right down. I wasn't myself, and I wasn't like no one else. I couldn't even remember what I had been too well. Hell, can *you* remember what color my eyes were? I couldn't sleep. I lost twenty pounds of weight. It all passed, in time. But I don't see as how it would've if Dance hadn't kept me on his team. And because that was for real, I shaped up just as quick as I could.

"But meantime, he's also taking care of other shit that could of messed with my mind. He was sending money to my folks while he hassled the army for the proper pension, stuff like that. He moved me in with him and Jenny—which is where I still am. And these aids and tools, the sonic guide, the

Optacon, they really help, but they ain't cheap. He sprung for 'em, no questions. Said it was against my wages. If that's so, I reckon I owe my soul to the company store," Bob grinned wryly.

"So by and by I come to some kind of terms with it. Ol' Dance would listen patient enough when I'd fall to sounding off, but he never let me get word one in if'n he thought I was just feeling sorry for myself. So I finally got there. I'm a blind man, I always will be. But I wasn't going to let it take my work away from me, and I was going to do my best by Dance. And I by God have tried to do those things. Because the frame for writing and the long cane and the speech outputs have all been good, but it was Dance that mostly got me through this thing."

He sighed, and after a last drag handed his cigarette butt to Cleaver to extinguish.

"And now this thing comes up," he went on quietly. "It's long odds. We both know it. Dance, he'll be up at the front, he always is, that's his way. He could go down, easy. And me, I'll be left here, with nothing, not one Goddamn thing I can do."

Cleaver held onto himself: Bob's words had touched a deep feeling in him, a profound sense of the things that life had thrown at them all. Then he made himself speak calmly.

"You've done it already. You're still the best wrench. We go down there knowing our bikes are a hundred percent."

"Yeah, but John, how about the bikes? I mean, we're talking that old time religion here—I know you'd rather fix than switch, but Harleys, Triumphs, them old four-stroke twins, they're grand for the soul but they don't hardly cut it on the street no more. The XR Harley still makes out on the dirt track, but that's a one-off. Gotta be four cylinders, maybe six— these modern crotch-rockets push out over one hundred bhp, one hundred forty plus in delivery trim, and that's leaving out tuning, turbos, all of that."

"Don't worry," said Cleaver, glad to be back on solid ground. "The bikes are only part of it. Mostly what they have to take care of is the Truckers, or what's left of them. And on the back roads, rough roads, handling's going to count for more than top speed. Plus, I've been checking with G. W. Brooks—and in those parts, God still rides a Harley. Down to you, we never yet met one of them that our own couldn't blow off."

"Yeah, well," Bob shrugged, "but how about that Sheriff? As I recall, they said he liked to play them car wars."

"That's down to Dance. How about his Harley? Is it ready for that?"

"Well—it's basically the street bike I built up for him—kind of half-race. It's mostly XR, but we run S and S con-rods, Sifton drag cams, smooth-bore Mikunis, an Andrews close-ratio cluster, and Barnett clutch and belt primary. Dance says it's got plenty of grunt, it's not too fierce for the road, and quick enough at the top end—around a hundred thirty.

"The rest of it's down to the usual—tuning the suspension, gearing, carburetion, tires. But I'm working in the dark," he smiled briefly, "if you take my meaning; I've had to do some heavy guessing. You sure the weather's going to be the way you said? Mist just lifting and all that?"

"It better be, for Levon and Leroy's sake," said Cleaver grimly, and then went on, "There is maybe another thing that you can do to help. But it's trickier. We've had to consider the possibility that maybe one or two of the guys had something to do with what happened to the Judge's kids down there. Now me and Krass have been asking around in a quiet way, but we've come up with nothing. The ones who weren't covered were the twins, the Dude, Six, Kemp and Tor. Kemp we can't do anything about, but we feel he wouldn't be helping the way he is if he had something to hide. But the others, we can't tell one way or the other. If any of them did it, we can't rely on them down there. And that's where I was hoping you could help."

"What you want me to do?" said Bob flatly.

"Listen," said Cleaver. "Just that. I don't mean to patronize or lay any sixth-sense shit on you, but I've noticed how you concentrate when people are talking, and I have to guess you've learned to pick up a lot from a person's voice."

"Yeah," said Bob with a slow smile, "there is that old built-in bullshit-detector. The ones who come on too quick and firm; too good to be true. The deep and slow ones; they can be lazy, but they're mostly nice with it. The gabblers—can be their minds are going too fast for their mouths—or it can be that they're talking so much 'cause they've really got nothing to say. . . ."

"All that from voices?"

"And vibes," laughed Bob, "them vibes, like the Dude would say. You can get a sense. Yeah, well, I'll try and do it. When?"

"After supper tonight, I lay the whole plan on everyone. Then we'll talk about it. You listen in. You and I can talk after that.

"Now, a couple more things. Was Six in here? I'm looking for him."

"He was here, doing something on his Harley, I don't know what, but he was cutting and welding some. All I told him was to lay off his engine, it was right. He went off maybe ten minutes before you came."

"Okay, I'll go look for him inside. Here's the last thing. Please don't tell anyone about this, not even Dance. It won't do anyone's confidence any good, wondering who they can trust. And I'm pretty sure none of our guys would have done it. But I have to do everything I can."

And take the weight, thought Bob. That was Cleaver. That was the man.

The Dude was singing quietly to his guitar:

> "By the old wood stove our hats was hung
> Our tales were told and our songs were sung
> Ten thousand dollars at the drop of a hat
> I'd give it all gladly, if our lives could be like that."

It was after supper. Cleaver had delivered his plan, and now there was a pause as the men took it in, while a big coffee pot and bottles of tequila and bourbon circulated.

As the song ended, Six said loudly, "Shit, you ever listen to that Dylan now? Not me, man, not me."

Cleaver felt a twinge of guilt at the stacks of records and the expensive but mostly unused stereo equipment back at his home. But then the Dude was talking, "Now Six, I know what you're thinking, man—what you'd like us to think—like, weren't all the things we dug then just a bunch of crap?

"I mean the stuff we all believed in when we were together may look pretty pitiful now, but I'm not ready to dump on flowers and music, love and freedom, just because they're out of fucking fashion. You want to understand why they look a little thin right now, then listen up—this here's Doc Dude's history class.

"Now after we split up, there was the seventies, and at first they didn't look too different to what had gone before. Plenty of music, only maybe a little heavier, pushing the loud button, the power button; but still some good stuff. Plenty of dope, and the same way, the volume up—STP, smack, PCP, coke. But still the same assumptions; that the hipsters had IT, that there was something you could never know by just thinking, a secret which you could feel your way into because it was a natural thing, something that opened all the doors.

"It was just that, like, by then the ways of getting there were separating out, and the further away they got from each other, the more each of them seemed to be liable to give you a big mother of a headache. Gurus—just hand it all over to me and Stay Up All the Time! Coke—another kind of—nonaddictive!—blissed-out pauperhood. The SLA and like that; spent more time listening to themselves than up against the real wall.

"Then sometime around '74, '75, came—the Maximum Yawp. A big uncertainty. Maybe it really did start when the Abs put their foot on the pipeline; because one of our articles was, you know, a good time on next to no bread. Then times start getting tough, people start looking out for themselves and suddenly, you don't know who you are anymore.

"The punks jumped in. All that fuckin' brainless noise and despair. Mutilation and gob, glue, sulfate and scag . . ."

"Maybe they're just us twenty years ago," Krass offered tentatively.

"Bullshit! It's the difference between just distrusting the supremacy of intellect, and a fucking lobotomy. But you could say, who can blame them? The Inheritors! 'Cause you look at what's left of our scene and what have you got?

"Fat rock cats—twenty-dollar tickets, two hours late, one-hour set, no encores, they don't even bother to play in tune. Castaneda a fake, and right now a tedious one, too. Chicks who hate men. Jonestown, Guyana. *Heavy metal!* Levis that come apart after a couple of hard months. Them AMF Harleys for a while, plus pretty well no more Brits, and no more VW Beetles or air-cool vans neither. Born-again Dylan. Short fucking hair. I could go on."

"You will, man, you will," muttered Six wearily, and Krass was saying something about hip conservatives, when from the armchair, Bob finished a pull of tequila and cut in flatly,

"I can't go with all that shitting on everything since the sixties. There's been good things happen, progress, as I well know. Five years ago there weren't no Optacon.

"And if you want to bring it closer to home, you're talking about motorcycles, well how about them? We've got disc brakes that really stop you, suspension you can tune to suit, tires that stick to the road, electrics that work; if you really think back to how it was, you'll see how far we've come on."

The Dude swept on.

"That's true, but you got to look at the big picture, man. Most of the world's running scared now, throwing away their freedom with both hands, trying to say that freedom never really happened. Take me in your navy, your factory, your fucking pension plan! Country's too cold in winter and the street's too cold, all the time," he concluded unhappily, and lapsed into silence.

"You just made the one big mistake, boy," said Leroy from the couch. "You took it all serious."

"Or maybe it's just an idea whose time has gone?" asked Laura quietly.

But from across the room, Krass was saying loudly, almost shouting.

"Jesus, Dude, you do bring it all back. Those endless rap-sessions—about what? What are you really saying? Or more to the point, what would you actually *do?*"

At this, the Dude rekindled.

"All right, let's get to cases. Like, the way you guys are intending to go about this thing. It seems all wrong to me, and I'll tell you for why. . . ."

"We're going in," grated Levon, "and that's all she wrote."

"You're going in!" the Dude caroled. "Feels great, I bet. Real righteous. But it's the same thing every time, every time a cop pulls his gun or a politician gets on the hot line to the military. Fuck the rest of the world, fuck the innocent bystanders, we're *going in*. It's the by God natural thing to do, ain't it? American as apple pie. Blow away the bad guys." At that point, the Dude felt the force of Cleaver's gaze, and turning to him, continued hastily, "I mean, it's a beautiful plan, man, but it misses out the one thing I been saying all along."

"Which is what?" said Cleaver.

"The girl. Emily. She's the one to concentrate your mind on. She could tell us who really did it."

There was a long silence. Finally, Cleaver said, "Perhaps she did know, still does even. But as I understand it, she's crazy, she's been locked away for thirteen years and she's gone schizo. G. W. Brooks told me himself he thinks she's lost her memory."

"No," said the Dude, "listen. Did G. W. tell you what she looked like now, how she was?"

"Well," said Cleaver slowly, "he said she was okay physically—still sweet—I think he said; but she didn't hardly talk at all. . . ."

"Right," said the Dude. "Now if she was a true schizophrenic, after thirteen years' isolation, she'd likely be sexless, skinny, flat-chested, mustachioed, with a real unattractive personality; she wouldn't have known love to begin with, she would have had little enough affect then, and by now she would have withdrawn nearly totally, withdrawn into fantasy. No, no," he overrode as Cleaver began to object, "I know what I'm talking about—the Doc tag may be a joke, but I took what I've done over the last several years serious enough, and I've read enough and seen enough crazies to know what I'm saying. . . ."

"It's true," said Cherry unexpectedly. "Like, get off his case and listen to the man."

"No," the Dude continued, "Emily's no schizo, she's another thing, a psychoneurotic."

"Fuckin' five-dollar words," sneered Six.

145

"Yeah, but they mean something," the Dude shot back, "and the difference is important. Now after what happened to her and what she must have seen, she was in shock, like when we found her; a totally natural thing, like if she'd escaped from a fire or a bad accident or gone down to combat fatigue. Pretty soon she'd come out of that rigid silence, but she'd stay apathetic and withdrawn. But recovery would take, like, days, or at the outside weeks. No way thirteen years."

After the silence that followed, the Dude's quiet, hypnotically fluent voice continued, "There has to be something else, see, another factor must have come into play to make her keep quiet. Sure G.W. thinks maybe she's lost her memory, but in my experience, short of physical injury, that doesn't finally happen. My guess is she's known all the time what happened, and she remembers well enough now; it's just convenient for her to have people think her memory's gone. Because thinking about it is too painful. And because she feels talking about it is too dangerous."

There was a pause, and then Krass asked, "You mean you think she's paranoid?"

"Maybe. Or maybe it's what we used to feel about the government; that old *justified* paranoia," the Dude grinned briefly and then went on, "What I mean is, maybe somebody's threatening her."

"With what?" said Cleaver.

"Well the usual thing is, like, if you tell them that, you're a mad, wicked girl and we'll put you in the padded cell and throw away the key," said the Dude. "But under the circumstances, it could be something a whole hell of a lot more direct, I guess."

In the silence that followed, Six cleared his throat noisily and said, "Too thin, Dude. It's all just your half-assed ideas based on the word of some tame spade—uh, sorry, brothers," he added hastily to Levon and Leroy.

"Six, park your mouth," said Krass. "Dude, if all that was true, what would you do to get Emily to talk?"

"Yeah, hypnotize her, or what?" sneered Six.

"Don't laugh, he does that," Cherry interjected, but the Dude just smiled and said, "No—more often than not, I've found that a sympathetic person, one who suspects the true story, is all that it takes." He looked into the fire. "She had such a natural grace, Emily; you must all remember that. With someone like that it just takes gentleness, and perhaps a little cunning, to protect and free it. Now I know it's easier for you to concentrate on zapping the bad guys. Maybe," he continued carefully, "some of us might have done something they'd rather not remember that night. But if we ignore this chance to help Emily and find out what really happened, we all run the risk that maybe some of us," and here he nodded at Levon and Leroy, "have fallen into already."

"What you talkin'?" bristled Levon.

"Becoming like what we fear," the Dude answered him, but it was Cleaver on whom his eyes were fixed.

Cleaver realized instantly what the Dude meant. He felt a surge of anger at this continuing challenge to his plans and the disruption of the mood he wanted to generate. But he allowed none of this to show on his face as he stared back at the Dude and said levelly, "I think I know what you're talking about, Dude, and if so, let's get it out front."

Every eye in the room was on Cleaver as he went on,

"I think you were around after we found them that night, and you saw me do something when Krass went to get the others."

The Dude, his wide eyes unblinking, nodded once.

"You saw me pull a blade out of Jimmy's chest and heave it in the bayou."

There was dead silence as the Dude swallowed and then nodded once again.

"I'll tell you why," said Cleaver. "It was my knife, with the JC initials just to make it airtight. I knew they'd have nailed me for sure with that. So I dumped it.

"Ariel, Dance, Bob—you saw me and Krass by the fire up to five, maybe seven minutes before the body was found. Do you think we could have done it?"

"Not unless you're real fast workers," came Dance's clipped reply. "No, I don't think so at all."

"My knife was missing," Cleaver went on. "Someone had

boosted it and left it there. That's why I did what I did. I'm not proud of it, and it was one more reason to run. . . ."

"Ah man, knife or no knife, we had to get out of there. We didn't have a flying fuck's chance with them redneck peckerwoods baying for blood," Tor rumbled, and there was a murmur of assent from around the room that secretly delighted Cleaver. He pushed on relentlessly.

"Okay, that's my sad story. Now if anyone else has anything they saw or did, doesn't matter what it was, they better spit it out now."

The voice came from an unexpected quarter.

"I see something," said Cooch's singsong, with a lisp due to his missing teeth, from the shadows by the fireplace.

"But you were with them by the fire, weren't you?" said Cleaver.

"All the time. Except when I go to take a piss. I go behind the clubhouse. Down in the trees close to the water back there. That's when I see him."

"Saw who?" said Cleaver.

"The Sheriff," Cooch replied calmly, "that Rampike."

"But . . . he was on the road."

"Not when I see him. He was on the water. In a rubber boat. Alone, real quiet. Looking to the island, but he no see me. Paddle on round."

"When was that?"

"Half an hour, maybe twenty minutes, before the light go out."

"Why didn't you tell anyone?"

"Then, didn't think nothing of it. Later, we separate. It was finish. Who do I tell?"

Cleaver nodded slowly.

"All right, the timing's about right. It had all happened pretty soon before we found them. The kid was still warm and his blood wasn't . . ."

"Coagulated," Krass supplied.

"Right," said Cleaver. "It has to have happened in that half an hour, forty minutes, while the lights were out. Now if Rampike was gone all that time his deputies at least would have to know about it, and one of them would likely have gone to the

Judge. Besides, even allowing he was some kind of psycho or pervert, which no way did he seem to be, Duane always said that he was stuck on the old man. It doesn't sound right that he'd turn around and off the guy's kids. He was likely just sniffing around, actually keeping an eye out for them."

The others nodded agreement. There was silence, which was broken by Dance's quiet, reflective voice.

"You know, you have to have at least two things going for you in my line. A good memory, and real good eyesight. They say that's why we Okies got the edge on the rest of the world; those long flat plains train up your eyes just fine."

"Okay, Superman," snorted Six, "what're you saying—you see through the dark of the night and the trees so you see who did it?"

"No," came Dance's dangerously lazy reply. "What I'm saying is, I saw come stains all over the front of your jeans when you showed up that night. Smelt it, too, if you want to know."

A babble of talk broke out—cut through by a roar from Six.

"I do not believe this, I do not fucking believe it! You know what you are, you're like a buncha fucking cops. They think, guy makes a couple mistakes, after that they can hang anything on him, up to and including, shoot the fucking President. . . ."

Cleaver's voice cut him off.

"What about it, Six?"

"All right, all right," the squat gunman grumbled, popping the cap of a bottle of dark Modelo beer and gulping half of it down before going on, "So I had cream on my jeans. Some guys were turning out a chick back there in the bushes." He belched once, then went on, keeping his eyes away from Laura. "So I joined in. That's all of it." He looked up and around at the circle of blank, silent stares and finally appealed, "Don't any of you remember how it was that night? Very crazy, most of us loaded and like that? Hell, Tor, you can tell them—it was you told me about the chick. . . ."

"I told you so you'd stay away," Tor shot back. "But yeah, I saw you there. Pretty soon after the lights went out. I don't see how even a horny little scumbag like you could have done both,

I guess." There was a ripple of relieved laughter and Tor went on, "But since I'm talking, I'll say one thing that's been on my mind. Has it occurred to you that Jimmy might have raped his own sister?"

"And then done hara-kiri?" said Krass. But Cleaver said, "Go on, Tor."

"Well," the muscular figure began, then sighed and was silent for several beats before starting again. "Well, you all know that I'm gay. With many people it's not an either/or thing, but I think that Jimmy Lafayette was coming to that place in himself that evening. I know I was; he pushed me closer to knowing. And because I didn't understand what was happening, it upset the hell out of me. Now you take a nice young kid, high on Kemp's STP for the first time, getting feelings he can't handle. He might turn to someone close for reassurance. He might even go ape and *grab* himself some reassurance from them."

"And then kill himself?" Krass persisted.

"Naw," Tor shrugged, "But someone could have found him at it and got mad enough to do what they did. And being her brother would also maybe explain why Emily still isn't talking about it."

"How about her other brother?" suggested Six. "That Cal seemed like one real salty-looking dude."

"No show," said Krass. "Our guys by the fire reckoned he and Cannonball were locked up in the compound round the clubhouse till they came out of that gate and nearly nailed us."

"And Jimmy doesn't really fit the bill," came the Dude's voice again, "unless he had some help. Because I found out from G.W. that the cop reports showed at least two different men had attacked Emily."

The longest silence yet fell on the room. Finally it was broken by a voice dark and sweet as molasses.

"Brother Levon, 'pears to me no one is lookin' our way, right now. Now why do you think that might be?"

"Why, brother Leroy, I'd have to guess that the gentlemen are putting it together in their heads that, 'less they seeing double already on account of the juice, there be two of us."

"Yeah," said Leroy. "And you got a white woman raped by two guys, and say, here's two niggers that nobody knows where

150

they were at when the lights went out—them being so black and all."

"And they showed up real close and real soon after," Levon agreed judicially. "But of course there is just one or two things might be bothering the more educated of the gentlemen."

"Yeah," growled Leroy, his anger finally breaking out, "the motherfuckin' honkies might be wondering why we're here at all, why we spend the last two days dangling under a bag of hot air by a pair of suspenders, and just why we're giving up our Saturday to put our asses on the line for them where we can't do no one no harm but ourselves!"

"All right," said Cleaver, "all right," but Leroy ignored him and concluded, "Now, if I was a white man with all them bucks and all that education, I could be asking myself who's, right now, trying to stop us doing what we got to do.'

And both Levon and Leroy turned flat hostile scowls on the Dude.

"I was up a tree," said the tall figure, nervously pacing before the fire, "out of my brain on Kemp's pills, howling at the moon in my head. And I got the strongest flash that something was going down, something that would pull us apart and then bring us together again a long time later. So I climbed down and, zap, I walked straight to where Jimmy's body was. I saw Cleaver throw away his knife, and the rest of it, and then we split. But however high I was, there still weren't two of me."

The others nodded and the Dude continued, "Now how about it? The only way we can find out the truth is not by getting in a fire fight with these guys, but to find Emily and help her. That way we might even get to see that pattern I sensed then, get to that place where will and chance are seen to be one. . . ."

There was another long silence. Cleaver forced himself to stay quiet. It had to come from someone else. Finally it was Dance who cleared his throat and said softly,

"That girl—she was nice. But Duane, he was one of us. He's what we have to go for."

"Oh man," said the Dude despairingly, "oh man, haven't we learned anything, getting older?" He looked around the circle of their faces. "I'll tell you, that's the thing that's saddened me about us, and the time passing. It's not losing hair, putting on a few pounds, not even the troubles that have come our way. It's how most of us seem to have," he searched for words, "less warmth than we used to."

"It's a hard world," said Six.

"Always was," the Dude came back. "But the hell with it."

Cherry stood and, going to him, whispered something in his ear. The Dude excused himself, and they both left the room. Cleaver saw Laura slip out after them and felt a twinge of relief. Then he raised his voice and said,

"All right. You've all had your say; you've got it out front, and now we know we can trust each other.

"The Dude feels bad about the fact there may be some trouble. He's right. After we've got Duane and his family, we have to avoid it wherever we can. We'll do this with what we were always the best at; being fast up here," tapping his forehead, "and fast out on the road."

There was a murmur of assent.

"But let's not forget one thing," Cleaver's hand shot out and he held aloft a 13 ring.

"This is what they sent us: Duane's ring, and they held him down and sliced off his finger so they could do it. Now I say we take it back to them and ram it down their fucking throats!"

A sound like a growl was rising in the room. Hands went up all around and on each of them, Cleaver saw the 13 ring was glinting. He felt the lift in his chest, the familiar feeling when in the past his words had forged their individual weaknesses into a collective strength. He surged on,

"They're not worth the steam on our piss! And if any of those degenerate scumbags gets in our way, we'll blow their balls halfway across the fucking bayou!"

It was half an hour later, and the room was hotter, the atmosphere thick with smoke and happy noise as they partied down, a mirror circulating with the coke that Kemp had sent, voices ringing loud, vying with one another above the pulsing undertow of Tom Petty's hard rock on the stereo. In the center

Cleaver, egged on and assisted by a whooping, gesticulating Cooch, was retelling the story of their trip to Mexico.

Dance was the only one who noticed the Dude standing in the doorway, and no one paid him any attention until the racer reached over and turned down the sound.

"Thanks, man," said the Dude apologetically. "I'm going into town, got a couple of last arrangements to make with some guys about this place.

"But Cherry's asked me to say that she's receiving visitors in the bedroom as of now. And she'd particularly like it if Bob was first."

With that he grinned once, shyly, and ducked out of the room. Only when the sound of his pickup came from outside did Six say, uncharacteristically unsure, "Is that for real?"

Bob drained his glass.

"Well," he said with a slight tremor in his voice, "I ain't sitting here guessing." And hauling himself to his feet, he swept his way to the door with the long cane, and as they watched in silence, went out.

Cleaver cleared his throat and said,

"Well, as your Fuehrer, I guess it's down to me to go next. . . ." but his speech was cut short as, like a whirlwind, Laura entered the room again, grabbed him by the shirt front, jerked him to his feet and, amid laughing applause, pulled him from the room.

As they walked down the passage with their arms around each other, Cleaver heard Six's voice yell,

"Damn, Tor, this is some break, eh?" and the answering burst of quick deep laughter that followed.

Good, he smiled to himself. That's good.

In their room they lay on the bed in the dark. They had made love once with a quick wordless hunger, so that Laura was only half undressed. In a strip of pale moonlight falling through the half-drawn curtains, Cleaver, naked, saw his wife's still beautiful breasts rising and falling as she lay beside him. He leaned over and they kissed deeply. Cleaver wanted her again, but Laura twisted gently away and said, "Just two questions, John," and when he grunted reluctantly, sat up and went on, "What happens, even if you win? If you get them out? Those people down there won't stop, and they know where to find us now. What then?"

Cleaver sighed and lay back.

"Then we do what I'd have preferred to do all along, only with the Judge's connections it would have put Duane at risk. Turn it over to the law, and stand up to whatever we have coming for running away like we did."

"All right. Then there's the other thing. Why? Why do *you* have to do it, John, taking all the weight on yourself, risking everything?"

"Because if I didn't, who would? Who would get Duane and his wife and kid out of this? Which of the guys here would do it, do it right, I mean?"

Out of the silence that followed and the dark came Laura's quiet voice,

"John, I love you."

Everything dissolved, the tensions of the evening, the memory of his momentary freeze-up in Mexico, the thoughts of what was to come. He reached for her blindly, fumbling to strip her skirt down over her hips and buttocks and flat belly, as she locked her mouth to his wetly and pulled him tenderly but firmly on top of her. She felt him rock hard and hot against her thighs, and felt herself, still moist from before, responding once again, flooding with fresh wetness and breathless excitement as his fingers found her again.

She gasped as he entered her with a deliberate abruptness, thrust once quickly and deep, then almost withdrew, lying just inside her with a stillness that excited her until she found herself bucking eagerly beneath him, words babbling from her lips, "You're my man, mine, mine, oh my man. John! Oh!" then a stream of adoring obscenities, words that made him forget everything in the rhythm, the deep satisfying thrusts. She met them eagerly, arched her body as his head dipped tenderly, caressing her breasts with his tongue, locking hungrily on her nipples. For long minutes they were lost, deep in the silent exchange of pleasure, with no sound but the slap of their flesh or a quiet moan as Laura twisted her body, wrapped her long legs around him, straining her sex to be even closer, to have his cock even deeper, himself more at one with her. It built and built until finally, helplessly, the wave in them broke and together they convulsed, Cleaver's long roaring groan drowning her cries. Then they lay, still locked together, exhausted and satisfied. She heard Cleaver whisper gently, "Yes," and there was a ring of light in her head just before she slept.

Before dawn, in the strange, luminous, metallic blue darkness, Cleaver, the collar of his leather jacket turned up against the cold, moved from the gently shaking transporter truck warming up by the barn and trotted over to the bunkhouse wing.

He knocked once and announced himself, so that in the room, Bob had time to slip on his dark glasses before Cleaver entered. Cleaver felt a surge of affection for the slight, pale, red-haired figure sitting up in bed with his head cocked toward him.

"How are you this merry morning?" Cleaver asked. "Tuckered out?"

"Some," grunted Bob with a trace of a smile.

"We have to leave," said Cleaver simply. "You got anything to tell me?"

"Nothing for definite sure," said Bob reluctantly, "but . . ."

Cleaver waited patiently and finally Bob said,

"Hell, it was the Dude. Not all the time. But toward the end, after he'd been put down a little bit. I don't know. I just got the feeling he has plans of his own. But then that stuff with Cherry kind of muddied the water."

"He's in the truck with us now," said Cleaver slowly. "I don't know."

"Do you trust him?"

"I don't know. He was always a bullshitter, but he was *our* bullshitter. In the end I guess it's a case of what won out with him, the Lord's grace or the Devil's style."

"Well, y'all be careful down there. That JC stands for John Cleaver, not Jesus Christ. Watch your ass."

Cleaver took the blind man's hand and shook it once.

"Sure. We'll see you on Sunday, with Duane," he said, and turning, let himself out. Walking quickly to the truck, he swung up into the cab beside Krass and Dance at the wheel. The racer grunted,

"Amarillo, Wichita Falls, Dallas, and points south and east," and let in the clutch.

Cleaver waved once to Ariel, Levon and Leroy in the loaded pickup beside them, and as the transporter began to roll, once to the solitary figure outside the door of their room. Laura raised her hand. Then the dust swirled out as they picked up speed, and Cleaver turned his eyes to the road ahead.

Around noon, Laura was in the kitchen when Cherry came in slowly, wrapped in a cream and pink silk kimono which trailed on the ground behind her.

"I guess I slept late?" she murmured.

"Coffee," said Laura.

Cherry nodded and slopped over to a stool. Laura poured her a mug of coffee, brought it over to her at the bar and sat down beside the younger woman. Before them a low wood-framed window gave a view of the paddock, and a lively ap-aloosa colt pacing the windswept dust. Laura looked at the girl's bowed head and said softly, "Are you okay?"

Cherry looked up and then smiled radiantly.

"Oh yes. They were sweet, all of them, creeping in in the dark, so gentle."

There was a silence, and finally Laura said hesitantly, "Just tell me one thing."

"Uh-huh."

"How did you tell Levon and Leroy apart?"

"I *think* Levon tried to talk a little bit meaner. But to tell you the truth, I never tried," she said sweetly. Laura's hand flew to her mouth, and girl and woman doubled over giggling.

"And that Six?" gasped Laura at length.

"Okay, but you can't, like, fake it, can you? And I think he was running some movie in his head. But it must have been a one-reeler," she spluttered, "'cause it didn't last too long!

"No," she went on, "the only drag was that Dance didn't show."

Good for him, thought Laura, another point for Team

Matrimony. It turned her thoughts and she said quietly, "Forgive me for asking, but—how does he feel? The Dude?"

Cherry's eyes, big and dark, met hers.

"He really can handle it, the way I am. And not because none of it means anything to him, or cause it turns him on. It hurt him to begin with. But he *really* believes in freedom; for him it's not just a word. With him I'm really free. And it's his strongest guarantee; whoever else I go with, how am I not going to come back to the person who loves me and lets me be free? I'll live with him and I'd die for him, I love him so. We're one."

"Oh honey," said Laura, and she hugged the girl close.

"How about you and Cleaver?" asked Cherry.

"Well—it's different. People are. Him and me go back a long way. We have lots in common, including the kids; mostly we feel the same way about things, and we've done a lot of stuff together. It's a marriage, not a bad one. You get the stale patches, but when it's good, there's nothing deeper or sweeter, no one more interesting than the other person, nothing to touch it. Maybe you'll get to something like that, maybe not. But for now you're young and healthy and going off in all different directions. And as long as it doesn't become just a habit, I say more power to you."

"Yeah, but tell the truth," said Cherry with a sideways look, "aren't you glad I'm not your daughter?"

"Perhaps," said Laura slowly, "but back in Montana where I grew up, I always did want a sister who was maybe a little bit wild."

Then they were silent. Outside the window, the swirling dust blew steadily now across the sage, and in the paddock the apaloosa colt stood patiently with his tail to the wind. For both the women, and for Bob in his bunkhouse room, the waiting had begun.

15

They leveled out above the cloud, under the half-moon and the glittering stars, and when they were cruising at a steady one eighty, Kemp handed over to the kid. He unstrapped himself and eased up with a grimace from the lumpy parachute he had been sitting on. Some things never changed.

He moved rearward, feeling the uneven drone of the twin Pratt and Whitneys shaking the plane, but it was reassuring music to his ears; all his senses told him that someone back there had done a Grade One reconditioning job on the old junker, which had been the best one of the three. He paused for a moment and stood with his head in the plexiglass bubble of the dome located on top of the fuselage, above and behind the cockpit. Despite his flying jacket and coveralls, it was icy cold. Beyond the transparency, veined with spider webs of filigree flaws and scratches, the stars, impassive, surrounded his head.

For Kemp, the worst of it was over. The winds and weather were as predicted. The plane was jake. The kid he knew he could trust—someone he had worked with in the late days in Cambodia, someone he had kept on ice, a fine flyer but an amateur, completely cut off from the corporation, and right now eager for a piece of change and some action. And the main hurdle had been passed. Outside Daytona Beach, with time in hand for Kemp to radio down and relay a message to Cleaver to cancel it if there had been any trouble, they had overflown their clearing point. On the ground, Sergio Acosta with a radio had checked their tail for possible airborne navy or customs tails sniffing out dopers. Sergio was Colombian, and Kemp hadn't liked to use him, but the guy was experienced at this, and for domestic reasons to do with immigration, Kemp had him in his pocket. On the radio, the South American's pleasant voice had briefly confirmed that they were clear, and then they were climbing, heading north and west.

Kemp worked his way along the drumming metal body into the hold. Here he had had bucket seats bolted along the sides of the compartment. With a troop-carrying potential of nearly thirty, the old goony bird was not going to be stretched by the complement of eleven plus two that they hoped to be picking up.

There was only one other chore to come, Kemp reminded himself as he made his way back to the cockpit. Before dawn they were dropping down to refuel out in the country, south of Jackson, Mississippi, at a road improvement site, the same as their projected LZ in Louisiana. No way was he going to have his flight plan showing, or the C-47 logged refueling at a regular field in the area, in case the Lousiana business went public later. If they did their sums right and located the place, hired help on the ground would light flares marking the improvised runway on the highway. The C-47's range of 1500 miles might just have scraped the round trip, but Kemp had never liked unnecessary chances, and he wanted to be sure of landing at their secure strip back in Florida. There might, after all, be dead or wounded aboard.

He stepped into the cabin again. The kid glanced up and nodded briefly when Kemp slid back into his seat. As he did so, his foot nudged the flight bag on the deck beside the younger man, his toe glancing off the hard barrel of the stubby AR-15 assault rifle that he knew was inside. That was the only problem with the kid, he thought. He was still just a little bit gung-ho.

"I'll take it," said Kemp.

In the predawn mist, Rampike tipped back his old hat and spoke softly and deliberately into the CB handset.

"I don't care none if they're not answering, Gabe. You and your boys jes stay where you are till I tell you to do different. You got that? Do you *copy?*"

A voice of grudging assent cracked through the headset, and Rampike grunted.

"And another thing, Gabe, don't you boys forget. If they do show up, keep your damn guns cased like I told you, less they don't give you no choice. Do you copy *that?*"

A laugh made harsher by static was most of the response he got, and Rampike broke the connection. He sighed, hung up the microphone and, slipping open his car door, stood up in the faintly glimmering darkness.

He was parked at the western end of the dilapidated wooden road bridge leading over the river into Badwater town. All around him, thick, shifting mist rose from the dark waters, out of sight beneath the trembling bridge, gurgling and lapping gently southward. The town laying brooding on the far side; three miles down the road in the other direction was the turning for the island and the clubhouse where they were holding the prisoners.

Rampike grunted and stretched after long hours in the confines of the car; close to sixty, his stocky body was still muscular, solid as a roll of quarters. And in himself he was ready. It came back to him, the feeling from nearly forty years ago, that terrible winter as a young PFC huddling beneath the lethal tree bursts in the forests of Bastogne, waiting for the next Kraut attack. The readiness.

Because they would be coming soon; nothing could stop it now. That Cleaver had called a couple of times, first trying to stall, then saying he'd bring them in at midday, but Rampike wasn't buying it. He had gone beyond protest to the Judge, and mental reservation. Now with a resolution coming, he was ready. He recognized relief there, too, an end to the long years of blaming himself for letting Emily and James onto the island.

With deliberate steps, his boot heels thudding lightly on

the planks of the bridge, Rampike strode evenly to the north side and stood with his hands on the rail, the breeze from the south playing on his collar, his mind probing the mist. Along the river, three miles to the north, stood the Judge's mansion, and Rampike knew with certainty that the old man too was awake and alert, knowing as he did that the thing they had all awaited for so long was approaching, with every minute that passed toward the deadline at midday. He would have bet money that right this moment, the old man would be seated, motionless and erect, in the drive below the porch in his son Cal's Jaguar (as usual, a corner of Rampike's mind momentarily pursed its lips at the boy's imported auto, though conceding it was a sweet machine), with Cal at the wheel, ready to roll to wherever the CB told him the action went down.

Rampike stood, thinking hard, but feeling the weight of expectation from the mansion and from the hushed town behind him. Every soul in the county knew what was going on, and not one of them would quarrel with the Judge's way of handling it. His boy killed and his daughter sick and shamed, to them that cried out for blood. That's not Christian, thought Rampike, but it was the country way, that he did know. In the long years since that night, an affection had built in the county for the old man, as the people had watched him wait and patiently endure his pain. So let it come, get it over with and clear the air. Then the old man would maybe pass on in peace. And above all, Duane and his family would get clear.

The Judge, the crazy old coot, so strong for the truth, he would likely have held his trial if the bike fellows had turned themselves in, though Rampike didn't doubt that it would have been interrupted with shooting, pretty soon and for good. Every man in the county who could leave his house and carry a gun would have been out there now, if Rampike hadn't kept it to people he could halfway rely on. Thirty or more of them in punts and powerboats were in the channels and bayou south of the island, blocking off the water in case any of the outsiders should try sneaking in that way. Another twenty were dug in by their trucks and bikes at the focal point on both sides of the causeway to the island, the only landward approach. Added to which Rampike had kept himself and his deputies, with the dogs in case of fugitives to track, here on the bridge, covering the approach from the east and acting as a mobile reserve. Plus there was that Cannonball and his bag of tricks, if it came to it. It was set the way Rampike wanted it, the way his war had taught him about defense, not too tight around the objective, but not too damn loose either.

There had been one more disposition. Rampike had put five men (and since it was a little exposed, had taken care that they should all be some of the remaining Truckers) at the three-way crossroads, the first junction west of the causeway and the way the bikers would have to pass if they came in by road. He'd had them dig pits, camouflage their machines and keep their heads right down, staying in touch by CB with the main group at the causeway, checking in every hour. No way would the outsiders spot them, not knowing they were there.

That was what Gabe at the causeway had had to tell. For the last hour the Truckers at the crossroads had failed to call in. Gabe, of course, was hot to take a bunch of boys and check out the crossroads. Rampike had put the lid on that one, quick. Most likely the radios were just acting up; that always happened when it mattered. But if the Yankees had jumped the guys at the crossroads, sending more men out there was the last thing Rampike was about to do; it would be just what these guys would hope for, pissing away his forces in bits and pieces in the mist and confusion. No sir, not this hoss, grunted Rampike.

Rousing himself from a last sifting scrutiny of the mist, the Sheriff turned on his heel and walked swiftly to his car. He was satisfied, filled with a conviction that it was going down, here and now, because in the mist as the dawn came, as he had known all along, was the time that would favor them best. He would drive on out to Gabe and keep the ranks dressed.

He climbed behind the wheel, a long-barreled .38 worn in the old style, high on his belt and tilted forward, and a Remington pump clipped vertically, barrel-up, beside the wheel. He turned the key and instantly the 440 Magnum mill rumbled into life. A 165-mph automobile, it was no wheelchair, Rampike reflected as he spoke quietly into the mike, informing his deputies and Gabe of his intended movements. But driving was kind to old-timers, and a lot of of the top NASCAR men, Foyt and them, were pushing fifty. If that Cleaver and his friends wanted to make a run of it again, Rampike felt ready.

Snicking into first, he eased the big car away from the bridge, west along the familiar road to the causeway, nosing carefully through the mist. Squinting sideways away from the lights, through the side window Rampike thought he detected a glimmer of rose light. Dawn was coming. The car moved forward faster.

Deep in the dawn mist of the bayou, the pale shape of an egret was picking its way slowly, with dignified hesitancy, through the shallows. Suddenly it froze.

For long moments it stood with one leg still lifted, its curved neck drawn back, the plumed head as immobile as if captured in a print by Audubon.

Then in a flurry, the bird launched into flight on wide wings, at first awkward, then graceful, and was gone into the mist.

The thing that had disturbed it came again. Above the mist, fire breathed.

Two hundred feet up, in absolute silence after the burn, save for the hiss of wind in their flying wires and the soft flare of their burner's pilots, in sunlight three silver shapes linked by a slim cord drifted on the northward wind. Ariel, Levon and Leroy rode the breeze from the Gulf above the mist toward the island. In a beautiful phenomenon, the sun, shining through the wet air onto the mist, surrounded each swelling silver pear-drop shape with the colors of the rainbow.

Ariel had eyes for none of this. He was concentrating as hard as he ever had in his life, attention flickering between the altimeter, the compass on his right wrist, his watch, the fuel level, but above all, working his memory of the briefing information coupled with his flyer's instincts. His task was made harder by the fact that above the vapor there was no sensation of movement, no shadow driving below them on top of the mist.

He was suspended in a sitting position, by broad harness and shoulder brackets, beneath the thirty-foot-tall, smooth-gore silicone-proofed polyester envelope of a Colt Cloudhopper, a one-man basketless balloon. On his back was slung a three-foot high cylinder of propane gas. Above it a burner unit, mounted on a swivel ring, connected to the collar of the fuel tank. That was all that held him in the air.

Ariel stared at the surface of the mist below the heels of his thick, smooth-soled jump boots, probing for the breaks which had begun to come now, as to their right, in silence, the pale white orange orb of the sun rose imperceptibly, haloed in soft color.

Ariel was tense, his moon face set with the knowledge that there would be no second chances. The Cloudhoppers, while controllable up and down with great accuracy, were not truly dirigible; they went with the air, rather than driving through it. So since they could not come back, he had to drop the three of them down on the island correctly the first time. And conduct their flight to precise time limits, with the mist at first concealing them from the guns below, and then breaking up to reveal their target as they approached it. Ariel knew the accuracy of which he was capable—he had won twenty-mile competitions to the inch; but that had been in full daylight on a clear afternoon. Still, early was the best time to go in summer, before the ground heated and thermals rose. And thank Christ, the wind was as predicted, light and steady.

So they had positioned themselves at the outset correctly to take advantage of it. A call from G. W. Brooks had confirmed that their launch area was clear of the Judge's men. Then in the predawn darkness, they had gone in by truck, and just before dawn rapidly assembled and inflated the envelopes five miles to the south and east of the island. They had been sheltered by the massive road-making machines scattered along the highway development, which was to be their pickup point as well. When dawn broke they had taken off, climbing out, lift correct, to meet the six knot breeze, then burning to counteract the wind shear and loss of false lift, coming up through the mist into the new-made morning.

Now Ariel craned his neck to check the other two. Their takeoff performance had been outstanding considering the short training period, though their parachute experience had helped. In flight there had been no problem with the connecting cord going round anyone's neck, and only once had Ariel had to use his short afterburn to counteract the inevitable tendency of the last two in the chain to go up and down more than the leader. He looked at Levon's set face where he crouched in his harness fifty yards away beneath the rainbow-covered canopy, in olive drab crash helmet and tiger-striped coveralls, with a pack of heavy equipment slung across his chest, topped by the slim tube of his machine-pistol, and felt a momentary twinge of sympathy for the Truckers below; if he, Ariel, managed to deliver the brothers there right.

Then his attention was fully engaged, as to his right, above the tattered mist, reared the limbs of a single massive oak tree, overgrown with fern and Spanish moss. Beyond lay a stand of cypress. With a thrill of recognition, Ariel registered the landmark from the photographs and maps their contact on the ground had provided. Their line was close to correct, just a little off to the west. His gloved left hand rose to the burner control, and a sharp pencil-like tongue of flame gouted from the burner unit up into the envelope, carrying him up and to the right. He checked behind to see Levon and Leroy doing as he had done. They were on line, and less than five minutes from the island.

With trembling fingers, from a pocket of his coveralls Ariel fished out the walkie-talkie set, thumbed the button and was about to speak when his eyes bulged and he half-choked. The mist was evaporating fast now, and directly below them among the dank vapors, concealed by reeds, Ariel had spotted a flat-bottomed boat with four men crouched in it, the barrels of their guns raised skyward. But their eyes were fixed intently on the surface level of the water in the direction the three had already come from.

Totally vulnerable, the three men and balloons floated silently above the guns of the boat, and slowly away. It was a thing Ariel had noticed before, how people, adults anyhow, never looked up. But this was the first time his life had depended on it.

A minute later, his round face drenched with sweat despite

the morning chill, Ariel thumbed the button on his handset again and spoke softly into it.

"Red One, Red One, this is Red Three, do you copy?"

There was no reply.

He repeated the call twice and then the flat voice of Cleaver was crackling close to his ear.

"Red Three, this is Red One, we copy. Are you close? Over."

"Red One, we're right on line and about three minutes from the place, over."

"Red Three, that's good work, you're dead on the stopwatch. We'll start the ball rolling now. You be lucky. Over and out."

Ariel swallowed and stowed the set in his pocket again. As he did so there came a sight that clutched at his heart. Drifting in ahead and just to their right, about three hundred yards across the bayou, he made out the black hump of the tree-covered island rising from the flat water, and in its center the low shape of the hut, the windowless log frame and moss-covered slope of the roof making it seem to have grown from the island itself. A single wisp of smoke rose from the chimney at one end, a magnet to his eye.

Ariel made an urgent hand signal to Levon, who relayed it to Leroy. Then with no time to lose, his right hand rose to the six-millimeter cord above him, operating the parachute valve controlling deflation.

Just as they started forward and down, the silence was shattered. From their left, in the distance to the west, came the stutter of high-powered motors. But these were quickly drowned by an eerie guttural growl of a siren starting up, that built quickly to an ear-splitting banshee wail.

The cabin was drifting up closer, agonizingly slowly. Then the first shots slammed out.

When the sound of the bike engines first came to the men at the causeway, Rampike, in his car, just had time to bellow through his bullhorn:

"HOLD YOUR FIRE!" as bolts rattled and safeties snicked off. Every eye was fixed westward down the misty road, the men crouched in the dirt on both sides of the causeway's end or kneeling beside their trucks, rifles and shotguns ready, as the sound grew.

Then it was cut by the blood-freezing shriek of the siren, and Rampike's yells of:

"STEADY!" as he saw panic and confusion in some of the faces around him, and guns begin to come up.

Then from down the misty highway, the first wave of bikes appeared, headlights blazing, rolling steadily, quite slowly toward them, the siren screaming louder and louder. Even as he stared incredulously, something about the first riders nagged at Rampike.

Just as he had it, several things happened at once. At about fifty yards, one of the riders coming toward them swerved his machine and deliberately crashed, laying it down on the road as best he could. Perhaps reflexively, this caused the first shot to be fired, the bullet sparking off the road between the two machines. Despite Rampike's yells and gestures a ragged volley of largely unaimed fire followed. The front line of motorcycles came crashing down, though only one man had been hit, in the arm; the rest followed the first rider's example and dropped their machines deliberately to dive for cover.

"DON'T FIRE!" bellowed Rampike into the bullhorn, "THEY'RE TRUCKERS!"

He was right. Captured at the crossroads in the hours before dawn, the five luckless bikers were being pushed forward as a human shield. As the first rank went down they revealed a second row of riders, two of whom had been training weapons on the bikers in front of them, forcing them forward. Now they all threw their machines in a U-turn, one hurling aside the siren which ran down to a halt so Rampike's words through the horn could be heard clearly:

"THOSE ARE THE MEN WE WANT. LET'S GET AFTER THEM!"

Gabe and his people needed no urging. Already all around trucks and bikes were bursting to life. Even with the horn, Rampike was only just able to make himself heard as he yelled and pointed:

"YOU, GABE, STOP RIGHT THERE. THEY'LL

MAYBE TRY SOMETHING ELSE," before the pack streamed off, swerving round the fallen Truckers in a roaring torrent, down the road, after the vanishing motorcycles, with Rampike weaving his way through the fired-up traffic, leaving only a haze of road dust and a disgruntled Gabe and friend to mind the store.

Inside the cabin, when the sound of the engines had first approached, Spider's one eye blinked as he reached for the twelve gauge by the table and said,

"Kill 'em now."

At the other end of the darkened cabin, Duane's arms moved slowly to hug his wife Mary and his little girl to him.

Curtis, the second Trucker, licked his lips.

"Judge won't like it. . . . ," he began to say, but the ragging noise of the siren came, and he too went quickly toward a deer rifle slung on a nail on the wall.

Spider, jacking a round into the pumpgun's chamber, began to say,

"Well, anyone comes through the door I'm gonna . . ."

But he got no further.

A second before, hovering four feet above the roof, Levon and Leroy's hands had gone to the Capewell quick-release locks on their shoulder straps. Meeting each other's eyes, together they wrenched the buckles open.

As the balloons, freed from their load, rocketed upward in the stable air, the two laden figures, yelling the marine battle cry "KILL OR DIE!" plummeted downward, gripping their weapons across their chests, smashing feet-first through the rotten shingles of the roof and with a rending noise plunging from the morning light in a hail of debris ten feet down into the shadows of the room.

Levon achieved a stand-up landing, and even before his eyes had gotten accustomed to the dark, with a practiced move sprayed a thumping stutter of silenced fire in a wide arc six inches above head height. At the other end of the room, Leroy's fall was broken by Curtis; barely pausing to butt-stroke the winded Trucker with his weapon, Leroy hurled himself on top of Duane and his family, dragging them to the ground and covering their bodies with his own.

Spider, shattered by the suddenness of the assault, had frozen on the trigger over by the table. The barrel of his shotgun was beginning to come up when Levon, firing on movement, lowered his aim a foot and let go with the rest of the Sidewinder's magazine in one burst.

Most of the equivalent of four full .45 pistol magazines found their target in just over a second. Ten feet away, Spider, hosed by the bullets, jigging horribly, was flung, screaming once, against the wall and collapsed, bullet-riddled and dead before he hit the floor.

The first sound in the stillness was the tinkle of Levon's empty magazine and the smack as he rammed home a new one.

Leroy checked the smoke-laden air of the cabin with a quick, careful gaze before slowly rising. Then for the first time, he looked down at Duane, his wife and the little girl, taking in their filthy clothes and hair, dirty bandages, pale faces, wide unblinking eyes and trembling limbs. In the silence the little girl began to whimper.

Leroy was careful to make no move to touch her.

"Well all right," he said softly, almost crooning, "don't you fret now."

Duane's voice came as a croak,

"Leroy?" After a second, his hand reached out and grasped the Marine's black fist tightly.

At that moment from the causeway came the roar of a vehicle approaching. Levon leapt to the door, but it was locked, with no key visible. Unhesitatingly he whirled to the wall and fell on the body of the dead Trucker. As Duane watched in horror, one arm of the riddled body came away in Levon's hand as he wrenched at it. The battle-rage on him, Levon flung the limb aside and came up with what he sought, Spider's pump-gun.

Back at the door he ignored the lock and, as the motor outside came closer, with a deafening roar fired twice, flame and sparks from the gaping barrel showing clearly in the darkened room, and blew both hinges off the door.

169

Drawing back his booted foot, Levon lashed out once, and as the hinges went, flung himself forward like a black artillery shell and hit the door, knocking it out of its frame and somersaulting through with the shotgun cradled tightly to his body. Fifty feet away, on the far side of the chain-link fence, Gabe's truck, alerted by the sight of Ariel's silver canopy hung on a tree, was slewing to a halt in a pall of dust.

Levon came up firing, but the chain-link, blurring where the pellets hit, deflected the shotgun round, and he flung himself flat as from the truck's cab, two rifles banged out, bullets kicking up dust close to him. He yelled hoarsely,

"Grenade!"

Back in the cabin, Leroy wrenched a grenade off his harness, tore out the pin and, ducking briefly around the doorway, tossed the live egg to his brother. With the finest of margins Leroy caught it right-handed and in the same motion lofted it clean and high over the fence to land in front of the truck and roll on under the vehicle.

There was a flat explosion, and the front wheels of the truck briefly lifted clear of the ground. Black smoke began to billow from the engine. After several seconds Levon rose cautiously and, holding the shotgun on the truck's cab, came out through the gate in fence with Leroy covering him.

There was no movement in the cab; the two figures there were concussed and unconscious, blood trickling from their ears and noses. The brothers hauled them out and dragged them clear of the burning vehicle.

From around the building, Ariel emerged; he had landed at a distance deliberately, as the black Marines wanted him well clear of the action. His face was ashen. In the light, Levon's coveralls could be seen clearly, covered with blood.

Duane, with his wife Mary carrying the little girl, emerged from the cabin cautiously, blinking in the sunlight. Leroy gestured them over urgently to the two trucks parked at one side of the cabin.

"We better move before someone gets to noticing all this," he said. "Kemp's coming for us in an aer-o-plane down the road apiece. Ariel's gonna take you there in this old Dodge.

We'll take the Ford and draw off anything evil. Good luck to you."

"Thank you," said Mary simply. Duane nodded and then helped her into the cab of the old truck. Ariel stripped off his coveralls to reveal worn work clothes.

"Dressing the part," he explained, with a shaky attempt at a grin.

Levon and Leroy unclipped the packs from their chests and laid them in the back of the Ford, Levon vaulting in next to them while Leroy slid behind the wheel. He pumped his hand once, and the little convoy drove away from the island down the causeway to the main road, once there turning left and heading west, with the brothers bringing up the rear.

Five minutes later, drawn by the sound of the firing and explosion and the confused gabble on the CB, the first of the boats nosed its way onto the back of the island. Led by a tall, black-bearded figure, the four men from it approached the cabin cautiously, rifles leveled.

Round at the front they found Curtis, the second Trucker, sitting with his back against the wall beside the shattered door, holding his head in his hands. He looked up and groaned.

"Don't go in there, Bud. Your brother Spider's dead. It ain't pretty. Two black fellers with machine guns fell out of the sky. They really killed him. They took Duane and them, and lit off in our trucks down the road west."

Bud, the black-bearded one, began to curse thickly. He was Spider's older brother, an ex-Trucker, and he had a reputation as the mean one in the family. The other three men were also his brothers.

"Junior," he growled, "get on the CB and tell that Cannonball to get up and after a black Ford pickup and an old blue Dodge. Tell him to nail them good. We'll take the powerboat down to the road south of the bayou and cut 'em off if they head that way."

"But Rampike said . . . ," Curtis protested feebly.

"Fuck that rock-ribbed bastard. It ain't his kin that's dead," snarled Bud, grimly leading the others at a run back to the boat.

Rampike had worked his way to the front of the pack of vehicles pursuing the 13 a few hundred yards before the crossroads. From there he had seen the figure in black and white racing leathers at the rear of the bikes they were pursuing deliberately raise his visor, grin mockingly, and gave him the finger.

Rampike was unused to this treatment, since for many years in Badwater, racing with the Sheriff had been considered equivalent to playing Russian roulette with an automatic pistol. He recognized the slim boy who had raced the Truckers all those years back, and when the crossroads came up and the tail-end bike peeled over all the way and tore off along the right-hand road, Rampike swung the wheel and drifted the big Chevy in a power slide after him.

"You for me, boy," he grated, released into action.

Cleaver snapped a glance behind him in time to see the Sheriff drawn in pursuit of Dance, as they had hoped would happen. In his mirror he saw Six and Cooch hurl into the left-hand turn and get away clear, as the rest of the pack took the easier option and hurtled straight over the crossroads after himself, Krass and Tor.

There should have been a seventh rider, but an hour before dawn they had discovered that the Dude had slipped away. Cleaver had taken the difficult decision and continued with the plan as before, risking the fact that the Dude might have betrayed them. In the event it seemed not likely, and wherever he was now, Cleaver had no time to worry about it.

They hit one hundred on the short, empty straight beyond the crossroads, the deserted road steaming as the sun came up, trees and telegraph poles blurring by close in on the edge of the two-lane blacktop, the wail of Cleaver's triple and the roar of Krass' eight-valve Triumph twin and Tor's Harley XR-1000 blurring into one wall of sound as bugs smashed on their visors and the first turn flickered closer, an S-bend. Cleaver left the braking late, slamming down into fourth, feeling the discs bite and the front end dive as he went all the way over, tight into the first right-hander, chamfered footrests scraping the black-top, and wide out, using all the road, gambling on the early morning emptiness, hauling the big machine all the way from full right to full left lean, the back end pattering on the bumps in the turn's apex, but the bike going round on rails.

He came out of the S-bend far over to the left and snapped a glance back to see one truck, a real trier, hunkered down on its suspension and still close up with them, with bikes straggling behind it, the truck too close, knows the roads, and yes, better do it now.

They flashed past a tall ramshackle wooden structure, an old sawmill. A long gentle meander of road was coming up and Cleaver hit his button. As the Windtones bleated in the hundred-and-ten-mile-an-hour breeze, he and Krass spread out, and Tor drove between. Cleaver, slowing fractionally, reached inside his jacket left-handed, and as the leading truck behind them loomed dramatically in his mirror, closing up to twenty feet, a fraction of a second at those speeds, he and Krass lofted their prepared cartons behind them to shatter on its windshield.

From clear vision of the fleeing bikes, at a hundred miles an hour the truck driver's view turned in an instant to black as the oil-filled cartons exploded over his windshield.

When he hit the brakes on instinct the two Trucker bikes close to his rear had no time to avoid him. The one to the left glanced the truck's left side, lost control of his shimmying front end and aviated off the road, clear over the ditch, to crash to earth sixty feet further off in the field beyond, the rider somer-saulting clear another thirty yards over the dirt. The biker to the right was less lucky, his Harley smacking straight into the rear of the truck and the rider being flung over it, tumbling hard into the ditch.

The truck slowed, fishtailing violently, brakes screeching, and the driver had his fist drawn back to punch out the wind-shield when a further massive impact catapulted him and the whole vehicle forward. A second truck, accelerating out of the turn and greeted with the sight of the braking, slow-moving vehicle ahead, had lost control and slammed into the back end of it. The lead truck was rammed blindly forward to crash nose-down into the ditch. The one that had struck it, the driver screaming, skidded through two full turns and came to rest facing in the opposite direction, its front end stoved in, the horn jammed on, and water gushing from a fractured radiator onto the road.

After the next curves, Cleaver snapped a glance in his mirror and thought they were clear. He checked the trip odometer; just four more miles to their turn onto the unmarked dirt road which G. W. Brooks had found to take them back east and link up with the road running south to the pickup point.

Then he took a final look in the mirror and with a shock registered the single dot there, closing fast with them. He cranked on the throttle and pushed the big triple hard ahead, blurring through the gentle curves, trusting the other two to stay with him. A glance snapped to the rear showed that despite their hundred-plus speeds on the snaking two-lane, the bike behind had gained dramatically. This was no ordinary Harley.

In fact it was no Harley at all, but what Bob had feared, a modern high-performance four-cylinder motorcycle with every possible go-faster aid. The rider was a young independent, not a Trucker, a tough solitary individual, and his nitrous-assisted GPz 1100 Kawasaki had run in the low tens at standing quarter-mile events for street-legal machines. In a cold fury at what he had just seen happen to his friends, he pulled steadily up on the three machines ahead, in total concentration, at speeds nudging 130. He wanted to get them in range of the pair of automatic shotguns he had clipped on bumper bars, low down and facing forward.

With two miles to go to the turn, his mirror told Cleaver that the Kawasaki had closed up alarmingly, and a long straight was coming up. Then the first shot banged out above the engine roar, pellets kicking dust for a moment to Cleaver's right, near Krass' rear tire. Frantically Cleaver hit his horn button twice, and then with Krass drove past on either side of Tor as the big man's machine fell back.

Two things happened at once as they hit the straight. The rider, determined to get up close for an effective shot, hit the button activating his N_2O canister, and the power-assisted Kawasaki leapt forward. At that moment Tor wrenched at a lever on his tank and dumped the gallon of oil, suspended in a pouch on his sissy bar clear of his own rear tire, to splash all over the road behind.

As the extra impulse from the nitrous oxide pushed him forward, there was no time for the rider to swerve. Momentarily, miraculously, it seemed speed had carried him through and that he would maintain control. Then the wheels went out from under him abruptly, and he rocketed sideways off the road to the left, rider and machine separating in midair, turning end over end to hit the dirt far off in the field beyond, the rider continuing to tumble, sliding over the earth for a full seventy yards, the Pro-Tek chest and back protectors and inserts in his racing leathers at shoulders, knees and elbows taking the worst of the impacts and abrasions. He came to a halt and miraculously staggered to his feet before collapsing in shock and disorientation halfway across the largest of the pieces of twisted scrap metal that had been his machine.

Cleaver never looked back. Less than a minute later, their visors, eyes and noses clogged with beige dust, they were bumping fast down the dirt track east and south.

Lying half-submerged in the waters of the rice field, the Dude felt the sight and the warmth of the sunrise soak through him like deep chords of moving music. Ignoring the discomfort, breathing deeply, steadily, his mind and body fingered their way forward into this day, and the thing that he must do.

The river lay behind him, and close to his right, lawns and outbuildings rose to the shimmering white colonnaded bulk of Beau Mont mansion standing still and silent among the oak trees. The sun, rising behind the house, threw shadows toward him.

In the new light, on the curve of the gravel drive before the building, the Dude watched two burly men sitting on the hood of a Ford coupe, their heads cocked to a CB set. Despite the chill damp and the dirt, with long practice he let his body relax after the tension of the flight from Cleaver and the others. He had carefully navigated the back roads to the spot two miles or more away where he concealed the Shadow and hiked on, with fast and cautious broken movement through the fields in the half-light of dawn, his high boots waterlogged, going to ground when the first distant sound of gunfire and the siren came, and the big cars had roared out from the drive and down the road by the river heading for the junction at Badwater town. But he had kept moving, silently, elliptically, always nearer the mansion.

Now he stiffened and grimaced as, like far-off firecrackers, the sound of gunshots wafted to him indistinctly on the breeze from the south for the second time. Away on the drive the guards, too, tensed. After a moment, their CB set squawked into life. The two men exchanged a look; they glanced back once at the mansion, then, without a word spoken, both jumped in the car and with the sound of doors slamming and fat tires gouging into the gravel, the Ford powered away, sliding fast past the spot where the Dude lay motionless, close to the road.

After a minute had passed, the tall scarecrow figure slipped to his feet in silence and, picking his way forward, jumped the ditch and set his boot heels on the road. After another moment, he started out, quickly but calmly, a lone pilgrim, unarmed, toward the imposing mansion.

"Got to climb that stairway to heaven," he muttered to himself as the still bulk of Beau Mont loomed nearer. At an open window, a curtain fluttered once and then subsided.

He walked on the grass to the side of the drive, and when he reached the house, circled it and passed to the rear. By a flower bed, he paused once to watch in silent fascination as, lanced by the sun's rays, a dragonfly hovered, translucent, above a dew-laden white rose.

He walked on, rounded the corner and came up short, looking down the gaping barrel of a long-barreled shotgun.

After a long moment the Dude murmured softly, "G.W.?"

The elderly black man was in his shirt sleeves, with red-rimmed eyes and white stubble standing out from his dark, withered cheeks and chin. The trembling hands continued to hold the gun centered waveringly on the Dude's chest. Looking at the old man, the Dude finally realized what kind of a strain

Brooks had been under as he deceived his old friend and employer and secretly helped the outsiders.

Now he spoke hoarsely, querulously.

"What you come sneaking round here for, bother the Judge this way?"

All right, thought the Dude, fighting to steady his breath, *take me. Take me if that's what it needs. But let her be well.*

Standing still, he said simply, "How is she?"

For long moments, G. W. Brooks didn't answer. Then slowly he nodded his grizzled head.

"Yeah. Yeah, that's it, ain't it? Has been all along. The kids. Poor Jimmy, now Duane, and Miss Emily most especially. That's it. Yeah."

Lowering the shotgun, wearily he rubbed a hand rasping across his unshaven features.

"She's all right. Maybe a little bit agitated, just now. I'd guess she feels that something's going on."

"She's nothing but right," nodded the Dude. "Today's the day it's all going down, okay."

They both looked for a moment at the low brick house standing between the back of the mansion and the river, and then together began to walk toward it. There was a porch, and on it a cane-bottomed chair standing with a guitar propped against the wall nearby, a little way from the single green door.

The Dude stopped short of the porch for a long moment. The sun, rising behind the brick house, circled it with a golden glow.

"Daughter of the night—sister of the sun," thought the Dude. *"Let me. Just let me."*

"That your axe, G.W.?" he asked, gesturing at the guitar, and when the old man nodded yes, went on, "May I?"

G. W. Brooks nodded again, slowly, understanding, as beneath the blank windows of the little house, the Dude stepped up on to the porch, and seating himself on the chair, commenced to tune the twelve-string to his satisfaction, absorbed, even when the silence of the still garden was broken by the sound of an explosion off in the distance.

Then, quietly, almost tentatively at first, the Dude was playing, the music flowing from his fingers, "Love in Vain," the same blues he had played for Emily that night in Duane's yard so long ago. After a while the sound of the hypnotic flow of music and a foot tapping time was joined by his quiet, almost terse voice; until the moment when the guitar broke loose again and sang its high steel song.

Neither the Dude nor Brooks realized when the door opened slowly, or saw at first the pale figure standing there in a shapeless dress of faded cotton. Tears slid down her cheeks unheeded in a continuous flow. She looked at the Dude. Her lips parted.

The thick trees of the bayou clustered in to their left as Ariel nursed the ancient Dodge truck at a steady fifty-five down the empty road running south. They were heading for the junction where he was to take a left turn and run along beside the levee and the river, to the road improvement site and the pickup point.

He had provided candy for the little girl, now asleep in Duane's arms, a comb for her mother, and a flow of nervous talk across to Duane, as much for his own benefit as for that of the tense and emaciated southerner. For previously, when they had reached the crossroads, Levon and Leroy's truck had abruptly shot away straight across the junction, leaving the Dodge to swing left unaccompanied, the escort gone. Anything could happen. And Ariel, deliberately, was unarmed.

With relief he recognized the sign for a bridge ahead, crossed it and saw the left turn coming up. As he swung the blunt-nosed truck into the turn, putting the river beyond the levee to their left, the engine faltered, and as they rolled on, spluttered and died.

Sweat broke out on Ariel's forehead, but he attempted a cheery grin as he coasted in to the side and turned to confront the anxiety-stricken faces of Duane and Mary.

"Don't worry—there's nothing I can't fix," he said. "Duane'll tell you it's true." Except for an empty gas tank, he added to himself. He had hoped that the old truck's gauge had been broken. He opened the door and swung down into the morning light, and the silence.

*   *   *

Rampike was respectful but not impressed by the speed of both the rider and machine in front of him. There was nothing vainglorious in his attitude; he simply saw them as something to be mastered.

The rider was very good, there was no denying it. Three miles after the crossroads, he hung a frighteningly fast right onto a dirt road, which Rampike matched with a full-lock slide, splintering a couple of fence posts with his left fender as he went, but boring out of the turn close in the dust that the Harley threw.

As the toughened-up suspension smashed over the corrugated surface, from the haze, curves rushed at them, and Rampike, his hat pulled down low, coolly handling the wheel, caught fleeting glimpses of the rider throwing his machine front end sideways with no braking, feathering the throttle to the limits of the tires' adhesion, his foot going down to flirt with the dirt tearing by beneath at speeds of seventy and eighty, coaxing and wrestling the big bike, its frame stretching and flexing, through the corners, at speeds that the Chevy's roaring engine could easily match but its weight and suspension could not.

After a last tight turn around some bushes, the Harley did what it did best, the pulses of the low-set vee-twin's eccentric firing order powering it out of the corner with maximum traction from right down low, giving the rider, his body taut and far back on the saddle, the power to pull back on the bars and leap into the air out from the dirt road and up onto the blacktop at the T-junction ahead, rear tire kicking dust as it smashed back to earth, swinging in a squealing zig-zagging arc to the left.

Rampike stayed in second, his wheels too leaving the ground, and braced his body for the impact, wrestling the wheel as the car slammed onto asphalt and fired out of the turn, tires squealing and smoking in half-moons, and hitting his lights and siren, slammed smoothly up into third. Here was where the big engine would really come into its own, he thought, sprinting ahead after the motorcycle seen dimly through the dusty windshield as they raced for the next bend at terrifying speed, both leaving the braking till the last moment and beyond, the Chevrolet doing a nose-stand as it braked hard on the corner, the Harley grounding everything, footrests, matt black silencer, the rider's knee, and yes, as they screamed round and out with the power right back on, the kid could do it on the road as well as the dirt, and Rampike wondered if he knew he was heading back toward Badwater town. Probably, the Sheriff considered dispassionately, since he's in control of everything else, as they ran between fields, eating up a long shimmering straight, Rampike watching the red needle climb past 130 and changing up again, only then beginning to gain on the roaring V-twin ahead, by *God* he's pulling tall gears and someone had put that motor together right, but one more straight and I've maybe got you, thought Rampike. Though it seemed more likely that he would have to keep running on the raw edge and wait for the man to throw a shoe or make a mistake, because he had it, authority, it shone through in every move he made.

After the next fast, gentle curve the road unwound straight again in front of them but undulating, so that they could only see to the top of the next rise. The rider was going flat out, crouched right down with his chin on the tank for minimum resistance as they breasted a crest and flickering up ahead, shocking on the so-far empty road, came the back of a lumbering trailer full of farm produce hauled behind a tractor, going their way. The rider went round it in the time it took to blink an eye, and Rampike followed, registered the mule frozen in the middle of the left-hand lane close in front of him, and in a momentary failure of reflex wrenched the wheel a fraction too hard, missing the country hazard but sending the big car into a shrieking skid which he was unable to prevent turning into a series of 360-degree slides.

In the center of the screaming, blurred vortex, Rampike calmly drove the circling car, turning into the spin, keeping mastery of the wheel and his position on the road. He might have succeeded had the highway not swung right a hundred yards further on.

At fifty miles an hour, the Chevrolet spun off the road to the left, over the ditch and into the big field of cut hay beyond. Its left wheels dug into the dirt and the car flipped, crushing the lights on the roof before turning one more half-circle and tipping with a crash back onto its wheels.

There was a long moment's silence. Rampike waited, still in his safety belt, his ears singing, getting his breath back, checking for the smell of gasoline. To his right, the tractor and trailer had slewed to a halt across the highway, and the over-alled farmer was scrambling into the ditch to come across and help him. But Rampike's eyes were fixed on the spot far down the road where the Harley had pulled to a halt and the rider sat turned in the saddle, looking back at him.

Deliberately, Rampike's wrinkled hand reached out and turned the ignition key. The engine coughed and refused, once, and again. On the third attempt it caught, and Rampike, idling the motor gently, punched out the rest of the shattered windshield and reached for a pair of sunglasses to protect his eyes against flying splinters. As he put them on, the farmer, approaching, saw the Sheriff suddenly clutch wildly at his head, so that the man thought he was hurt. The truth was worse; Rampike was realizing that during the course of the wreck, he had lost his hat.

His face set grimly, just as the farmer was approaching the car, Rampike began to reverse slowly and carefully over the stubble until he was four hundred yards from the ditch. Then he began to roll forward. With the car rattling and clanking he had reached nearly eighty when he brushed through the field fence and, wire trailing, took off over the ditch at an angle and hit the road again, as in the distance the Harley began to roll toward Badwater.

Gunning up fast through the gears, Rampike gained on him. As he drove he tried the radio, but the impact had knocked it out, so he was unable to call ahead and tell his deputy Otis to block off the bridge.

They rounded the last curve before town, and beside the rickety bridge, Otis, standing by his cruiser, saw the scarlet bike flashing toward him as the Sheriff's Chevrolet appeared round the corner, slithering, right down on its suspension, then firing out of the turn, wisps of charcoal-colored dust puffing from beneath the tires. The bike roared past Otis while he was still dithering between his pistol and the cruiser's steering wheel.

Brakes smoking, the Chevrolet, with its dents, scrapes and trailing wire, shattered windshield and broken lights, screeched to a halt on the bridge. Hatless, the grizzled Sheriff presented an alien face to his deputy. Blood from cuts on Rampike's hand and head smeared the steering wheel. But his voice was level as he called across, "Radio that car two to close off the road east out of town. Then you get down into town after me and help me catch this feller."

Otis swallowed hard and reached for his hand mike, as the Sheriff's battered car shot off toward the town of Badwater faster than the deputy had ever seen an auto move.

Levon and Leroy, following the old Dodge in their black Ford pickup, were reaching the first crossroads when Levon spotted the helicopter.

He pounded on the roof of the truck's cab and yelled to his brother, "Chopper coming! Pull him off the Dodge."

The Ford surged forward, and at the crossroads, with the wok-wok of the low-flying copter's blades becoming clearly audible to them both, Leroy drove straight ahead, leaving the Dodge to bumble south. Less than a hundred yards further on, the Bell helicopter, with its plexiglass bubble, burst into sight between the telegraph poles above and behind them, and Levon, kneeling braced and ready in the bouncing back of the Ford, loosed off a long burst from his now unsilenced Sidewinder, an ineffectual gesture but one which succeeded in attracting the chopper's attention.

Throwing itself sideways and standing on one rotor blade, the Bell swept deafeningly forward, tilting from one side of the road to the other, and then a burst of automatic fire from an M16 raked the road around the pickup, punching holes in its metal flanks where Levon cowered over the packs.

Up in the sky, firing from the hip with the weapon braced on a sling around his shoulders, Cannonball watched the black tiger-striped figure cover his head and whooped, "Coon hunt! Go get 'em, boy!' at the pilot, who grinned with relish and pushed the helicopter forward ahead of the truck, then hovered broadside low above the road as Leroy negotiated the first bends and flashed out from the trees into a hail of fire from Cannonball. The windshield shattered and bullet holes perforated the hood. As they drove beneath the chopper, steam began to gush from the punctured radiator, blowing back into the cab, while in the flatbed, Levon frantically worked over the packs.

"Gotta find somewhere to set up before she dies!" he roared at Leroy, who nodded hard and then yelled, as to their left along the road, the tall ramshackle shape of the sawmill came into view. With the Bell turning to barrel down the road after them, Leroy screamed left across the road on two wheels, and the truck disappeared round the corner of the mill.

"Gone to ground," yelled Cannonball, and he hoisted himself out of the bubble cockpit as the Bell flashed down the road less than ten feet above the surface. The big Trucker rested his good leg on one of the skids and leveled the M16 forward, as the chopper slowed in front of the sawmill, and edged round the corner, hunting the truck.

Cannonball spotted the black truck forty feet away in the shadow of the building, and began to raise the automatic rifle to his shoulder. Suddenly he found himself looking down the gaping maw, outsize to his widening eyes, of a short, tubular rocket launcher clamped on Levon's shoulder where he knelt in the flatbed. Every detail of the scene was etched on Cannonball's consciousness. Then the black marine fired.

Trailing a brief tail of smoke, the rocket streaked across the short distance and with a flash and a thunderous concussion blew the Bell's main rotors off at the head. The bird crashed deafeningly straight down to earth, hurling Cannonball off the skid.

Flames licked at the cockpit. Leroy ran forward to the pilot but he hung limp and lifeless in his harness, his neck broken in the crash, and Leroy sprinted away and flung himself flat as the gas tanks blew and black smoke billowed up into the still morning air.

Cannonball came to in a ditch by the roadside and was starting to crawl away instinctively when the cold tube of a Sidewinder's silencer gently touched the back of his fleshy neck.

"You the Cann'ball, huh, the man that likes to eat stuff so

much?" grated a black voice. "Well, turn around now and eat this."

On his knees, inch by inch, Cannonball turned his head until he faced the silver tube of the silencer.

"Eat it," Levon repeated. Slowly Cannonball closed his fleshy lips about the metal.

"Now remember," Levon went on, "I could blow the back of your head clean into Alabama. So you better move."

With the gun still stuck in his mouth, Levon forced the big Trucker up off his knees and out of the ditch.

"The truck's all shot up," Leroy called across, "Done for."

"So we march," said Levon shortly, extracting the silencer from Cannonball's mouth with an audible plop, then wrinkling his nose and adding in disgust, "Oh hell, big boy here just dropped a packet in his pants."

Leroy had a map and compass out and was pointing away over the fields behind the deserted mill.

"This way looks to be it. We're gonna have to shake it if we want to get there on time."

At this, fresh dread dawned in Cannonball's eyes.

"Oh no," said Levon when he noticed. "A quick bullet would be too easy for you. You march with us, you big bag of jello, war wound and everything. And while you're marching, you can tell us a couple of things."

In Badwater, Dance was going like the hammers of hell with both Rampike and his deputy's cruiser hot on his tail.

After the noise filled the few streets, and the first turns from asphalt to gravel side roads had showered them with gravel from a plume behind the bike twenty feet high, the town's pack of snarling, hungry dogs had given up all ideas of participation and slunk for cover.

As Dance had burst out onto Main Street for the second time, a venerable citizen had blasted off at him with an antique double-barreled fowling piece, but had only succeeded in shattering the plate window of Grafton's General Mercantile Co. across the street, and the withering look he had got from Rampike as the Chevy swept past had sent the graybeard scuttling indoors again like the rest of the town. The few trucks or cars

184

unknowingly entering the town that early during the chase, confronted head-on by the heart-stopping speed of the roaring scarlet motorcycle and the cruisers weaving round them in pursuit, would not soon forget the experience.

After ten minutes, when Rampike began to think they might have him soon if he ran short of gas, Dance broke from the little town's square where Rampike had been keeping his distance, looking to block him out, and rode flat out back toward the bridge. Crouched over the tank, knees and elbows tucked in, he ran the big twin up through the revs to the redline in each gear. Two hundred yards behind, Rampike, his own speed mounting, watched calmly as the rider temporarily drew ahead. A mistake at last, thought the Sheriff—the open road would favor the Chevy's muscle; and then the bike was slowing as it reached the bridge, and he saw the rider's left hand extend deliberately and a black package drop bouncing onto the wooden bridge, and Dance pulled a wheelie away. Without thought Rampike slammed on his brakes, Otis behind and to his right being forced to follow suit. The two cars shimmied and squealed to a halt within inches of each other, and fifty yards short of the bridge. Three seconds later the charge that Levon and Leroy had provided for Dance exploded, and the bridge blew.

Streamers of smoke shot into the morning sky as flame blossomed, and the matchwood that had been the planks of bridge cascaded out and up. Ducking at the roar of the explosion, Rampike and Otis stayed crouched beneath their dashes as a hail of debris, chunks of sleeper, and hanks of cable rained down around their vehicles. It was a full half-minute later before either emerged.

Rampike, who rarely swore, looked at where the bridge had been.

"Well, shit," he said economically.

"Who *are* these guys?" said Otis.

"Don't rightly know. But they're going to be mighty darned sorry they pulled this stuff in my county," said Rampike. "Get Cannonball and the chopper."

"They haven't been able to raise him on the air for a while now. He already took off when he heard about Spider."

"Heard what about Spider?"

"Oh hell, Harlan, I thought you knew. Out to the club-house, two of them got in, killed Spider and took back Duane and the woman and child."

Rampike began to nod slowly, absorbing the information and thinking hard. Finally he looked up at Otis and said,

"South. They're headed south. He knew what he was doing, that fellow. They'll know we can get north or west quick enough on the back roads. Blowing the bridge keeps us from the crossroads and the road south."

"You want me to have the office call the state troopers?"

"Nope," said Rampike, "get them to call the Judge and tell him where we're headed. Do it as we go. Now follow me," he called, and the 440 Magnum engine rumbled into life again.

Ariel turned nervously at the sound of the explosion off in the distance when Cannonball's helicopter went down.

The family remained in the truck, the woman with her eyes closed, the little girl eating candy, never looking up. Duane had stayed with them to be close, knowing that the moon-faced flyer would do anything that could be done with the truck.

He had his head under the hood when Duane said softly, "Ariel," in such a way that the flesh crawled on the nape of the flyer's neck as he straightened, and turned slowly to look behind him as Duane had indicated.

Over the top of the levee, four men in hunting clothes were advancing, rifles and pumpguns pointed at the truck. Leading them, a tall black-bearded man with mean glittering eyes kept his rifle leveled at Ariel.

Duane's wife opened her eyes.

"Oh no," she breathed, "oh no."

"Little engine trouble, huh?" the bearded one asked with a contorted grin. "That's my brother Spider's truck. He never was worth a damn with an engine."

Duane spoke quietly from the truck.

"Bud, let my family go."

"Put your hands where I can see 'em, Duane," barked the bearded one. "Junior, check them out for weapons."

The youngest of them, with thick black sideburns and a lowering forehead, held a gleaming deer rifle topped with a telescopic sight on Duane as he opened the truck door and searched carefully.

"Can't let them go, Duane," said the bearded one when he was satisfied. "Your friends that killed my brother, they came to get you and yours. Here you be. They'll be back for you. Then we'll nail 'em. Now you sit tight in the truck because," he cocked his head, "if I ain't much mistaken, that's motors coming. And remember," he added with a mean grin, as the four of them faded back to the top of the levee and, spreading out, sank into the long grass there—"one wrong move out of any of you and I will personally put a bullet in your woman's ear."

Down the road from the direction they had been traveling toward, the sound of engines came clearer. A cloud of dust could be seen by Ariel as he stood motionless by the truck's raised hood. Sweat beaded his upper lip. Finally he watched Six and Cooch riding up fast toward them and drawing to a halt close to the truck.

Six astride his Harley switched off, kicked down the stand, and lifting the visor of his black full-face helmet said, "Christ on a crutch, what did you do, run outta gas. . . . ," but then turned, following Ariel's tortured eyes, to see the black-bearded man rise up from the grass above and behind him with a rifle trained on his back, and the others, guns aimed, visible but staying low.

Six tried to bluff it out.

"Hey cousin, point that peashooter someplace else, will you? We just stopped to help these folks," he called, relaxing in his saddle, his hands casually leaving the bars. But the bearded man said, "Get your hands up and your helmets off, both of you."

Slowly, under the guns, Six and the Mexican pulled off their helmets and let them drop.

"Nice try," said Bud, advancing down the slope, "But I was on th'island that night. I *know* you, boy. And the greaser, too. Your friends jest killed my brother Spider."

"*Ay, que porquería,*" muttered Cooch in disgust, while his eyes concentrated unobtrusively, gauging distances as the four men came down the slope toward them. But Six said loudly, "Spider? That one-eyed piece of *caca de vaca,* as my Mexican friend would say? *He* was your brother? Well it figures, I guess."

Bud's face was contorting with rage as he came closer.

"Just keep your hands up," he grated.

"Still and all," Six went on calmly, "it's always the wrong ones that get blown away." Bud had one foot on the road now, his brother Junior to his left and the other two to his right, his eyes never leaving Six's face.

"Yeah," sneered the squat gunman, "it should have been you, you sorry son of a bitch."

They all heard the sharp intake of Bud's breath and the click as the safety catch came off on his rifle.

Six, hands high, spat on the road and continued deliberately.

"Better keep your distance, pea picker—a long gun's the only thing that gives your kind an edge, you know?'

"Oh no," panted Bud, the rifle raised, circling Six's Harley pace by pace, "Oh no. I want to be right close to you when I open you up."

His last step sideways put him level with the right end of Six's handlebars. At that moment Six, hands still high, closed his right knee firmly on the rubber tank pad, putting pressure on a solenoid concealed inside it.

With no warning at all, a gout of flame exploded from the end of the handlebars, the blast of the single shotgun shell housed inside it taking Bud full in the chest at point-blank range. His finger squeezed the rifle trigger convulsively as he went over, and Six tumbled off his machine with a bullet in his left shoulder.

Ariel dived beneath the truck and Duane in the cab flung himself to protect his wife and child as the scene erupted into violent action.

At the sound of the first shot, Cooch's right hand had streaked in a smooth arc to his boot top, sweeping on and up and releasing a knife in a powerful underhanded throw at the man nearest him. So smoothly that it looked inevitable, the blade flickered across the intervening distance in an instant and sliced into his target's throat up to the hilt. The man died gurgling on the road.

But Junior, balked of a shot at Six concealed on the ground behind his machine, fired fast across it at Cooch, the high velocity bullet catching the slight figure in his right ribs and crossing his body to smash into his heart. The brave Mexican's life ended abruptly there by the levee.

Six, slowed fractionally by his wound, had his Smith and Wesson automatic out now and fired twice across Cooch at the last man in the line, who was wincing away from the gunfire. The shots slammed out, and both bullets hit the man in the back. Bright blood spurted like a geyser from his open mouth as he went spinning down, triggering his shotgun as he fell and by ill chance sending a load of 00 buckshot smashing into Six's right shoulder. As Six's pistol went flying, to his right, Junior, the only one still standing, frantically worked the bolt of his hunting rifle and leaning over the Harley, shot him in the chest, close to.

While Six lay writhing on the road and Duane held tightly to his wife and little daughter, Junior, the rifle pointed high, ran frantically from one to another of his brothers.

"Dead! They're all dead! You killed them all, you little son of a bitch!" he screamed, whirling and striding to where Six lay, "You're all going to die," he ranted, waving the rifle at the truck. "But you first."

Putting the muzzle to Six's forehead as he lay bleeding and screaming on the road, he jerked the trigger.

Nothing happened. Junior had forgotten to work the bolt and reload. Cursing, he wrenched at the action. As he did so, Six's eyes came open; he mastered his moans of agony, and his left hand raised, snail-slow, in something like benediction. Junior slammed the bolt home and lowered the gun to his head again, but the shattered figure's movements arrested him, and Six's eyes, jammed wide in his bloody face, mutely engaged his own.

Junior watched as, infinitely slowly, the gunman's left hand dipped to his ruined chest and slid inside his blood-drenched jacket. With the rifle barrel at his forehead, slowly, slowly his hand emerged again with something clasped between two fingers.

It was his wallet.

Junior's eyes bulged.

"You killed my whole family and you're looking to buy me off? Why you . . . ," he screamed reversing the rifle and going to club Six's face in with the butt.

But it never came to that. With a last supreme effort the squat gunman had grasped and raised the black wallet. As Junior swung down on him, the sharp sound of a shot snapped out. A disc of leather was punched from the end of the wallet as the Hi-standard derringer built into it loosed a single round, and three feet away, a neat hole perforated Junior's forehead. The last of the brothers tottered back and over, the rifle clattering to the ground as he fell, twitched for long moments, and lay still.

There was a minute of absolute stillness, with just the breeze eddying the pungent haze of gunsmoke that hung over the bodies. By the time Ariel and Duane forced themselves forward and reached him, Six was dead.

Looking round the scene of slaughter Duane called shakily,

"Don't come out now, honey. It's all right now, but don't you let her see."

"Gas," piped Ariel incongruously, "We got to get gas. Kemp'll be there in about fifteen minutes."

As Duane began to drag the corpses of the brothers off the road into the long grass, Ariel, swallowing hard in the silence, gently lifted the slight body of the Mexican from his machine, and unbolting its gas tank, carried it to the truck and slopped gas roughly into the filler cap. Without a word, he and Duane helped each other carry the bodies of Six and Cooch to the back of the truck where they lay them down and covered them with a tarpaulin. Then they climbed into the cab, Duane white-faced and shaking, but now with a rifle clamped in his fist. In perfect concentration, Ariel gradually coaxed the motor into life. They moved off eastward down the straight road running beside the levee.

Halfway to the rendezvous Dance rode up from behind

and fell in with them, and then Cleaver and Krass, alerted by the shooting, came out to meet them. Duane squeezed his wife's hand, feeling a lump rising in his chest at the sight of his friends riding alongside. Less than five minutes later they were there.

The road improvement site was widening the two-lane to four. To their right, the road had been cut back to the very edge of a rough wooded area, while to the left, where the levee rose to the river, it was scattered with the heavy road-making machinery, diggers, dump trucks and cats, deserted on this early Saturday morning. Below them, the blanked-off new section of the road, completed but unopened, would be Kemp's runway.

Ariel pulled the truck close in to the road-making machines, and the three bikes pulled up nearby. Immediately, Cleaver sent Tor and Dance with two of the M16s that they had cached there, on along to the furthest vehicle to the east, to cover the side where trouble would start if it was going to come.

Ariel climbed out. Walking to the rear of the truck, the flyer lifted the tarpaulin wordlessly as Cleaver and Krass stood and stared. Cleaver's face was expressionless as he said, "How many more?"

"Five that I know about," muttered Ariel. There was a silence.

"Where's Levon and Leroy?" asked Cleaver at length.

"Last we saw, they were taking off west with the hammer right down. Later we heard kind of an explosion from that way. . . ."

"They're grown-ups," said Krass reassuringly. "They'll hack it."

Duane was helping Mary and the little girl from the cab. Cleaver turned and went to them. Duane reached out and clasped his right arm without speaking. Cleaver smiled and said to the woman, "I'm forgetting my manners. I'm John Cleaver, and you must be Mary and Annie."

For long moments the woman struggled for words, staring at Cleaver's kind smile, overcome by the way that, despite the desperate situation, he could be so polite. Finally, she said simply,

"Thank you. From all of us."

Cleaver waved her words away, and bending to the little girl said, "Did you ever ride in an airplane before?"

Wide-eyed, Annie shook her head.

"Well you're going to like it, it's lots of fun. And there'll be cookies and milk and good stuff to eat up there too. And maybe something stronger for the grown-ups," he added with a grin to Duane.

"Excuse me, John," said Krass, "but we best get down for now."

Cleaver nodded, and arming Ariel and Krass, sent them off to take cover in the direction they had come from. Then he, Duane and his family got down in the long grass, concealed by the truck on one side and a yellow Caterpillar tractor on the other, with the crest of the levee and the river beyond it behind. They fell silent. The deserted road stretched away on both sides. Cleaver lay facing front, a flare pistol and the radio by his right hand, beside the M16, his left wrist forward so he could see his watch, his ears and eyes tuned to the mild blue sky above. With agonizing slowness, the minutes silently began to pass.

Cleaver never told them when the deadline for Kemp's arrival had gone. His face betrayed none of his mounting anxiety while, as coolly as he could, he began to review his remaining options. There were not many.

Together in the shadow of the machines they hugged the earth, gazing at the clear, silent sky.

16

Mississippi, Saturday, 5:30 A.M.

"Foul deeds will rise
Though all the world o'erwhelm them to men's
eyes."

—*Macbeth*, William Shakespeare

The flares blurred by Kemp's window in a line as he eased the C-47 down to refuel, front wheels kissing lightly, holding her steady until the tail wheel touched and they were down, and the flares flicked by singly as they slowed in the predawn darkness.

They rolled to a halt with plenty in hand. Kemp was smiling sideways at the kid when the light smote them.

The light was a thirty-million candlepower spot. It was suspended beneath the customs Bell Cobra assault helicopter hovering above them in the dark, and it hit them with the shock of an electric fist. Every rivet on the C-47's wings stood out in its pitless glare. Kemp felt it like a hand on the scruff of his neck, as above the throb of his engines, a metallic amplified voice blared out:

". . . IN THE C–47. YOU IN THE C–47. DON'T MOVE. DON'T MOVE. THIS IS THE CUSTOMS AIR WING. KILL YOUR MOTORS."

"Snake-bit." Kemp forced the words out with a bitter

laugh. The Cobra was the tip of the iceberg. Before that, he knew, they would have been picked up by a Navy E2-C's sophisticated airborne radar and then tailed by a customs Cessna Citation; which when they went to land would call up the Cobra with its lights, its weapons and even infrared sensing equipment to track fugitives on foot. They were nailed.

And their clearing point, which should have warned them? Ah, Sergio, thought Kemp almost wryly, Sergio. Had the feds got to the Colombian, or had it been the corporation that had got wind of the flight, misinterpreted it as private enterprise on Kemp's part, leaned on Sergio and tipped the customs? It didn't matter. Either way, Kemp was finished.

Beside him the kid unfroze, reaching for his AR-15. Kemp knocked his hand away.

"Don't you remember, fool—we're clean!"

That was the irony of it. But Kemp knew he was finished anyway. In the next two hours, while they impounded and searched the plane, there was no way for him to contact Cleaver. And by the time it was sorted out, the corporation would have got to hear of it, if they didn't know already, and Kemp was dead.

The inevitability of it clicked calmly in his head. He was never meant to help the others, had never been any good for them or anybody else. And now the pig pilots had won.

Rising swiftly, Kemp stepped to the hatch in the deck, opened it and dropped down the ladder to the tarmac below. He stepped out from under the wing into the assault of noise from above and the pitiless light. The bullhorn blared out instantly, but Kemp, feeling a giggle welling helplessly up in him, in the shadowless light took a step, and another. Then, like the figure at the start of his dream, he began to run.

Badwater, Saturday, 7:30 A.M.

Cleaver was halfway to his feet when the sound of the engines came. It was fifteen minutes past the deadline, and he had decided their best hope lay with the old truck and their bikes.

Now he froze, trying to will the sound into aircraft engines. But from his left came Tor's shout, "Cars, coming fast!"

"Keep down, don't shoot," he yelled as the Sheriff's battered Chevrolet with the deputy's cruiser close behind hurtled in from the east. For a moment it looked as if the cars would pass them, but then Rampike spotted the old truck and stood on his brakes, broadsiding the Chevy and blocking off the highway.

For the next minutes, with a sick feeling in his stomach, Cleaver watched as vehicle after vehicle arrived from both directions, their armed occupants, under Rampike's direction, taking cover in the ditch across the highway and up the flanks of the levee on both sides, blocking them in to east and west.

Duane spoke softly, for the first time.

"Looks like maybe Kemp was the one after all."

Maybe, thought Cleaver, but it looked as if it wasn't going to matter too much now. He glanced across at the frightened faces of Duane's wife and child and felt a stab of anguish. Whatever happened, he knew, they must come first. Mentally he prepared for surrender, and whatever might follow it.

Finally they saw a big maroon Jaguar drive up swiftly from the left and pull to a halt fast and smooth beside the Sheriff's Chevrolet. The Judge had arrived.

Hunched in the back of the big car, a traveling rug over his knees, the tiny figure of André Lafayette was filled with a delirious elation. He knew that the thing he had awaited for so long, the sense of the secret that life had hidden from him, the shape of his life itself, was about to be revealed to him. He had known the sickness when the prisoners had slipped away, but now he had them in his hand again, them and the others. He was an old man, but the tenacity of his will was about to pay off.

At the wheel, his son Cal, in a hunter's jacket and high-laced boots, reached for the Magnum in the glove compartment, and, dark eyes fixed on the levee, slipped from his door and knelt by the front fender as Rampike, carrying a shotgun and bullhorn, ran across from the Chevrolet in a half crouch.

"Harlan," said Cal loudly, "nice work. Now when do we start blasting?"

Rampike calmly shifted a wad of gum in his mouth, but cursed inwardly. The mood of the armed men around him, even of his deputies, was ugly. News of the auto wrecks and the blown bridge and of Spider's death had got around, and it was known that Cannonball was missing. Neither man had been well liked, but they were from the county. And now Cal was starting to rebel-rouse.

"I been waiting till now," said the Sheriff, "till we got them bottled up tight. And they didn't fire on us yet. Now I'm gonna tell them to come out."

"You do that and they'll make a break for it," said Cal. "You're putting your own men at risk, Harlan—I've seen it happen often enough, in 'Nam. These are dangerous men, killers. You don't reason with a mad dog. You give it a quick bullet."

"The woman and child are up there," Rampike reminded him.

"You know Harlan, little baby rats grow into big rats. We can't take chances with killers. Or killers' women."

The sun was getting up, and Rampike felt it hot and oppressive on his unprotected head, felt the wave of silent approval for Cal's words among the men. Staring Cal in the face, he said steadily,

"What does your Daddy think?"

From the back of the car, frail but clear, the Judge's voice carried to those around,

"Get them out. Get them out alive. We must hear what they have to tell us. We must hear the truth."

Cal ignored him. Instead he shouted to the ex-Truckers nearest to him, "Lee! Gregg! You going to let the scum that killed Spider and my brother walk away from here?"

Coldly, the Judge said,

"Stop him, Harlan."

"And you," Cal cried, turning on his father with increasing frenzy, "have you forgotten what they did to Emily and Jim?"

"THEY DID NOTHING!" came a clear voice from the top of the levee. "JUDGE! JUDGE! LISTEN TO YOUR DAUGHTER!"

Both the Badwater men and the party on the levee looked

up in astonishment. Silhouetted against the top of the levee, unarmed and defenseless, side by side stood a tall scarecrow figure in a white shirt and black waistcoat and pants, and a trembling woman beside him clutching a raincoat around her.

"He's got Emily!" Cal screamed, "kill him! Lee, Gregg, you Truckers, kill him!" he ranted, the Magnum coming up.

The tension raised several notches as, off to the left, a rifle bolt rattled. But Rampike swiftly raised both the shotgun and the bullhorn and spoke into the horn for the first time:

"OTIS, PACER, YOU DEPUTIES—THE FIRST MAN THAT PULLS A TRIGGER, SHOOT HIM. YOU GOT THAT?"

Across behind their cars or in the ditch, his men readied their weapons and nodded. Whatever they were feeling, not to obey one of Rampike's rare direct orders would be unthinkable.

"NOW EMILY—SAY WHAT YOU HAVE TO SAY," Rampike went on.

In the crumpled raincoat, her fair hair lank and her fine features drawn, the woman on the levee was still recognizably the same lovely girl of thirteen summers before. When she spoke, it was to her father in the car on the road, the intensity of her emotion eliminating the distance between them.

"It wasn't them, Daddy! It never was! All they ever did was to protect themselves and look out for each other." She paused, every eye on her, struggling with her feelings, and then the words ripped out—

"It was Cannonball and Cal!" she screamed. "Your son, Daddy. My brother. They killed Jimmy and, and . . ."

As the emotion overcame her, Cal's voice, deep and smooth, intervened, "You can't believe this, any of you. That man has snatched her from her home, used tricks or drugs, playing on a sick girl's mind. . . ."

The Dude's ringing voice spoke up.

"I don't have a gun and I don't have any tricks—the only power I have is the power of an honest heart. I went to your mansion after you left this morning, and when I told her who I was, Emily came with me freely. We took your boat down the river to here—it's true I was meaning to help her get away from this place with my friends, and hoping that what she could tell us would help us clear ourselves. But that's all of it."

"It's true, Daddy," said the woman. "And what I said is true. On the island that night they came on us in the dark, Cal and Cannonball. He gagged Jimmy and tied him up and made him watch as he, and then Cannonball, did those—things to me." She hugged the coat tight around her, her voice shuddering, and then rising to a shriek as she relived the horror.

"And then they—O Christ Jesus—they—*Jimmy* . . ."

The long sobbing wail that came from her froze the blood of the listening men, the unmistakable grief and outrage transmitting the truth of what she said even more clearly than her words.

Rampike's attention, like the others', was fixed on her, and Cal seized the opportunity. Lashing out with his foot, he kicked the pumpgun from the Sheriff's hands and shouting, "Lies!" raised the Magnum.

"Don't do it!" barked a paralyzing voice of command from the levee to his left. "Not unless you want you and your daddy and your fancy automobile blown clear to hell! That's right, asshole, drop it!"

Looking up, they saw the kneeling figure of Levon in his bloodstained tiger stripes leveling the stubby rocket launcher down at the Jaguar, while further back knelt his brother, with a Sidewinder raised so that the muzzle rested behind Cannonball's ear.

"We caught us a ride on some farmer's truck, but when we see all the fun out here, we came along the river on foot again," grated Levon. Turning to Cannonball, he continued. "Okay hard-on, it's your nickel. Tell the nice men what you tell us on the way over."

Cannonball stood swaying, his flying suit torn and sweat-darkened, tears rolling helplessly down his face and hanging off his nose as he blubbered. "All right, it's true. We did it. But it was his idea, that crazy Cal. . . ."

Down by the car, ignoring the shotgun Rampike had casually leveled at him, Cal's calm, low-pitched voice came.

"I don't know what kind of a beating these murdering savages gave him to make him talk this way, but it's a lie. You

Truckers, you remember—there was only one way out from the clubhouse, and he and I were inside all the time when my brother and sister were attacked."

"We weren't and you know it," screamed Cannonball. "We had this crawl trench under the back fence, the way I'd seen them do in 'Nam. Only you and me knew about it. After you messed up the generator we went under the wire and did it. I just did what you told me. . . ."

From along the levee, Emily's clear voice asked simply,

"How could you do it, Cal? How could you do it to me?"

There was a long silence. Finally Cal raised his eyes to meet hers, and they all heard him say,

"I didn't kill you, did I?"

Emily shuddered and looked away.

In the silence, Leroy cleared his throat, spat, wrinkled his nose in disgust, and gripping Cannonball's arm, said,

"Here, you folks have him—I can't take the smell no more."

With a powerful shove, he propelled the gross Trucker stumbling down the slope onto the road to collapse in a heap by the side of the Jaguar.

Behind him, the car door opened and, moving for the first time since the terrible revelation, the short figure of the Judge heaved itself from the back of the Jaguar and stood, swaying slightly, above the sobbing Trucker. Only then did they see that from beneath the traveling rug he had produced a long-barreled Frontier Colt, one of a matched pair, an inheritance. A terrible coldness lay on his twisted face as he looked down at Cannonball and, gesturing with the gun, whispered, "*Va t'en, cochon.* Move!"

After a moment paralyzed with fear, Cannonball began to scramble wildly away under the long-barreled gun. Reaching the newly made stretch of road, he clambered awkwardly to his feet and hopped half-comically across the empty tarmac. Halfway across, he yelped as the big pistol boomed and a bullet, and then another, kicked up dust around his heels. As he neared the far edge, the Judge steadied his aim and shot him deliberately low down in the right leg. Cannonball shrieked, went down, then desperately dragged himself off the road and over the verge toward the shelter of the woods, leaving a trail of blood across the scrubless clay. Then quickly he reached the brush, and disappeared.

The Judge, trembling, raised his voice and said two words. "The dogs."

Rampike met his eyes, and then nodded slightly. His watching deputies threw up the tailgate of their wagon, and in a cascade, the black and tan bloodhounds and two Doberman assault dogs, in a frenzy from the shooting and the smell of blood, poured from the interior and at a word from the deputies, streaked across the road for the woods, the hounds howling eerily, the Dobermans running in silence.

Up on the levee, with memories of La Mesa Drive triggered, Cleaver shivered in uncontrollable revulsion, muttering thickly to Duane beside him, "I hate those things. Hate them."

The dogs disappeared from sight, and there was a long minute's silence, broken only by the questing baying. Then the voices of the hounds rose to a crescendo and mingled with great screaming shouts of human agony. Only gradually did they die away to nothing.

When the Judge turned his eyes away from the contemplation of the woods, his daughter was close by his side. He gazed into her face, and then addressed her directly for the first time, speaking quietly,

"Emily—why didn't you tell me this before?"

The woman gestured across to where her brother stood calmly under Rampike's gun.

"Cal told me he'd have me put away, taken away from the last thing I had, living at Beau Mont. And he said he'd kill me if I made more trouble for him. I was so alone." She began to sob quietly, gesturing up at the Dude. "This man guessed, Daddy. Why couldn't you?"

The Judge's dark eyes flared a fraction wider as he turned to stare at his son. Quietly he said,

"Why, Cal? Why did you do it?"

"But I was only doing what you always said, Daddy," Cal shot back mockingly. "'For all things have been blessed in the well of eternity and are beyond good and evil'—remember?

That was the difference, though. You just said it. I did it, did it all."

He threw back his head and laughed richly, the sound turning to a roar of fury as he shouted. "You blind old fool! I could have done anything and you'd never have known. Because I was invisible to you. It was only them you wanted, them you loved. Jimmy and Emily, they were your favorites; you sent me away while you fawned and doted on them. I hated them. I always had. So I bided my time. And then did something about it. Took their pride, and that unthinking way they had, and rolled it in the dirt. Got away with it, too, laid it on those smartass Yankees. And it felt so fine!"

He took a shuddering breath, exalted, "And everything that's happened here is down to you, *Judge*, to your blindness. All of them that have died today, they were fighting your war. But I'm glad it's out now, glad, do you hear? So that before you die, just once you'll know how much I've always hated you."

Cal stood there before his father's gun, seemingly invulnerable, absolutely mad and absolutely unafraid, and even Rampike felt himself quail before the thundering natural force of him.

The Judge had stood stock still through Cal's speech. Now he tottered, barely steadying himself against the car. Inwardly directed words, fragments from his past, trickled from his lips.

"'Away with me,'" he muttered. "'The lust to rule, the terrible teacher of the greatest contempt . . . it finally cries out of them themselves, Away with *me*.'

"Was this what it all amounted to? My struggles, my life? James dead, these other boys, too, my other son no son, a devil in my image, the devil in my mirror, a *devil!* . . . And my daughter with her life half-wasted . . ."

He staggered again, a sob bursting from him.

Man wasn't built to be torn this way, thought Rampike. He stepped forward and gently removed the pistol from the old man's fingers, then turned to the woman and said,

"Would you see to your daddy, Emily?" and as she continued to stare at her father's stricken face, the Sheriff murmured, "He did always mean things for the best."

Slowly Emily reached out to take her father's arm. Her touch seemed to bring him to himself for a moment. He blinked several times, his eyes searching hers, and finally spoke,

"Can you forgive an old man, forgive your father? Forgive me?" he sobbed.

Then he was released. Differences, and the pain of time passing, dissolved now in the light that filled his head, and it was his wife's name he murmured as he let Emily surround him with her loving embrace.

When he had seen her help the old man into the car again and settle herself by him inside, the Sheriff straightened and turned back to the Judge's son.

"Well now, Cal," said Rampike softly, "what we going to do about you, boy?"

"I have an idea," came the voice from up on the levee.

They turned to look, as the tall leather-jacketed figure walked out from behind the old Dodge truck and started down toward them with measured paces, the M16 held by its carrying handle down by his side. After a moment, a big man with a cowlick of blond hair falling in his eyes came out and fell in two paces behind him. As the first man approached, Rampike took in the firm mouth beneath the mustache and the tired but steady blue eyes, and recognized the leader from thirteen years before. Cleaver halted by the car and said,

"Let's Cal and me go over to the woods yonder and have a talk."

"'Bout what?" said Rampike.

Cleaver's voice shook with suppressed fury.

"The way he tried to pin a rape and murder on us, on me in particular. The way his lies drove us to live like fugitives. The way his kidnapping and torturing our friend Duane led to at least two of us getting killed this morning."

Cal, sneering, gestured at the M16.

"You go in with that, and me unarmed?"

Rampike, nodding slowly as he realized what Cleaver wanted, looked at the forty men or more clustering around now. Taking care of your own grievances, man to man, was something the rough-hewn country faces could understand. It would keep the blood of his friend's son off his own hands. And it would earn the outsiders, after the things they had done that morning, their way out.

"Shotguns," said Rampike, "You each get one. Three rounds of 00 each. Otis, Pacer, see to it." It's rough justice, he thought, but it's the best we got right now. He went on, "There's men dead on both sides—enough blood's been spilled over this thing. Whichever one walks away from there, that's an end to it!" He looked around, into their faces, "Right?"

The last to nod was a worried-looking Krass, but a glance at Cleaver's set, closed face convinced him.

The deputies came up with two pumpguns. On Rampike's word they patted down Cal and Cleaver for weapons, removing Cleaver's knife.

"Anything clse?" said the Sheriff.

"You got a drink of water?" asked Cleaver. As a canteen was produced, Cal sneered,

"Mouth getting kind of dry, boy? You've come to a place where there's no Thirteen to back you up, no one else, just you. Think you can handle that?"

Cleaver ignored him, and continued drinking sparingly from the canteen. But Cal's throw had touched a nerve. His anger, and the need to resolve things, to finish what he had started himself, had brought him down off the levee and carried him this far. But looking at the sleekness of Cal, with his thick black hair and the mad assurance of his dark eyes, suddenly Cleaver was weary, feeling the weight not just of the action that morning but of the whole pressure-filled week that had preceded it.

He would not let the exhaustion get hold of his mind, however. Hell, no, he shook himself, I'm made of the stuff that lasts. Always have been.

Rampike handed them each three red shells and said, "Otis, take Mr. Cleaver here down about a hundred yards to the left along the road there, and the same distance again into the woods. When you hear me fire a shot, give him the pumpgun and get back here. Pacer, same thing for you with Cal, only you go the other way. All right now, get to it."

Cleaver met Cal's narrow overshadowed eyes and said quietly,

"Be seeing you."

"Will you?" sneered Cal.

Cleaver turned away, and walked with the deputy through the circle of men and down the empty road.

As he listened to the deputy walking quickly away, his booted feet noisy on the dead leaves of the forest floor, Cleaver checked the gun and its carrying strap again, and then prepared himself in other ways.

A city boy, he had come late to hunting and had had to discover the woods for himself. Now he checked his watch; he knew time could be used to gauge distance traveled. On the hike in, he had noticed some things—the breeze from the south, the streams meandering from the river that lay to the north so they would likely bisect his path forward through the trees now. These things might be useful to orient himself by later.

The ground in fact was damp underfoot, and it was cool in the shadows. Cleaver dumped the change from his pocket out on the ground, buckled up the belt on his heavy jacket, zipped up the front, the pockets and sleeves to avoid both noise and obstruction, and tucking his jeans into the top of his dull black leather boots, fastened the jingling buckles that topped them. Finally, grimacing, he stooped and rubbed dirt on his face and the back of his hands.

But the most important preparation was internal. The shadowed woods enfolded him, cool and deep, mysterious, potentially frightening, like the embrace of an unknown adult to a child. They were untouched and wild, big moss-draped oaks rearing from a floor beneath that was choked with bramble, briar and the shoots of saplings, and underfoot, a thick damp-smelling patina, the humus from decades, centuries of dead leaf and tree. Cleaver knew that if he was not to blunder noisily through like the departing deputy, and if he was to detect his enemy, there was a rhythm to find, uneven but quietly insistent, that would help him flow among the trees like a stream of water or the breeze itself. He sought for it now with all his senses.

With a careful last look around, finally he tried to think as Cal would. Facing east, coming at him, he guessed that the other man's impulse would be to circle to the right, and away from the road. Cleaver decided to meet him head on if that was the case. Taking his weariness into account, he wanted to finish the thing quickly. But he willed himself to be simply relaxed and ready, to move forward neither hurrying nor delaying. Coolness did it, not rushing, he knew.

Grasping the weapon high across his body, lightly he began to walk forward and to his left.

Ten minutes later he dropped to one knee. He was on the edge of a clearing, the light ahead of him green and subaqueous. In the distance a jay screeched. To his right lay the indentation of a tiny stream, and Cleaver's eyes checked the damp earth along its bank for a telltale boot print.

Then he looked up, and thirty yards away across the clearing, Cal appeared.

The dark-haired figure seemed alarmingly calm and confident, but Cleaver never hesitated. Still kneeling, he brought his gun up instantly, thumbing the safety as he raised it, and aiming centrally, fired.

As the concussion rocked the glade, he thought he saw Cal sway, and pumping fast, he fired again. Through the smoke he saw the leaves shake where Cal had been. But the glade was empty again.

Uncertainty gripped Cleaver as he pumped his last round into the chamber. But he was certain he had hit the man, at least with his first shot. He faded back into the trees, and with infinite patience began to work his way around to the left, away from the stream, toward the point where he had seen Cal.

Ten minutes of broken movement and patient, cautious listening worked him round to the far edge of the glade. When he was as sure as he could be that he was close to the spot where Cal had appeared, he dropped to one knee again to check for signs or bloodstains.

The movement saved his life. A pumpgun crashed out and shot pattered into the leaves just above his head.

Hurling himself sideways, Cleaver rolled to his right instinctively, covered the dozen feet to the stream and rolled over the lip of the bank into the shallow indentation, his face feeling the icy kiss of water.

From his left came a grimly jovial voice.

"Come out, come out, wherever you are!"

He's mad, a madman, thought Cleaver, fighting panic, as now there came the sound of footsteps advancing through the brush toward him, with no attempt at concealment. All right, he thought, and steadying himself, came up from the edge of the stream like lightning, whipped the gun up to sight straight on the figure less than forty feet away, ahead and to his right, and squeezed off his last round.

Cal took the charge in the chest, and with a leap of elation, Cleaver saw him go over hard. There followed long moments of ringing silence.

Then, as Cleaver had risen halfway out of the stream bed, the impossible happened. The body across from him sat up.

Cleaver froze. Gasping as if he had been punched, Cal's right hand swept out and closed on his weapon. His mocking eyes fixed on Cleaver's, he raised the shotgun in his right hand, with his left tapping his shredded jacket, and the lightweight body armor beneath it.

"You know what they call this wonderful stuff?" he said. "'Second Chance!'"

As he spoke, Cleaver had whirled, leaped the stream and begun to run despairingly. He heard Cal's voice say,

"But you don't get one," and then the shot hit him in the back throwing him forward into the bushes.

After the initial agony in his shattered right shoulder, there could be no calculation, only the fight against the overwhelming urge to sink down, lie still, give up, only the knowledge that if he could move, then he would.

Scrabbling blindly in the deep undergrowth, scarcely feeling the briars that ripped his face and hands, on his belly, on all fours, frantically he went forward. Rising to a crouch and stumbling when he was able, running from the terrifying extinction waiting just behind him, the laughter and the mocking voice that came sometimes, Cleaver covered a remarkable distance. Briar patch, stand of trees, a stream, another, he ploughed through with no sense of time or direction. By instinct, his left hand still clutched the empty weapon.

He came to a clearing with tall moss-hung oaks on the far side. He was halfway across when he almost stumbled on something which made him recoil with a horror that for a moment overcame even the fear driving him on.

It was a corpse, the mangled red and white face and chest barely recognizable as Cannonball now that the dogs had finished with him. A swarm of flies rose at Cleaver's approach. He crouched panting by the body for long seconds. He felt the numbness in his shoulder grow and spread, the weakness sapping him. That's me down there, he thought desperately, unless I can think of something funny, and quick.

From behind, Cal's voice came.

"They'll all die when I get out of here, you know that? Your friends, old Rampike too. And what we'll do to that woman and child out there, that'll just be a dress rehearsal for what I've got in mind for your kids, and your Laura."

Dumb, thought Cleaver with sudden clarity. If it was meant to frighten or anger him, it didn't work. The repellent, remorseless evil in his taunting voice made Cleaver know that Cal had to be stopped. And the thought of Laura only strengthened him.

Crouching there alone in the forest, beneath his pain, exhaustion and hopelessness, Cleaver discovered a bedrock of stubborness. Once again he forced himself to think. He needed a weapon. Turning back to Cannonball's body, he methodically went through the several pockets of his flyer's coveralls. Strapped to the right leg he discovered a survival knife with a four-inch blade.

Think. What would Cal do? What did I do? You see the body, you go to the body. Yes!

Left-handed, slipping and stumbling, Cleaver, gasping, dragged the corpse to the edge of the clearing so that it lay underneath one of the larger oaks. Slinging his shotgun over his good shoulder, he used the last of his strength to try and get up into the tree. At first it seemed impossible; he lost a fingernail scrabbling at the slippery bark, and was afraid he would pass out as his shoulder, twisting, sent waves of agony through him. Then Cal's voice came again, much closer, and he flung himself at the lowest bough and somehow pulled himself up, got his feet on it, crouched, half-unconscious, his boots ten feet above the forest floor.

He swayed and nearly fell, then with his left hand, unbuckled his belt, tossed it around a bough by his left arm and fastened it again, slipping his left arm through it in a kind of sling that held him to the tree. In a fury of concentration, he went through the pockets of his jacket, found the three-foot length of electrical wire and the reel of duct tape he carried there, and with his eyes flashing frequently to the clearing, balanced the shotgun butt down on the bough he was standing on, and with the wire and tape began to secure the knife to its barrel. It was slow, awkward work; twice the blade nearly slipped from his fingers, and at the end he was none too sure of the sturdiness of the arrangement.

Then he froze, as through the leaves fluttering close to his face he caught a glimpse of Cal, gun held high, stepping almost leisurely into the clearing.

With infinite patience and care, inch by inch Cleaver lifted the butt of his weapon and then lowered the muzzle, so that the knife blade at the end was pointing below him, at the grisly shape lying beneath the tree. Heart hammering, face and mustache drenched with sweat that he blinked from his eyes, breath panting through his mouth for silence, he jammed the gun butt under his limp right arm, grasped the barrel tightly in his left hand, and waited.

A stillness seemed to fall on the forest, and in it, Cleaver thought he heard the sharp intake of Cal's breath. Had he spotted the corpse, or his quarry in the tree?

For long moments Cleaver hovered in a coma of concentration, and then the dark-haired figure stepped into his circle of vision by the body below. Cleaver never hesitated. Slipping his left arm out of the sling and pushing off with his feet, he flung himself unblinking to topple forward and down from the tree, the bayonet's point at the end of the shotgun stiff-armed ahead of him. He saw the pale outline of Cal's shocked face, turning up to meet his, the gun coming up, and then he hit.

The sound of the sixth shot came to them on the road, and Krass twitched painfully. He blinked twice and then blurted out,

"That's it. I'm going in there. He may be hurt and need help."

"Then I come too, son," said Rampike.

It took them less than ten minutes to find what they were looking for; the final drama had been played out a hundred yards in from the highway.

The three bodies lay close together. Krass ran over to Cleaver lying on his side. He was breathing. His left arm had broken in the fall and the wound in his back was bleeding again but Cal's last shot had gone wide. As Krass knelt by him and felt for his pulse, Cleaver's eyes opened and stared into his friend's face.

"Did I get him?" he asked softly.

"You surely did," said Rampike, standing motionless, gazing at the grotesque sight at his feet.

His black eyes wide open, Cal lay as if silently screaming. The improvised spear was protruding from his mouth, impaling his skull to the earth.

"Well," said Rampike at length, "guess I'd better call up a body bag and a blood wagon."

"Not for John," said Krass shortly. "None of you people lays a hand on him."

An hour later, as Cleaver, bandaged by Krass and with his left arm in a sling, lay in the long grass of the levee again, the Dude came out and squatted by him.

"I'm sorry, John," he began, "for what I did this morning, sneaking off that way."

"You did right, Dude," Cleaver reassured him.

"We all did, seems like, in our own way."

Cleaver looked across at Krass tending Duane's hand now; at Tor carrying the little girl on his massive shoulders, explaining that he was an airplane, a jumbo jet in fact; and his eyes strayed beyond to the truck, and his thoughts to what lay inside. Yes, he thought, we did right. We didn't become junkies or shoe salesmen. We stayed together.

Rampike was walking across toward him when he stopped by Dançe, who sat patiently sideways on the scarlet Harley.

"You're the feller on the motorcycle this morning," said the Sheriff evenly.

"And you're the guy in the Chevrolet," said Dance with a trace of a smile. "Thought it was Barney Oldfield back there. Like our old friend Six would have said, for a porky bear, you pedal pretty fast."

"You do all right yourself," muttered Rampike, and he walked on over to where Cleaver lay.

He knelt stiffly and said, without preamble, "If you're fixed up, I reckon it'd be the best if you leave now. All of you."

"You know there's some tidying still to do out there," said Cleaver levelly. "I'm talking about Spider's brothers."

"I know," sighed Rampike. "We'll take care of it. Anything happens around here, we do."

"And the Judge?" said Cleaver. "Does he know about Cal?"

"Emily took him home. He don't realize. Maybe he never will. It's nearly over for him, and it's better this way."

The Sheriff sighed.

"He was a remarkable person. But a man can get too hung up on his own idea of himself, forget it was the Lord that made him and in the end only the Lord can ever know what he is." He looked Cleaver in the eye and concluded, "As leader of the pack, you might remember that, mister."

Cleaver nodded.

"God willing, this is our last go-round," he said.

Rampike rose to his feet.

"That's good, that's fine," he said coldly, his hand on his tilted pistol butt. "Because I got one more thing to say to you. Don't come back."

"You got it," said Cleaver. He raised his voice, and his words reached Duane and his family, Levon and Leroy, Dance, Ariel and the Dude, Krass and Tor.

"Get our bikes and the truck. We're getting out of this place. We're going home."